W9-CUN-304

RUSH OF SHADOWS

RUSH OF SHADOWS

 radicevole

CATHERINE BELL

Washington Writers' Publishing House
Washington, DC

Copyright © 2014 by Catherine Bell

All rights reserved

COVER DESIGN by David Costello

BOOK DESIGN and TYPESETTING by Barbara Shaw

LIBRARY OF CONGRESS CATALOGUING-IN-PUBLICATION DATA

Bell, Catherine, 1943-
  Rush of Shadows / Catherine Bell.
     pages cm
  ISBN 978-1-941551-02-8 (pbk. : alk. paper)
1. Frontier and pioneer life—California—Fiction.
2. Women pioneers—California—Fiction. 3. Whites—Relations
with Indians—Fiction. 4. California—19th century—Fiction.
5. Historical fiction. I. Title.
  PS3602.E645436R87 2014
  813'.6—dc23

                                        2014018916

Printed in the United States of America

WASHINGTON WRITERS' PUBLISHING HOUSE
P. O. Box 15271
Washington, D.C. 20003

TO
Emma
and the family for whom
she saved the story
Helen, Tom, Kate, Eliza, Ben, Sam, Will

Shadows and remembrance are the diffusion of light in silence, and at an eternal distance from the sun, as if our stories were shadows that rushed to that elusive union of shadows and light.

Gerald Vizenor
Manifest Manners:
Postindian Warriors of Survivance

Listen to my story.

So when I sit before you talking, talking, talking, talking, you know who I am. Listen because I carry our history, yours and mine, ours. Some of it, anyway. Whoever you are.

Talk back. Tell stories. Put food out, meat. I will eat it. I'm not here to harm. I'm talking, telling stories. Watch. Listen.

Then you'll know I'm no stranger.

Greg Sarris
Keeping Slug Woman Alive

1

COMING INTO THE COUNTRY

ॐ

MAY 1855

Mellie

It was a beautiful country, though I hated and feared it, coming over the mountains with the wagon staggering on a gimpy wheel, black crags towering over the track, the sky blue and thick as a flatiron, and the vultures turning and turning on the hot wind, waiting for somebody to die.

On the wagon front, Law worked the mules between twisted oaks, sweat stain spread all down his shirt. He wasn't a talker, and I hardly knew him, though I'd been married to him since Christmas and was big with his child. He was doing what he was born to do, picking his way around the gulches that broke the gleaming slopes of oat and barley grass, coaxing and cussing low and steady.

What a time we'd had in San Francisco. So many wagons at the wharves, the shops with every kind of thing, sugar in bales, rice, matting, oil, pianofortes, parasols, French carpets, sewing silk, cigars, pineapples from the Sandwich Isles. Music, operas, gambling in every street. We'd seen a man hanged for murder. They noosed him and stood him on a windowsill, everyone silent with hats off as he pleaded his innocence, then pushed him out. He dropped, snapped and twitched, tongue wrenched out, blackening. Three days north of there, we came past the last stage stop, and afterward to Santa Catarina, not even a post office then, only a little store with soap and coffee. After that, every human habitation seemed to drop away, and the land went on still, full of emptiness. Wild hogs scrambled in the brakes, dry hills rising to ridges dark with firs and knobs of black rock.

"Oh, it smells good, don't it, Mellie?" Law said. "Hot rocks and pepper trees and deep-root grass."

A few farms pushed out into Esmeralda valley with wheat and hops, and a woman there let me have some chickens and new peas. Beyond the farms, Indian humpback lodges strung out along a stream. Women beat at the oat grass with wicker paddles, swinging the seed into their baskets. They stopped, naked above the waist, and looked at us with square brown faces.

"Poor beggars," Law said. "They roast and eat it."

Children ran along the wagon in the smell of woodsmoke and reached out, catching at the spokes, till I worried for them.

"No need to fear," Law said. "They're peaceful. Indians won't hurt you."

At the ford of a creek, the birds had worked a dead deer down to ears and bone, pieces of bloody gut swinging from their beaks. I reached back in the water keg, sipped the warm stale stuff, and passed the gourd up to Law. He wouldn't say it, but I reckoned we could die before ever we saw Oak Valley. A bear could come out of the swale. Law coaxed me like one of his mules.

"This here's the halfway mountain. Indians won't bother you. They're well disposed. Not bright, of course."

Happiest people on earth, Father used to say, till we improved them.

"Brandt brothers been in a year," Law said. "Good men. They'll have a rooster for you, I expect."

The mules strained, following a dry wash into the hills. The mountains stretched away the more we climbed, and the wrinkled valley dropped behind, too big, too wild, too empty. I crawled into the back of the wagon, rolled in the quilts and closed my eyes against the land. Making out the slide and stretch of little heels and knees, I wept to my unborn child, too low for Law to hear.

"Will we die here, darling? Will you live? Will you keep me company?"

My sisters hadn't thought Law Pickett would make any kind of husband, a man who could hardly read, a man who said "the-ay-ter" and had never been inside one. When I went ahead and married him, they called us fools to go so far north. Even Nannie, who was afraid of nothing but men. She set her fists to her hips, thin with fretting over Father.

"Who will be by you when your time comes? Law doesn't know a thing, and nor do you."

She was too late. It was finished for me at Santiago, with the Padre dead and the Mission ruining, Father restless as ever, doctoring the Indians up and down the valley, and Bessie married to her Californio boy with the silver buttons. Law had seen a place up in the coast range and built a cabin. It was late to

5

plant, but we thought barley might make by winter, if we could get water to it.

The wagon bruised my hipbone, jerking this way, that. I turned to the other side, wishing for cool, for evening.

When evening came at the Mission in Santiago, Joaquín would pull his leather bag dripping from the well and sprinkle the *margaritas* and the *clavellinas* rich as cloves. *Mariposas* would flutter in white pairs above the paths where no big American girls ran down any more for mint and lemons before supper. Francisca would scuff her old, sore feet to the pump and the rosemary bush. Nothing to break their Indian quiet and the quiet of the ruined walls.

I opened my eyes, and brightness stabbed them. Oaks splayed like spiders on the hot hills, making splashes of shade if you could get to them, and a hawk rode the updrafts, hunting the slope ahead of his shadow.

Law reached back and shook my ankle.

"You're too big for him, Mell."

ℬↄ

MAY 1855

Law

Law heard a thump, a crack and crumble, and the right wagon front went down.

"Jesus God," he said.

He saw he'd hit the raw edge of a gully, pieces of wheel shattered over the ground.

"Threw a blessed spoke."

He got out and kicked the other wheel a lick, damned it all to hell, and went on from there, with Mellie looking at him like she didn't know he had it in him to cuss like that. In the quiet without the wagon running, the mules looked back at him, chewing their bits.

"We'll make out," she said. "You've done so well."

Lucky the buckeye was in flower. He could see it, pink along the woods. Buckeye makes good mend, light and strong. He hunted a shapely branch while she unhitched and brought the mules up the steep grass to the shade, trying to keep uphill of both of them. The air had a sleepy heat he hadn't looked for at the north. Must be the ranges broke the ocean fog. He shucked his shirt. Mellie helped him unload the bed and

7

dresser. He piled stones to set the wagon up while she emptied it, and he cut away the wheel where the rim split, dovetailed a sound piece, and whittled a new spoke. It took the afternoon. She helped him steady the wheel while he gathered the rim around the new piece and fitted the spokes, and they strapped it with rawhide soaked in their last water. Then she stood up and tipped over in the grass. Damn, he wasn't taking care of her. And he'd promised her father.

"I'm a fool," he said. "I should have got you in the shade before the mules."

He carried her under an oak and rode down the canyon for water, brought it back and opened her collar and splashed her neck and pulled up her skirts and let the breeze at her.

"I'm all right," she said.

He waited while her color came back and the rawhide dried and shrank tight around the rim. Then he tried the wheel. It went pretty well, with hardly a wobble, and they loaded everything, dresser, bed, sacks of salt and canning jars, seed and lamp, hoes, rakes, plow, dutch oven, fishhooks, bedding, sacks of wheat, chicken crate, nails and tack and sewing. She was holding up all right, and they started out slow. The wheel held, too, and they pushed on into the twilight on a piney summit. At thick dusk, they made a dry camp on a little flat, raking a bare patch for a fire.

She was strong, for a woman, but she had some of those fine ways of her father. That worried Law.

"Oak Valley's just the other side of this," he said. "But will you take to it, Mellie? Swell as your folks was?"

"Not so swell," she said. "Only Grandfather went in after the Creek War and took land."

He liked the sound of bacon in the pan, the smell of it, the coffee pot screeching on its wire. He told about the water at the ranch, how good it tasted, how it seeped and soaked all down the hill. Something he didn't want to say. Or think, either. No sooner come to the valley than he'd have to ride back south for stock. Get animals on the land before the green dried up.

"These potatoes aren't waiting to get in the ground before they sprout," Mellie said. "They'll be up and leafing by the time you're back."

Law wondered if she could read his mind, if she knew him that good already.

"I'll do it in a week," he said. "You'll have to tote a lot of water, planting this time of year, but the calves will be walking good, that's the other side to it."

"Best say two weeks," she said.

"I can get to Santa Catarina in two days."

"Why, it's eighty miles, and rough. You thought to be six weeks this winter cutting tanbark in the woods, and it went past three months."

"All right, put in a day to settle on a price. Can't be more than nine-ten days, all told." Dark fell, and the fog came over, blotting the stars. Law watered the mules again. They nuzzled him for more, but she'd used it all for her little fruit trees.

"Lucky it's too dark to see the poor, wilted things," she said.

He drank thick coffee and went to bed thirsty. She let him reach around her belly, warm as a cake out of the oven.

"Sam Brandt will help you," he said. "Jakob too."

She lay quiet, looking at the fire.

"Indians won't bother you," he said. "Diggers ain't got the gumption to make trouble."

"It's not them I'm afraid of."

"What, then?"

"Oh, the emptiness is all."

He laughed. "Emptiness can't hurt you, Mellie. What ain't there can't hurt."

Sparks wandered up through the trees, two or three at a time.

"Wait till you see the willows by the creek," he said, "the way they turn their leaves, first white, then green. Wait till you hear them rustle."

When he slid her down in the quilts, the sour went out of her, and they made their own sweet circle in the mountain night.

"Anyhow," Law said, "I beat the Brandt boys on the wife."

ॐ

JUNE 1855
Mellie

A cut let out of Kaikitsil valley to the east. We could see it divid-
ing the mountains. I was wondering in the sleepy heat whether
the wheel would hold, and curious if the east side would look
different from the rest of the country. Where I was looking out
of the wagon, a brushy hill came close, and something in there
disturbed the manzanita. I thought a turkey or wild pig, but a
human face looked out between the leaves, a dark face. It froze
me, from surprise, and from the fear I saw in it, the terror. The
face was a woman's, and it said, *Don't tell. Hide me.* A little pair
of eyes stared out below, where she held a baby against her col-
larbone. The wagon moved on. Law went on through into the
open cut. He hadn't seen. I didn't know where I'd put my
tongue.

Halfway across the opening, a broad savanna like the rest
of it, running east, dotted with oak trees, came an island in the
flat, a piece of high wooded land, and just there, where a dry
rill ran alongside the cliff, a man dropped out of the rocks and
trees, mouth open, yelling, running at us. I screamed. The
mules jerked back.

"Jesus Christ," Law said. "Steady, Meg. Steady."

Another man, naked, followed the first, half his face red with blood gouting over his shoulders, hair tossed and clinging.

The wild men veered away, scurrying down the valley, and were gone, so fast I wondered whether I'd seen or dreamed it. But the mules panted and Law gripped the seat beside him with one hand.

"What in hell?" he said. Once the mules stood still, he scrambled to me, touched my hair. He'd turned white. "We in one piece? I thought we was done, sure. Give me some water. I need a drink."

"What could have hurt them so?" I said, but I said nothing of the face in the manzanita. I couldn't. It was as if I'd promised her.

"Not us they want, I guess," Law said. "Thank God. Right on top of us. Surprised, I guess. Heard us too late, rattling down the rocks."

He started the mules on, laying the whip gently along Joe's flank where it flickered with nerves, steadying with his voice.

"Pass me that Sharps up here, Mellie, if there's going to be shooting. Whee, Bob, if them Indians had it in for us, we'd a been in trouble."

"The bloody one was stumbling."

It was the first I'd seen such blood, such wild hurt. Would he live, the one with blood over his shoulders like a cloak?

"Something's chasing them," Law said, "and maybe they deserve it."

We ate some nuts and jerky, collecting ourselves, wide awake now, and came to where we could see again up east, a pretty valley, sickle-shaped, and under the trees a couple of men on horseback, circling this way and that. They were running down a fellow in a red shirt. One of the riders swung a rope, trying to lasso him, but he dodged, and the lasso missed and missed again, till it caught his heel and he slid down hard. I saw his head bounce, and the man on horseback whooped and dug his heels into his pony and dragged him our way, till he saw us and pulled up.

"Christ," Law said. "You killing all the Indians in the country?"

The other man rode up. "Don't hurt him, Tom. He's got to work the hay."

The man called Tom pulled a rifle out of a saddle sling. He waved it to get the Indian to his feet and kept the gun on him.

"He run off a ranch out east a way there, hay harvest coming up. We come out to rustle up some ranch hands and found him hiding out at one of the rancherias, them Indian nests. This is him, all right. He stole that shirt."

The Indian stood head down, skinned raw on his knees and elbows, breathing hard, his rough, tow linen shirt torn through one shoulder.

"Shoulda seen the trouble they give us at that rancheria," the man with the rifle said to Law. He pointed up east with his chin. "Shot my brother in the foot."

"You didn't need to lose your temper," the other man said. "Why'd you have to cut loose?"

"He knows all about guns now, don't you, buck?" said the man with the rifle. He gave a yank on the lariat that made the Indian hop and totter. "Some escaped down there, where you come from. Didn't you see none? What you see, anyway?" he asked us.

I put my hand on Law's sleeve.

"Nothing so ugly as that," Law said, indicating the Indian. "Where's your ranch?"

"Twenty miles east. Past Coyote Valley."

"How you going to get him there?"

"Walk him." He swung the rifle, and the Indian, caught in the temple, fell in the grass.

I'd never seen a man be so mean to a poor Indian.

"Come on, Tom," said the other man. "We come to get ranch hands. The boss ain't paying us to kill Indians."

"Did you see Ben's foot? He got a arrow in it."

"Let's find him, then. He's riding herd on five of them. We better catch him up before the lake."

He got down, the second man, and stood the Indian up, tied his hands with a handkerchief behind his back, and put the lasso around his neck. The Indian stood quiet, didn't speak or look at anyone. They set off with him coming behind at a slow trot. Every so often he would stumble and be dragged a while, and they cussed and slowed down till he got up, and so they went on till it was just Law and me and the blue sky and hot grass again.

"What did he do?" I said. "I believe he just tried to go home."

"I hope they ain't too many rustlers out here," Law said, "disturbing the peace. They don't think what happens to women and children if the Indians go wild."

14

"What happens to Indian women and children?"

"Why, they take them for labor too."

"Of all the high-handed..."

"Don't get all indignant, Mellie. You heard him say they shot a white man."

"Why so would you, if he came after you."

Law hunched over the reins, and I didn't say any more.

In the morning, we came through firs, the tallest I'd ever seen, and looked out over a big flat. Bright sunburned hills rose to crests of dark trees. To the east, a ridge with a ragged red cut. Far off, a lonesome blue mountain with a rocky saddle.

"Fifth day of June," said Law. "Still green." He bit his pipestem with his hunger for the land. "Ready to see your cabin, Mrs. Pickett?"

What a fool I was to go to nowhere with an optimist. The stillness dried my tongue, but I hoped he would take my silence for awe. We rattled down the slope, startling a herd of antelope through an oak grove that spread along the flat – not twisted hill oaks, but stately, moss-bark trees. It was something beautiful, going under them. The flat ran east, widening along a creek, and around a bend, past a big rock, a raw wood cabin sat up on timbers, as if dropped there out of fright at all the wilderness around. I saw from Law's grinning it was ours. I couldn't help it. I took and sobbed until I made a wet place on the ground. Law's hands came and went, didn't know whether to touch me. At last he gave up and threw his hat down.

"It ain't much, I guess," he said. "Ain't much yet. But the place is ours. Will be, once we prove up on it."

He showed me where the spring ran out of the hill, cupped his hand so I could taste the water, made me climb down among the manzanita to the creek and up, the thistles tearing in my skirt, to where the firs stood dark and solemn, tops stirring in the sky. He kicked at the duff and turned his hat over, curling the brim.

"Oh Law," I said, and pulled his head down where I couldn't see his eyes.

I didn't want us tearing each other up so close, like Mother and Father. I made him show me the cabin. It had a door, a window, pegs for our things. He took the shutter down and said he'd find a piece of glass by winter, get a kitchen built before the rain.

"Meantime, I'll cook under this tree right here," I said. "Likely won't rain until October."

I started a ring of stones for a fire, Law cheered up, and we went to work to unload. The bed and dresser nearly filled the house.

"It'll be right cozy," I said, "come winter."

He stayed three days to plow and put in corn. We rode up to see the neighbors one afternoon, the Brandt boys, about four miles up the valley, through a little pass between two hills. Pepper trees spread out from their big boles, making whole worlds of shade and squirrels.

"They should be looking for us," Law said.

They had a log house with a stone chimney at one end, three glass windows, cooking pots upside down under a tree, but all was still and empty. From the dust on the coffee mugs, they'd been away some time.

"They might be over to the coast," Law said. "Can't be gone long." He picked up a mug and turned it over. "The planting won't wait, Mellie, and we can't do without stock."

"They could let you have some of theirs."

"They're not first rate. I mean to build a fine herd, not hurry things and have them turn up poor. It ain't worth it."

He left me alone and went to look at their little grist mill on the creek. There was no wind, but the sky around me seemed to boom and thunder. I would be alone in the whole valley. My mouth watered, and I vomited as when I was first with child. When Law came again, I was in one piece. He left a note, and we rode back through the resin smell and the humming of cicadas.

Next day, I felt him leave the bed at first light, heard the splash of water in the bucket. Meg stamped in the brush corral, and I went out with letters to my sisters and to Father. Law hugged me to him hard and quick, smelling of spring water. But I found a button on his shirt that ought to be sewn on better, and when that was done, he came to think I'd need more firewood, and by then it was late morning, and he said he'd plow over that one piece so I could put in beans, and go tomorrow.

I lay in bed with him that night, watching him sleep, the only man I had. All the same, tomorrow came, fog tangled in the tops of the tall trees. He brought me the shotgun, saddled Meg, told Joe, the other mule, to take care of me.

"The Brandt boys will be back directly. I don't expect the Indians to trouble you. Digger Indians won't start anything."

17

"Go on, then. They don't worry me."

"Nothing won't hurt you. Look for me in a week, Mellie."

"Two or three weeks, maybe."

He laughed. I let him mount and turn away in the swimming light. He was not unhappy, off to see the world. He waved his hat at the top of the rise. Mother would have begged Father to stay, and when he gave in, laughed at his softness. Father knew how spoiled she was, but he'd hear nothing against her, although he blamed her bitterly himself for leaving him alone, preferring death to pain that terrible hot night in Louisiana. I wept myself sick in the pitiless sun, but only after Law was gone.

୫୨

JUNE 1855
Law

Law walked into a saloon in Santa Catarina. He'd seen only spindling-assed cows that would frustrate any calf with a good head to it, and now he would have to go all the way down to Drake's Bay. It was mostly dairy men down there, but he thought he might do something. Beside him at the bar stood a man who paid for his whiskey out of a pimpled leather wallet he said was ostrich skin.

"Mexican had a horse kick his elbow," he said, "and it swole up three times the size and purple, but the padre prayed it down to nothing in a week."

"Oh, go on," Law said. He was tired, and it hurt him to think of a kicked elbow.

"High time," the man went on, "cause that Mexican was powerful thirsty. Couldn't lift no drink to his lips all week."

Some of the men along the bar laughed. One of them shifted his weight, and Law saw he had a bad leg.

"The padre was on the side of the spirits, I guess," Law said. That got a laugh.

"There was an American up to Kaikitsil got hurt a funny way," the lame man put in. "First settler, friendly with Indians

19

on his ranch. How much work they did, I don't know. He used to pile his wheat in the corral and drive unbroke horses in to thresh it."

"Something for nothing, sure," said the ostrich man. He poured more whiskey all around.

"Well, he did get something," the lame man said, "but not what he wanted. One them horses tried to break out, knocked off the top timber of the gate, hit this man across the mouth and broke his jaw."

"Ain't but so much luck a man can have before something hits him," the ostrich man said. "I bet them Indians was less friendlier than he thought right about then."

"No, sir, you're wrong. They carried him into the cabin."

"And took off. Stole everything, I imagine."

"Nope. Took care of him, fed him, nursed him to recovery."

"Don't you believe it. Sounds good, but it ain't so."

"I met this man, and he swore up and down it was."

The whiskey was yellow in the hanging lamp, in the bright glasses.

"Wasn't nobody there but them and him, to tell it," said the ostrich man. "And he's not around no more, is he."

"He's down to the city now," said the lame man.

"See? Ten dollars says it was them hurt him in the first place."

"Then why'd he let this story get around?" Law said. "Stands to reason he'd be embarrassed, bloodsucked by Indians on his own ranch."

"They don't want to work on no ranch," said another man,

a man with some kind of ticket in his hatband. "Don't want to work."

"Some of them do," the lame man said. "Get a little cash money, a shirt. Real food."

"No telling what they want," the man with the hat said. "Makes me nervous."

"They ain't mean," Law said. "Least I hope not. I'm going in, two three days north of the river."

"You're settling up there?"

"These fellas I know been in a year. Idea is, take up your land, let the Indians alone. Don't rile them up. Ain't that a plan?"

"You're right," said the lame man. "I've been fed by some of them on the road. They're all right. They don't imagine you got any reason to treat them bad."

"Then some of these volunteers go out," said the man with the hat. "Indian hunters. Bounty boys. Then they learn a lesson."

"You got to learn them," said the ostrich man. "They set the grass afire up near our place. We had to punish them. They'll be fixing to roast our cattle next, we don't."

He took his whiskey over to a table to play cards.

"What's that ticket you got?" Law said to the man with the hat.

"Took the train all the way from Baltimore to the Ohio River."

"Don't say."

"Wait'll we get the railroad out here, boy."

21

"Don't hold your breath on it," Law said. He paid up and readied to go, tightened his belt a notch.

"Well, good luck," said the railroad man. "You ain't taking no women up there, are you?"

"Fine place for a woman," Law said, "if you don't act mean to nobody. And I'll tell you something. It never hurt no grass to be burned over."

He tipped his hat and rode on down the valley. By God, he didn't like to leave Mellie on her own, but there was nothing for it. He meant to work his land himself and build a fine herd any man could respect. He wasn't looking for trouble, and he wanted no damnfools coming in to rustle cheap labor and stir up Indians. Still, you can get trouble anywhere, whether you look for it or not. Meantime, Indians might come on the land for grass seed, but they wouldn't bother Mellie. He hurried on down toward where he thought he could buy his cattle.

He was pleased about the abundance of water on his place. In March, when he'd gone through and built the cabin, he'd seen the north valley flooded. Now in June it was still green. Better not plant too low over winter, but the land was first-rate, the more he understood it, for wheat or pasture. Indians didn't know what to do with land. He and Mellie would fill the valley. Big barn on the hill, grain fields all the way south, children on her knee. A pony. Grapevines on the fence. A porch with a swing in it.

Still, he didn't like her being there alone. Not a stubborn woman, exactly, but she wouldn't see some things are best stayed out of. If she'd been a cow, she'd be the one that would think to get across a bog or down a gully for a little grass and never consider the trouble she could get into. He'd have to get a rope and fetch her out. He'd promised her father to take care of her. There was a man, now, her father. That book learning made him think too much, tangle up in everything, and she took after him. If there was a question in the world that ought to be let alone, them two would ask it.

៱

JUNE 1855
Mellie

I built up the fire for coffee and swept out the cabin, and I was getting kindling up under the dry trees when I noticed it had been some time since I'd felt the child move. Something had got at the radish tops in the night, so Law would have to fence. I cut and planted potatoes, the water buckets clanking against my legs and slopping, till noon baked the air to molten stone, and I had to rest, sitting in the shade of the big rock. How long since I'd felt the child? I dreamed back to Mississippi, the black bottom land, the road between white fences deep in dust, pump water splashing on the kitchen stone, and the watery eastern light. And woke with a pang.

"But not for you, Law," I said aloud, for luck.

Ten days gone. He must have had to go below Esmeralda for the herd. Nothing moved. Not the stone mountains, not the black firs on the ridge, not the flat sky, not the child. I was not used to fear and didn't like it.

All across Mexico, my sisters and I had never been afraid. From Matamoros through the swamps and up the mountain tracks, we skirted precipices on our burros' backs, counting the crosses where unwary travelers had plunged to their deaths. In the villages, Father saw anyone who was sick, and we shot marbles with the children and slept sound in adobe huts with the roof poles stuck through. Once I woke with voices arguing in the open door. The night was cold, but no one closed it. In the lamplight, Father crouched in his hammock with a pistol, watching. After we went on in the morning, I remembered the men's cheekbones, the warm colors of the serapes, as the place Father had been afraid.

Now in Oak Valley, I was alone. Where were the Brandt boys? When would they find Law's note and ride over and do something men would call easy and laugh at a woman for not thinking of? I dragged the brush corral closer to the cabin. I wanted to hear Joe breathe. Toward sundown, I stood stroking his rough flanks until he wondered why. I would not be shut up in the cabin till it was worse to see the fir shadows darken down the hill. Then I talked myself inside and read Mother's prayer book, "God be merciful unto us and bless us." If she'd had her way, I'd be in Mississippi still, with the heat haze on the fields and the smell of horses under the trees and war coming. That's what the papers said in San Francisco.

We had never been afraid, even on the ship from Mazatlan, when a storm damaged our rudder, and we drifted, low on water. Many were sick with cholera. Father forbade drinking out of barrels, made us catch rainwater streaming off the sails. Every morning there were one or two dead under a blanket, if someone had thought to pull one over them. Nannie and Bessie and I competed to recognize the narrow nose and slack skin that told of coming death.

"No test with cholera," Father said. "Too easy."

I was afraid now, always, and knew not why. On my way back from the field one day, a rattlesnake crossed my path, going swift and smooth, raised up knee high, a yard long and speckled in diamonds. I went on to the cabin, shot through with lightning, and set the gun in a corner close to hand, happy to know at last what to be afraid of. I would wake in the mornings free of fear, only to slide into it again like a seed under a furrow. Twelve days. If I counted to my age, eighteen, the child would have to move. Or twice eighteen. Or eighty-one. But it did not move. I mounted Joe, an awkward business in the shape I was, and rode up the valley to the Brandt boys, but their cabin was still empty, Law's note under a saucepan on the table outside: *My wife at ranch below for your help Pickett.* I'd ridden four miles in the heat to see a couple of missing bachelors about a baby. Might as well laugh. The child was dead in me, I reckoned.

Riding back, I saw movement far out in the savanna, a little line of figures going east. Women, maybe, with burdens. Smaller ones taking little running steps. Children, and I had none, hardly the hope of one. Alone in the cabin, I took a glass of whiskey to steady my nerves. Horrible stuff. And another. After dark, I heard little footsteps coming downhill, rustling in the grass like lost children or rats' feet, and clapped the pillow over my ears, but they came on still. I scrambled for the shotgun, set the barrels on the sill, and fired. Joe screamed. I heard a slump of bones and reeled back on the bed, plunged into nightmare. A hanged man swung and stared, tongue wrenched out, blackening. Padre Rafael washed his bare hands in the creek, shaking his head. No fish, no fish. I lay on my back in a cornfield, flailing with no legs or arms, calling with no voice for help, until Dacey stood above me, stern as daylight. "Enough, Miss Mellie. You ain't going to pieces here alone."

I stumbled to the window, like a corpse raised up in a coffin, threw up the whiskey, and went out to wash in the bucket. God, what a fool I was. I'd shot my mule. The firs stood tall against the splash of a million stars flowing westward, and something whickered from the corral. Alive? He must be down, terribly wounded. I felt my way toward him, stumbling over a dark form in the starlight this side of the brush fence, smooth-coated and small, a doe with round ears and open eyes already clouded. I had shot her? Across the fence, Joe's breath wondered over me, alive as ever. The ridge loomed black against the stars. I heard the owl, and the coyote barking. The resinous night came to me, dry and tart, the real smell of the place, no breath of nightmare.

"All right," I said to the child, if child there was. "Die if you must. I'm going ahead. You come along if you can."

In the morning I got the skin off the dead doe, buried the head and offal, and layered the meat in salt. I laid the hide over a rock the way Joaquín showed me at the Mission, scraping the stringy fat with the flat edge of the knife, thinking I could make water bags like his, hoping the work might scare up movement from the child. If it was dead, how long would it stay in me? How would it come? I dropped my knife and looked for Joe. I was sick of beans and soft potatoes. I wanted company, and I wasn't particular. Law expected me to stay put and keep the shotgun handy, but if the fear came back, how could I answer for myself?

The hills hunched like big cats as we rode, their tawny hides creased with swales. A skunk trundled along the creek bank, not the least bothered by Joe and me. Quail scuttled at the edges of the chapparal, their head feathers like blue question marks, and the creek trickled among stones, licking gravel edges under dark trees.

A few miles out, I smelled smoke. Around a bend, where the creek spread onto a wide gravel beach, we scared a flock of children out of the water, little ones two and three and four, with blue-black hair cut off above the eyes. They fled down the pebbles to a cook fire, to a woman, naked above a fibre skirt except for beads, and big with child, bigger than I. A little one backing away from us bumped its head on her belly. The woman looked at me grave and alert, like a fox met in the wild. It was I who looked away.

"*Hilleu ma tanin*," I called, the greeting Francisca taught me.

I slipped off Joe and slapped him into the shade.

"Yes," she called. "No."

Oh, I was disappointed. I'd been hoping they'd be wild. I came to the edge of the bank and sat, a stone's throw away.

"They play like ducks," I said.

She shushed a child and turned her head, listening.

"*Aki, aki*," I said. "Ducks. *Chu weyusha*, I am glad."

She crossed the cobbles to a brush shelter, the littlest children running along, holding to her skirt. They hovered behind each other, peeping out at me, while she ducked under the thatch, and I thought how a child's skin smells in the sun. She sent something to me by the biggest boy, teetering over the grass, naked but for white beads about his wrist. A small girl started to follow him, stopped, and hopped on one foot. He dropped his burden just beyond my reach and ran. The mother laughed. I caught it before it spilled, a little patterned basket full of water.

"Drink," she said.

At Santiago they made baskets of rough sticks, those who remembered how, but this was smooth and tight, a shallow, pleasing, bowl-shaped thing, patterned dark and light. The water tasted good, like my own spring, but nothing here was mine, and when I thought this, the tears came. She started toward me and led me to the lodge's shade, her brown breasts tattooed with leaves and branches, caught among shell necklaces. I shook off my weeping, and she brought dried meat and mush and a cool soup of berries.

"Eat," she said.

She should not have been beautiful, with her great belly and dark skin, but I thought so. I was sorry about my fingernails, bitten and filthy, but there was no help for it. The children sat on their heels to watch me, heads to one side. She cut tubers into a great basket, fishing red-hot stones out of the fire with long wooden spoons and dropping them in, so the basket bubbled, boiling. Worn out, I leaned against the thatch and fell asleep.

In my dream, Law insisted I was tall. He had to raise the roof because of it. I held a little basket curiously adorned with feathers. I had made it myself, but it was very heavy. Somebody rolled over next to me, and I surfaced out of sleep. A little heel or elbow fluttered, and I waited, wondering had I dreamed it, but it came again. The child. The child lived. I held my belly in my hands like a bunch of wild flowers.

When I sat up, the camp swarmed with squaws, yellow-gray and dark as blacks, half naked but for odd articles of men's clothing, shirts and hats. One creature shrugged off a load of sticks to greet a child that toddled toward her. One suckled a baby bound in a cradle basket up to the chin. Seeing me awake, they pointed and chattered. An old woman touched my shoe, showing teeth outlandish white in her wrinkled face. I was sitting on the ground with savages and wanted to be gone. I found my woman washing a child's bottom in the creek and gave her my handkerchief, a useless lace thing of Mother's, not very dirty. She smiled to feel her own fingers through the lace.

"Yes," she said.

Joe waited where the creek rushed loud under willows, and blackberry canes abounded with roses and green fruit. We cantered out to the wide flat among the mountains. That Indian boy had no backward look. That was a likely boy.

"I will call you Rose," I said to my child. "You will smell sweet in the sun and know where blackberries grow and run in and out of water like an Indian child. We'll have grapes on the fence, a pony. Father will come to visit and ride you on his shoulders."

Mother was dead. She would never know Rose. Impossible, anyway, to imagine her old enough to be a grandmother. Or sweet enough, either.

ॐ

JUNE 1855

Sam

When he saw the note, Sam wanted to go right over and find
the lady. Jakob was in one of his slow, silent spells. First he had
to pick a bunch of spinach and wrap it in a cloth. By the time
they came around the big rock at Law Pickett's place, it was late
afternoon. She flew out the door, a little thin thing with a big
belly, took one look and plopped down on the stoop. Sam knew
he should talk easy.

"Morning, Ma'am," he said. "You'll be Law's wife."

Jakob dismounted and gave her the greens.

"He's Jakob," Sam said. "I'm Sam. A person gets tired of
sauerkraut, don't they, ma'am?"

"We looked for you," she said.

"We been over to the coast to see about shipping meat to
San Francisco. Nothing doing, neither. Steep ravines every trail
we tried, and hell to pay when we got back, coyotes worrying
the calves."

"I heard you coming," she said, "and tried to make you into
Law."

Sam thought to keep talking, give her a chance to cheer up.
Pretty gal.

"He's built you a nice cabin here, right smart frame. Redwood goes gray, you know, over winter. You'll want a stove, but he'll bring you one, I shouldn't wonder."

"He's fetching stock."

"Next time, then."

"Don't wear her out, Sam," Jakob said. "She don't want to think about a next time."

Sam got down from the saddle, and turned his horse in to the corral, with Jakob's. She must have wants.

"What do you need, ma'am? You need anything?"

"I need to know when the rains come."

"About November. You can put your wheat in then. Winter's not hard, not if you ever been up to Wisconsin."

He saw she had plenty of wood. Jakob brought water, and she asked them in. Sam wished he'd had time to clean up. Her breasts were bigger than apples, not as big as melons. About like a good-sized turnip. Been a long time since Sam had seen a white woman. He made to brush against her going through, but she backed out of the way. It was only the one room with a bed and dresser and a quilt she was piecing.

"That's nice," Jakob said.

"Just a nine-patch."

"Grandma made me one like that with a bit of red in it. She said boys like red, and I guess they do."

"Mine is a girl," she said. "I don't know how I know."

Sam was no fool for woman stuff, so he went out. Jakob came after, and she gave them coffee, let them have the chairs while she sat on a log. She was in a sad case for bread, her potatoes too old for salt rising. She admitted to frying bannocks in a skillet.

"Dear Lord," Sam said, "you do need help. Folks around here use sourdough."

"By folks," she said, "I guess you mean Jakob."

Jakob grinned at that, like he would. Sam saw the sun was sliding toward the hill, the hawks settling.

"How long you say your man's been gone?" he said.

"Two weeks and some."

"You could stay with us till he gets back. Bring your mule. We got a rooster for you."

She could cook, probably. Make a change from Jakob. But she shook her head.

"Don't you want to? That's a long time for a gal to be alone."

"I'm all right," she said. "Thank you. You'll be needing to get home."

Sam nodded toward the corral and Jakob went to bring the horses up.

"No coyote's coming after a big barrel-back mule," Sam told the gal. "When you have lambs, you can fret then about coyotes. The land's good, and the Indians well disposed. Ain't it so, Jakob?"

"It is," Jakob said, looping his reins.

"About the Indians," the little gal said, her stomach near as big as she was, "how do they get their English?"

It worried Sam to think she'd been talking to Indians. "They come around here?" he said. He mounted and looked at Jakob.

"I rode down the creek, " she said.

"They trade a little at the coast towns," Jakob said.

"I wouldn't ride around," Sam said. "Not just anywhere."

"You're safe enough," said Jakob.

"I wouldn't say safe, Jakob."

"I do say it, Sam. Don't worry her for nothing."

Sam's horse danced backward so he had to scold him quiet. He wished his brother would let him handle this. "They're good Indians, but they're Indians, Jakob."

"What should I worry about?" she said, looking up at them.

"If you're mean," said Jakob, "that's the only thing could get you in trouble."

"What kind of trouble would it be?"

"There was a killing at Clear Lake," Sam told her. "Indians turned on a couple of men."

"Two of the meanest sons of bitches ever starved a poor Indian," Jakob said.

"You can't look at it like that," Sam said. "The squaw poured water down their gun barrels. That's treachery."

Jakob circled his horse and it let go a big pat in her yard. "Just shows she knew how to act human."

"Don't talk like a damn fool," Sam said. "You can't have Indians killing whites."

"You will, so long as whites kill Indians."

"Who's killing Indians?" she said.

"Now talk serious," Sam said to Jakob. "You can't let it happen. That's why the army had to go up there."

"And massacre so many? I suppose that made peace in the country."

34

"You going to clean up that horseshit, Jakob, or let Ms. Pickett do it?"

"Don't trouble about that," she said. Sam wished he could get a feel of that belly. It was huge. She pulled a couple of homemade leather bags off the fence and hung them over her mule. "I've got to water my fruit trees."

"That'll stretch all out," Sam said. "You'd do better to take the wagon down and fill your barrel."

"I walk my mule in the creek and fill them, and he carries to the field."

Sam kicked his horse into a walk.

"Darnedest idea," he said, low, to Jakob. "Take a woman to think of it."

"I dare say it answers."

"We'll be back with a cow," Sam called. "For the little fella. Not before Thursday."

"Oh. Thank you. What day is it today?"

"Tuesday."

She'd lost track of the day of the week. By God, somebody ought to be taking care of her.

ॐ

JUNE 1855

Mellie

Toward mid-morning of a hot day after I'd stopped counting, Joe and I were bringing the water bags dripping to the beans when he balked and laid his ears back. I looked for something in the field, maybe a snake, but there was nothing, only dust rising over the dry track to the south. Dust and no wind. Then came a little thunder in the ground, so I began to guess at it, and then they poured around the black rock and barreled to the water, handsome red and white cows with Law behind them in a new hat with a silver buckle. He caught me up to his saddle, skirts all gone to glory. He was glued to his clothes with sweat, bristle-faced, sour with chewed tobacco. I made him get down in the creek and wash. He wanted me to scrub him here, there, everywhere, tugged me in, ducked and kissed me till I splashed a storm at him and made the bank.

"Do I know you?" I said.

I could not abide to be so in love with him when he could come and go just as he pleased.

"Ho, Mellie. Do you?"

"A man left out of here, said he'd be gone a week. I thought he was no liar."

"And got what he went for." Law scrubbed up his armpits. "A dozen three-year-olds with calves, seven heifers to breed next year, and six cows bred and settled over winter."

"Couldn't be three weeks," I said. "Couldn't be more than nine ten days. Oh no."

"Did you miss me, Mellie? Wait'll you hear what I had to do to get them. Gol, you're big, girl." He waded toward me, waist deep, naked but for his hat. "Cut it out, now. Don't get my hat wet, or I'll skin you."

"Where you been, Law? Down to the city for the bright lights?"

"Why, I'd no mind for anything but stock. Nothing doing in Santa Catarina, nor Esmeralda either."

"Yes, I noticed how nobody has stock in the whole country."

"Not good enough for us, though, Mel. We're going to build us a real herd. Don't want some narrow cow won't slip a square-built calf. All right, Sharper."

All this while, a black and white collie stood on the bank watching the stock water. Now he went down and drank.

"Good as a man," Law said. "I found a sea farm, Mellie, along the ocean fog. Scotch fella with a beautiful herd. Didn't want to sell me a dog, let alone a cow, till he knew I wasn't going in anywhere near him. 'Used to be a man could ride all day and never a fence,' he said, 'and now it's all you young fellas.' Five dollars a head he started, would have ate me alive." Law called to his dog, "Go on, Sharper."

The dog turned the cattle out up hill and lay with his nose down, watching.

37

"I had to make a show of taking myself off, and then he allowed he could do business. Three dollars and six bits each, with calves. Don't they have nice, broad faces, though?"

He came out of the water stark naked, wet and affectionate, made to dance with me and kissed me everywhere.

"You're different," I said, for there was a taste of the road about him.

"And you're the same, sweetheart, only better," he said, kissing me and more than kissing.

"Law," I said. "Right out in daylight?"

"Gather round, everybody."

He made me laugh, pulled me down on the creek bank. Oh God, the feel of him.

When we'd got reacquainted and he'd put his pants back on, he was solemn struck with how I'd got ahead, fruit trees turning their leaves in the little breeze, corn showing green, deer meat down in salt. He petted Joe a long time for taking care of me. Then he whistled up his dog and went to work, felled a young redwood and broke out posts for fence. In the evening firelight he carved a scythe handle out of oak, smoothing the white wood where he meant to dovetail in a grip, watching whether I liked it. He was a whirlwind. I near burst with pride at him that day.

"I met a couple of bucks on the road down," he told me. "They let me have some venison, but you want to give them a berth. They ain't like us. They'll have two squaws sometimes."

It was true, Indians were different. In Santiago, a squaw would go down to the beach and couple with sailors, come back with money enough to get drunk and sleep in the street. An Indian could get killed for nothing. Once, on a dare, a white man stabbed an Indian's pony, and the Indian turned and killed him with a knife. Got hanged the same day. "Everybody righteous as hell about it," Father said. Francisca of course was Indian, but not so as you'd notice, the tattoos down her chin more faded than wild-looking. Though when the Padre died she tarred her head and shrieked in the field four days. After I married Law, and he went up on the Russian River to strip tanbark, it was only me and Francisca. I went on chopping wood with the rain dripping down the tiles and the Padre's sad old dog for company. I missed Law in the bed at night, what he did then, what I let him do. Francisca made me play guessing games, gambling games, and when spring came, and a sickness in the mornings made me gag, she boiled tea from herbs she hunted on the hills, roots of blue-eyed grass and *yerba buena,* which brought sleep. She tempted me with clover, miners' lettuce, shoots of columbine and milkweed, mushrooms sprinkled with dried seaweed, tart. She taught me to say *chu weyusha,* I am glad.

But Law had the fear put into him coming across from Missouri, the fear the whole country was sick with, though he never met an Indian on the plains, only a couple of old men wanting blankets.

I meant to tell him I'd seen Indians, but I didn't seem to find the time to do it.

ॐ

AUGUST 1855

Mellie

Come late summer, the gold sinking out of the hills, I didn't
know how I could get any bigger. Sam wanted Law to haul lumber from the sawmill at the coast. That was near fifty miles,
some of it steep and the road not good. Law said he wouldn't
go, with my time near. Told me Sam had ten ideas a week, and
he'd catch one of the later ones.

I was at the fire one morning, warming milk for clabber
cheese, when I heard a cracking from the hill above the house.
They were beating the oak trees with sticks, women mostly. They
would gather around a tree and sing a little, whack it with sticks,
and turn their backs against the rain of nuts. Children climbed
up and shook the branches, fell down, laughed, and chased
each other, pounced on acorns in the grass. I stirred the milk,
tested it with a finger, poured it into a flat pan, set it on an up-
turned bucket in the sun. They were watching me, of course, as
I watched them. Law had gone to look over his stock in the
south valley. I could not resist. I picked a bowl of blackberries
and climbed the hill, and they watched, square-faced, dark and
short, outlandish in their broad, bare feet and bits of clothing,
never the right size. Wisps of summer-baked straw clung to their

hair where they'd lain on the ground or scrabbled for acorns. The woman I knew was among them, slim now, with an infant on her back. I gave her the bowl and caught my breath.

"Berries," I said. "Blackberries."

All gathered to eat as though I'd brought something special, though blackberries grew everywhere in the country. The children's fingers turned purple. The woman swung the cradle off to show the little one, round-cheeked and tiny, safely born. The baby stirred, opened deep eyes black as the fruit, and the mother loosened its ties and took away the soiled moss between its legs. A girl.

"Pretty baby," I said.

"Baby," the woman repeated. "Pretty baby," her voice uncertain over the P and T. She fed her child at her breast, tattooed with leaves. I had never shown my breast to anyone. When I reached for some of the fruit, she stopped me with a hand on my wrist, put the bowl behind her back, made ugly faces.

"No," she said, laying a hand on my belly. "Pretty baby."

Did she imagine the berries would spoil the looks of my child? I reached for the fruit, laughing, insisting, but she was in earnest and would not let me eat.

I slid off acorn caps with the children, finding them curious but unafraid, as though I had been a strange aunt come from away. We tossed the nuts into a basket near a white-eyed, blind old man who used his amazing good teeth to bite off any caps that stuck. The woman sat by me and asked the names not for the things but for what we did, lifting her chin. "Toss," "bite," "slide." When a very small child tripped on a root and cried, she comforted it, her face a perfect mirror of the small surprise and sorrow.

Someone unearthed a quantity of worms at the roots of a big tree. An old woman shook them in a basket to remove the dirt, and all fell on them with relish, crunching and sucking their teeth. My stomach turned, but before I left, I wanted that woman's name.

"Mellie," I said, pointing to myself. "What are you called?"

She didn't understand the simplest thing.

"Mellie," I repeated, gesturing. "Who are you?"

Everyone said their intelligence was low. I showed her things. "Tree. Basket. Acorn. Baby." I pointed to myself, "Mellie" and then to her.

She took my meaning, and she did not like it. She drew herself up, her tattoo of leaves and branches rippling. I went hot. Why had I sunk to sitting in the dirt with Digger Indians? They ate worms and bitter acorns and bound their babies in cruel baskets. I must get back to my clabber milk, lest leaves blow in or anything upset it. I turned and went right down the hill. Only the steepness of the slope kept me from running. I tripped and heard their laughter.

They stayed all morning. When Law rode in, I went out to meet him, and by that time they were gone.

"The grass is pretty well dried up," he said, "but it still makes good feed. The two-year-olds have got their weight up good. What's the matter?"

"Some Indians came after acorns on the hill. I went up to look."

"What you do that for?"

"Curiosity got the best of me."

He swung out of the saddle, and I walked along with him to the corral.

"No reason to think they'll do us any harm," he said, "but why test it?"

"The children heartened me for what's to come."

"They ain't fit companions, Mellie. They don't build nothing. Eat grass like beasts."

"Not like beasts. They roast the seed."

He pulled the saddle off and slung it on the fence.

"Don't take me up so, Mellie. It's the same with snakes or bears or wasps. You don't want to bother them."

He began to rub Joe down, making big circles on the flank, and I thought of all that wriggling.

"Oh Law," I said. "They eat worms."

"I know it. What did I tell you? How you going to be friendly with that?"

ॐ

Law

Law noticed the Indian women taking acorns on the hills, coming early and leaving before the heat. He didn't begrudge the acorns. Let them go. He wouldn't need them till he had hogs. Indians were the least of his worries.

"If talk is work," he told Mellie at breakfast out under the oak tree, "Sam works as hard as Jakob or I do. He has a list of jobs for me long as your arm. He pays fair, though."

"Just do what you can," she said.

Another thing, he was still sore about the big ranchers down below, the way they tried to show him how small he was.

"I don't like how they think," he told Mellie. "Keep the range open or get your hands on it. If I did like them, I'd get hold of every spring in the valley and make the newcomers pay for water."

"Then your land would be worth more than you."

A high-minded wife was good for a man, Law believed. Keep him going the right way.

"Haven't told you the worst, Mellie. I put everything on the stock. We don't have much hay. If we need feed, we can't pay for it."

She dried her hands on a red cloth she kept hanging from a branch. "We'll get through the best we can. They're good cattle, Law. You've done right. Maybe it won't snow deep."

On his way up to where he was building a smokehouse, Law noticed a squaw woman on the creek bank, where Mellie went with her water bags. Tan-oak leaves curled up brittle and crunched underfoot. While he nailed shingle on the roof, he watched her fill in the skeleton of a basket, weaving onto a circle of fibers wide as an armspan, with a reed she straightened through her teeth.

"Who is she?" he said, when he went down for Mellie to give him coffee.

"I don't know her name."

"What does she want? Did you speak to her?"

"I thought you wouldn't like me to."

"I wouldn't."

She reached for a knife to peel potatoes. "Well, I didn't."

Law saw where down at the creek the squaw strapped a cradle basket on her back, collected her reeds, and started off.

"Find out what she wants," he said, "if she comes back. Get her to put on clothes before she comes around here again."

AUGUST 1855

Mellie

The next time I saw her come near the creek, I picked up a shirt of Law's I was mending and went out. Wind stirred the tall grass, everything very dry, a little herd of deer grazing.

"Don't look at me," I told them. "I'm not letting you at my turnip tops."

She sat under a tree, weaving, her baby near.

"Man?" she said.

"Up the ridge. Not home."

I wondered if I should have let her know I was alone, but could conceive no fear of her. What she was making with her hands was fine. The laurel tree, that we called pepperwood, swept the ground, making a fragrant shelter for the birds and squirrels when the red hawks flew over from the tall firs. *Bahé* she called it. I had a time sitting down, big as I was. The blue jay cocked his head, cheerful and safe with us. Black-capped sparrows hopped and mated through the grass. I played smiling games with her little one to see the fresh light come into the black eyes. We swapped words: "hop" and "sit" and "fly," "tree," "sky," "mouth" and "milk," "acorn". When a cramp came across the top of my belly, she showed me how to rub it out.

Back in Mississippi, long ago, Father was curious about Indians and thought they knew a deal of medicine. Mother had no use for his enthusiasms. She hated the northern ways he'd learned at Philadelphia. Why must he whitewash the slave cabins against cholera, talk of free labor, write letters to the newspapers? "Slavery's doomed, my dear," he would insist, "but not soon enough to spare my children." He was denounced from the pulpit and threatened in the road. He thought he would go on to Texas. She had never wished to be anywhere but Bracken, but when he went down with fever the second time, she must have seen she stood to lose him. She let him sell up and go West.

"I mislike taking Dacey into New Orleans," she said. "Her son Bert was sold away down there. It's the only thing she's ever held against us."

"Dacey stays," Father told her. "I'll keep no more slaves."

"Only a hard man," she told us girls, "would drag a woman to a wilderness and take all comfort from her."

Why did I never take her part? In the end, Mother made Father hire Dacey for a dollar a day, so she came with us, and Mother flourished at New Orleans among the music and the books and talk. But when she saw Father meant to go on into Texas, she grew desperate. He warned her of the woodchuck holes, but though she was with child, she galloped along the river, reckless, threading the line of trees, head down, ducking the branches. I saw it, standing in my pinafore by the fence. There was a halt in Ragner's stride, only a little, but she pitched forward, and the big red horse stumbled over her. She flailed

47

one wild arm before Father reached her. He carried her to the dooryard, where she flung loose, staggered to the gallery, and crawled upstairs, gripping the balusters one by one, rings clicking on the wood. The fall had twisted something inside and started the child coming too hard, too soon.

Now in Oak Valley the Indian woman touched my shoulder. I ceased daydreaming, and we got up and gathered our things among the dry, glossy leaves of the sheltering tree, the tree she called *bahé*.

"I'll call you Bahé," I said, of a sudden.

She looked pleased. That was all right, then. I don't know what got into me. I gave her that shirt of Law's.

ॐ

SEPTEMBER 1855

Law

Law was hammering siding onto the smokehouse, spacing to save nails, when Mellie happened along in her apron and looked up the ladder at him.

"They know how to birth children, Law."

"Reckon so?" he said, nails between his lips.

She had a rash on her face, and her belly all blown up. He hung his hammer on a rung, got down and wiped his face with his shirtsleeves.

"You won't be alone," he said. "I've birthed calves in my time."

"I'd a little rather have a woman by."

He didn't like to cross her, being delicate, but what else could he do?

"Haven't I said you don't never want to depend on no Indians?"

She looked at him like a mule not planning on cooperation. "Why wouldn't I want a woman by?"

"These squaws won't know nothing more than an animal."

"I guess I'm animal. I guess you think so if you talk of birthing calves."

"You ain't no animal, if you *are* burned black as an Indian."
He squinted at her, thinking to make her laugh. "Darned if I
ever thought my wife would look like a fat Digger squaw."

She balled her apron up and threw it at him.

"Here I've been," she said, "feeling sorry to be mad at you,"
and marched back to her fire.

He grabbed her wrist and wrestled her against a tree, playing she was so strong he could barely move her and so big he
could hardly get his arms around her. He went to kiss her, but
she got away and grabbed the kettle off the fire, sloshing the
boiling water all around, some of it on the coffee.

"Don't take on, Mellie. Now don't. I don't mean nothing by
it. Course you're white as anything."

"Regular boy in church," she said, "the way you're laughing."

"I'm sorry. Now Mellie, I am," he said, still laughing but
sorry now.

She pulled the beans off the fire and slammed eggs into the
skillet. Scraped her knuckles grating the squash in, he could
see the blood.

"They're strange to you," she said.

"Well, they *are* strange, Mellie. You know it yourself."

"And that's the way you like it." She raked the eggs with a
spoon. "This baby here's a girl, I know, and girls are stronger,
but it might be a slim chance for a child in the wilderness with
just a man."

That night he woke with her shivering in the bed. He
touched her, and she sat up screaming.

50

"In case I die..."

"You won't," he said. He tried to take her in his arms.

"...or go out of my mind... "

"You're not going that way."

He sat her up and put the pillow behind her. The night was black, only starlight leaking through the trees.

"Oh, Law, the head stuck, coming out."

"Wake up. It was a dream."

"No. Doña Inez. In Santiago. She screamed." Mellie's fingernails dug at his wrists.

"What happened? Tell."

"Her belly mounded all up. Father sent us for hot water and wrung cloths in it and put them on her. She sounded like Tabby when the tom got at her. Nanny said, '*I'll* never make a noise like that.' 'Don't be too sure,' said Father. 'Wait till she sings her other song.' He sent us for a knife and string, and when we came back, the baby was there, heaped red and sticky. 'Tie the cord in two places,' Father said, 'cut between, and wait for the flat pudding to come out.'"

"All right," Law said.

"But a lot comes before."

"What else? Tell me all you know."

"You lose your water."

"Water?"

"I don't know. It's a sign. Did Father say anything to you?"

"That about the cord, the same. Don't be scared of noise, he said. When she bears down, press below the opening. He asked me did I faint at blood. I told him I'd got weak with that

51

axe cut, and he said, sit down, then. That's no time for her to be worrying about you."

"Listen," Mellie said, her voice calm of a sudden in the dark. "Take care of the child."

"Now Mellie, don't."

"Take care of her."

"I'll get the doctor at Kaikitsil. It ain't but twenty-five miles."

"No. Don't leave me."

"I'll get Sam Brandt. Jakob can ride for the doctor."

"There won't be time."

ℬ

SEPTEMBER 1855
Mellie

Law fell asleep after dinner by the fire. I was washing up pots under the oak tree, thinking he'd have to take the mules up the valley in the morning to new grass, when I felt the burst of water down my leg and walked away from the firelight to steady myself. The dark stirred, and the black animals in the corral loomed like holes in the starlight. I went in the cabin and lit the lantern, and a pain stopped me. Then it was over and not too bad. I got cloths and a kettle and came out to finish the washing, and then had to stand still and gasp. Law woke and stared.

"Mellie? Can you hear me?"

Yes, I nodded, panting with the ache of it.

"I'll get Sam."

"No. Stay here."

Then I was all right, waiting. I soaped the skillet but had to leave it, couldn't help groaning.

Law gripped my hands, looking ten years old. "That woman. I'd better get that woman. What do you call her?"

"Bahé? Down by the..."

"I know where. Stay, Sharper."

He left me leaning on a chair and ran for Joe. Nothing I could do but try to float and not go under. In between, I finished washing up. Then it came again, strong, and I did go under. I tried to think of my child. I would see her at last. I could go under and come out again, only the waves built up rough, like a storm at sea.

I held to a tree through the next wave and the next, until Law came out of the darkness and Bahé soon after. The night was cool, and she wore clothes. She touched my knee, leaned her cradle basket against a tree, piled straw and made up the fire, reasonable and calm. Law took a blanket and went up to the fir grove with his dog.

When the labor came on, she kneaded my back and legs. In the quiet times, she put stones in the fire, and we watched her baby sleeping, head sweet on one side, how she woke and nursed and slept again. When the pains came dark and difficult, Bahé boiled an herb drink, bitter strong. She made me look at her, sang patterns for my breath, made me take breath for breath with her. I dozed between waves, and she waked me, ready for the next, made me get up and walk, and this steadied me. Deep in the night, when I lay too heavy with cramp to rise, she wrapped hot stones in wet skins and pressed them to my belly, loosening the pain. I held to her eyes, breathed to her breath. Dawn broke, and Law came down, pale and suffering.

"I guess I'd better milk," he said.

"Good," I said. "Go on and take the mules up the valley. I'm all right."

But new pains came, stronger, higher, and I went staggering up them and vomited and knew I would die and did not care. Bahé changed her song. The power came in cross-waves, and I sank exhausted in thick sleep within the troughs, only to be thrown up, fighting toward her face that was so like and not like faces I had known.

"*Ha é, Ha é,*" she sang.

When I could do no more, she made me squat and pull her wrists, called to me, gave strength with her eyes. Her face was the face of an angel. The only face. I pulled, rolled up over the big mass of belly and bore down, needing to, feeling better for it. Bahé pulled back with a new, quick song, and the core gathered and tore out of me, the sick pain gone. Seized and taken beyond anything, I bore down, shouting, and in a rush like a horserace the baby was there.

Oh, the wonder! Bahé tucked him into my arm, a little son, not Rose at all. But oh, he was perfect! He had all his tiny parts. He sucked a little and looked around at everything. The afterbirth sickened me a moment, then Bahé took it away. A burst of char at the fire, and it was gone. She made me walk trembling to the creek and wash myself and the little boy. The rising sun came through the fog in streams, the hills sliding between white and gold as the veils lifted and the water smoked, warmer than air.

Law met us on the way back, shivering, for he hadn't thought of clothes. He was so pleased with his son, his hands and knees, his black hair and little ears. Bahé wrapped us and put us to bed. She brought grits and berries and fed me with her own fingers. Law lay down beside us, and the little boy gazed long at him.

"Looks like he knows me," Law said.

We called him Matthew, after Father, and were close and comfortable, and then I must have slept, for I woke missing someone.

"Matthew?"

"Here," Law said.

"Bahe?"

"Told her to git."

"You never."

"Went up to cut firewood, and when I came back she was steaming the baby."

"Law! She wouldn't hurt him."

"Had a pit of hot stones covered thick with leaves and was laying him in it." He was laughing fit to kill. "I may not be much of a hand with babies, Mellie, but I do know not to cook 'em."

ॐ

OCTOBER 1855

Law

Law got Jakob Brandt to help him kill his bull calves when the
weather cooled. He reckoned he could get a good price for
jerked beef at the lumber camps. He and Jakob hung three car-
casses from poles between oak trees, laid two others over saw-
horses, and hunked off the meat. Mellie walked down to the
willow shelters.

"Get away from all this death," she said. "Find Bahé. Show
her the baby."

It embarrassed Law to have Jakob know Mellie was so taken
with a squaw woman.

"The dern squaw," he told Jakob, "sang one song till it was
all wore out."

"Oh well," Jakob said, "that's the way of it." He went on
butchering.

Mellie came back too soon. "Gone," she said. "Nothing but
black patches on the ground and the creek trickling. I worry
they've been burned out."

"They'll be up the ridge, I guess, already," Jakob said. "They
go up for the acorn dance and stay till spring. They fire the
summer place to keep down vermin."

"How many songs they got?" Law said, "if you know so much. Just the one? Not to mention I had to stop her roasting the baby."

"Law," Mellie said. "I'd like to give her something."

"I thought the less we had to do with them, the better."

She set her feet wide, rocking the baby. "Don't we pay our debts?"

"That acorn dance," Jakob said. "In a few weeks now. You don't want to miss that."

Law was surrounded. He went on cutting meat away from the ribs.

"Take her a loin strip, then. I'll go with you when you're fit."

Mellie took a knife and went to work cutting meat, while Jakob got on with burying the guts.

"It's something," he said, "that acorn dance." He drove his shovel. "Big drum, cloaks all of feathers, songs."

Law picked up the whetstone and ran his knife edge back and forth.

"They got a dance house up there big enough for hundreds," Jakob said. "Course they ain't got hundreds anymore."

Law tested Mellie's knife, touched it up on the stone.

"They'll feed you," Jakob said. "Plenty of meat. The cider ain't bad either."

Who asked you? Law thought. "Look here, Mellie, you don't want to do nothing without a sharp knife."

"Anyhow." Jakob leaned on his shovel and knocked his hat back. "This hole deep enough, Law, you reckon?"

That was a good deal of meat. Mellie cut strips, soaked them in brine, and strung them to hang in the smoke. Law fired up with too much manzanita, crackling and flaring with resin, and the whole smokehouse like to have gone if he hadn't made to rake some of the brush out, Mellie yelling at him and his eyebrows near to scorched off. The barley made a little patchy with short heads, but all right, and they worked to scythe and shock it and thresh it out, him flailing and her flailing, till they got a stock to put with the little wheat flour they had, so they were sure of the winter.

One morning that same week, Law saw salmon rushing upstream through the shallows of the east branch, big fellas ten and twelve pounds. He came home for his tackle, but they wouldn't take a hook, so he got a pitchfork and speared them out that way. Mellie came along and did the same with a hay rake, in between nursing Matthew. She took off her skirt, made it into a sack to carry fish, and went home in her petticoat.

Next day, they took a look at the south fork, and came on a party of Indians camped across the water by a fish dam. They'd sunk poles and woven withes through the flood, maybe twenty feet wide here. The weir led most of the fish angling into holding tanks built close to the far bank, with one side left open where fish could go on upstream. Boys stood knee-deep, scooping them out, and there were plenty. Two big piles, knee high. The women cleaned and split the fish and laid them on racks over fires, while the men smoked in the shade. Except one big fellow went back and forth, captaining the catch to one pile or another. Sometimes he dropped a fish on a smaller third pile. He picked two big silver salmon from the holding tank and waded across above the weir, splashed out of the stream, naked but for a little leather around his hips, and held the fish out to Mellie. She stood back a little, but he looked her in the eye.

"*Dika-sha,*" he said. "Eat."

He signalled Law to come with him and take from the holding tank. Law waded over and got a couple of fish. The captain offered more, but Law misliked taking too many. He didn't want to be owing anybody. He went on back to Mellie.

"We'll do them a turn someday," she said, settling down to clean.

"They ain't going to be here long," he said.

"Why not?"

"Why, because we're coming in."

From the far bank a delicious smell rose off the cooking fires. She laughed.

"What you laughing at, woman?"

"Plenty of room for us and them. Look at the size of the country."

Some things must be harder for a woman to understand.

"Ain't wanted to tell you, Mellie, 'cause you're soft-hearted, but we're going to have trouble. We got it already. The country's filling up. Sam brought news, last time he went down to Kaikitsil for the mail, says over on the coast, settlers are moving onto the reservation. Good water's scarce, they say, and nothing but the best for the Indians, while a white man has to take what he can find. All that spells trouble. Don't be getting used to no Indians."

"I can't believe it's necessary to quarrel among neighbors."

"Don't think that way. The races won't mix. They ain't your neighbors."

Meantime, some kind of fight was breaking out on the other bank. The people argued, churned around, stood over the third pile. The captain divided it, crossing from side to side. No good. The two camps drew apart. The captain worked them, back and forth, this side and that.

"There she is," Mellie said.

That squaw of Mellie's was doing some of the talking. Another woman shouted, spat on the fish, pushed at the captain. Voices rose in complaint, people showed knives. Law felt it was time to clear out, but Mellie hadn't finished gutting. Her squaw went back and forth now. She got an old woman to come to the middle and sit down. Got another one from the other side. Law wondered what was up. The two old squaws shook handfuls of sticks and dropped them. Be darned if they weren't gambling.

Everyone gathered to watch. "Ah," they said on one side at how the sticks came out, and "hah" on the other. It went on an hour. Then it was done, and the camp broke up. One side took the third pile of fish, and the other let them do it. They all packed up. Darned if the winners didn't throw some of their fish back to the losers, though. A lot of fish. Pretty near half, looked like.

౭౦

OCTOBER 1855

Father

Mrs. Vermella Pickett, near Kaikitsil, California (to be held at the post office)

September 18, 1855

My dearest child, Vermella,

Your sister Nannie and I are at Rough and Ready. Since I have not seen you, I have become a sad old man. Mellie, it is bad here, the gold played out and people in no good temper. The mines have destroyed the creeks. There is no fish, no game. A drove from Texas came in and dropped the stock price from thirty dollars a head to sixteen. But Mr. Pickett could make good money teaming, ten dollars a day, if he came over.

We hear that Bessie is tiring of her hacienda boy. She made her bed, but finds it not all silver and fandangoes. I fear she is unhappy.

Many Indians are starving here. I took a slug today out of a poor fellow's leg, with a dozen splinters of bone. Miners had seized his wife and were living with her. When he tried to get her back, they fired on him. People argue whether the Indian can be civilized, taught religion and spelling and such, and made to wear clothes. I say, civilize the white savage that will shoot a poor aborigine for meanness or for fun. That's the civilizing needs to be done.

I tell Nannie she should marry and let an old man fend for himself, but she won't leave me. I hope you are well and strong and ready to deliver a fine, handsome child. Perhaps by the time this makes its way to you, you will have him in your arms.

Your devoted father,

Matthew T. Roberts

OCTOBER 1855
Mellie

The miracle was still on me, like a dream too soon to wake from, of the Indian woman singing low and steady, her quiet face lifting me when I thought to fail. And I had not failed. The birth made me clumsy and new. The rush of milk soaked my dress, seemed fair to drown poor Matthew, and kept me from sleep, but now the milk was settled, I was keen to see the coast. Law had to make a run over. Sam would pay cash for lumber, and there were things we needed. The cattle were doing well on grass, and we could leave the cow and mules with the Brandt boys. I thought so. Law said it meant four or five days in the mountains, with the days getting short. That was nothing to him, being a teamster from so young, but he didn't know the road, it was bound to be rough, and he wouldn't undertake it with women and children. So I was disappointed and alone again.

I had never taken a present to Bahé, though I thought of her often and felt the debt. I didn't think to go against Law, but I was curious. Father would have been talking to her till he found out how long she steamed a baby and how to do it. I packed my saddlebags with smoked beef shoulder and jerky, tied Matthew in my crossed shawl, and rode across the south end of the valley toward the ridge. We came through a marshy place at the edge of a little lake, then big trees, Joe muscling up where the rise started steep, stones clattering down, oak chaparral catching at my skirt. Jakob had killed a wildcat in these hills. Then the pines began, and the land fell away sharp over the valley, above the hawks. I sought this way and that an hour or more, with no sign of a village, till I told myself finally it was foolish and dropped the reins to nurse my little son, squirming and twisting in his shawl. Joe backed through manzanita scrub and along a spur of blackberry brush where a track opened to a grassy flat, and there it was, a dozen cone houses of leaning bark around a center mound.

I laid Matthew over Joe's neck, dismounted and reached up for him. He was limp with sleep. The grass sparkled among the lodges, bark slabs set against frames of pole. No one was there, not even a dog. I looked in at one of the low, triangular doors. The house inside was circular, sand-floored, clean, with plenty of room in the center to stand. A mild light came through the smoke hole. Sticks lay ready for the fire, skins hung from cross poles, blankets. Around the rim of the circle, baskets held tools, bone awls, brushes, knives, and strange things of wood and feathers. Birds sang in the sun outside. Butterflies darted over the grass. I ran after one, with Matthew. I spun him in circles on the grass. We followed a path down around the center mound to its dug-out entrance, smelling of old fire. It must be the place Jakob talked of, that they danced. Behind a barred door in the gloom, rows of posts made of tree trunks held up their cut branches in attitudes all their own, like men.

Matthew fussed. I climbed back to the grassy place and pulled out a new cloth for him and looked around, uneasy, not liking to wipe the soiled one on the bright grass. Something about the light had changed, and I saw in the deep shade under a tree where three old people sat. One was the blind old man. The others saw well enough, and cackled. One was taken by a coughing fit, so hard she was laughing. I started away, but the old man gave a gesture, unperturbed, a wave of his hand.

I couldn't believe the Indians were going. They were the spirit of the place. If they ever disappeared, the land would cry out.

ॐ

OCTOBER 1855

Law

Mellie looked good to Law after five days on the road, and so did her scalloped potatoes. He had a bee hive in his wagon and a little boar and lumber for a kitchen, and still some cash left from Sam's payment for the freight. He had one thing they didn't need, a little dog he'd found wandering the country in the fog. Mellie laughed at his wise look and called him Plato. And Law had a surprise.

"You can't imagine the size of the logs they're getting at the coast," he told her, sitting out of a fine evening. Mathew was asleep in his basket. She was sewing a little shirt for him, her mouth full of pins. "Bigger around than a man is tall."

"How you talk," she said.

"All of them that big, easy. Some of them three times that. I seen one stump where six couple could dance a reel."

"How much of a fool do you take me for?"

"God's own truth."

She spat the pins into her hand. "How do they get them out, then?"

"Run chains around, put seven eight span of oxen to the

log. Cord the track. Crash them down to the creeks when the water's high, and float to the mill."

"I'll never believe it, Law, without you show me. Take me over there."

He liked her eager like this. Wanting him.

"You mightn't like it," he said. "Settlement's scared the game off. Street's full of begging Indians."

"Why are they begging?"

"They don't have a horse or gun. At least I hope not."

The baby fussed in the basket. Law picked him up and balanced him over his knee. He was strong already, trying to hold his head up.

"Got to get this little teamster fit to travel," Law said.

"What's the doings at the town?"

"Two three stores on the flat at the river mouth, and a plenty of saloons. Farms along the bench above the sea. Got a doctor there, Doc Gray. Church abuilding. Another sawmill going up. Fella with the livery stable freights up and down along the cliffs. I wouldn't want his job in a fog."

She put her work aside. The light was going. Not enough to sew by.

"What dress are they wearing?"

"Danish woman at the farm where I put up wore clogs and a pinafore."

"In the town. Big sleeves, or narrow? Come on, boy. Tell."

"Well, it ain't San Francisco. Except the ladies of the night."

"Which you don't know a thing about."

"I don't. And there's an end to it. Don't you want to know what I brought you, Mellie?"

"Why you brought a pig."

"I mean for you. Come on. Guess."

"All right then. Spanish apples."

"No."

"A weaving loom."

"Not that big."

"Mr. Dickens' book."

"Never thought of that."

Law shifted the boy, reached around to his bag, and brought out a dress length of cloth. Mellie gasped and pulled it open, letting it ripple to her feet in the sunset light. Green silk-cotton with a gold thread.

"Law, it's too fine."

"Not for you, it ain't." He bounced Matthew on his knee, singing *Ride a Cock Horse.* "Come on, little buster. You getting ready to ride with me? I do enjoy taking a team over the mountains."

"Don't jounce him so, Law. You'll rattle his stomach." Mellie picked the boy off Law's knee and settled him against his shoulder. "So, what will the Indians do, if they're hungry?"

"Starve. Or go in to the reserve."

"But that won't happen here, in our valley. We won't spoil their hunting. A few settlers won't."

"A few won't, but more's coming. That's what I'm trying to tell you."

The boy upchucked some milky froth. Mellie pawed at Law's shoulder with a cloth.

"It's not right," she said.

"Ain't right or wrong. Just is." What did she think? Hardly a glow in the west any more. Too dark to see her face good. "Whose side you going to be on, Mellie, when it comes down to it? Theirs or mine?"

❡

OCTOBER 1855

Mellie

I'd been cooking under the oak tree right along, setting the dutch oven in the fire or balancing a skillet between stones. I wanted a kitchen before the rains, and Law wasn't getting to it. Now he had to build Sam's shed. If I said "kitchen" and Sam said "shed", I knew who Law listened to. But I didn't say anything. Law had to help Sam out if he wanted the borrow of his bull. He said he'd stay at Sam's overnight, get the shed done inside two days, then start in on our kitchen.

After he left, I found a nice piece of smoked beef to take up to Bahé in Joe's saddlebags. We still had never done anything for her. It was a quiet time, the hills gone past gold and the sun done burning. Going up among the black oak, dusty with the pollen of a whole summer, Matthew and I came across a woman pounding acorns in the hollow of a boulder, corralling the nuts in a no-bottom basket held between her feet. Another woman came to collect the coarse meal and sift it in a basket. Then it was Bahé who took the fine yellow flour, spread it on a flat, sandy place and poured water through it.

"Dance," she said. "Lotta days."

She sniffed the smoked meat. Half a dozen women came

71

around and poked at it, and she cut off pieces for them all. The woman I had seen shouting and spitting at the fish camp came back for another piece and another. On her fourth try, Bahé turned away from her and kept turning. The woman kicked over a meal basket, and with a strike of her head like a snake, took herself off. Bahé slid wary eyes after her.

"Poison," she said.

I helped her scrape up what meal we could, and she went back to pouring water through the acorn on the sand. The children played with Matthew's toes. He wriggled, all eyes. She gave him a name, *Dika-sha*. Fish. She poured again. Her own child, loose in the cradle basket, reached for my face. *Dashuwé*, she was called. I liked to think of her as Rose, who could have been my daughter. Bahé poured patiently, time after time. The first flour puckered your mouth, but after much leaching the acorn was no longer bitter, but nut-tasting and mild.

A party of men came in with a big buck, cut meat in a buzz of talk and laughter, and speared it on stakes around a fire. They were nearly naked, with leather pouches instead of trousers. I received curious, frank looks, and stayed close among the women. When meat was shared, I got the first.

When shadows lay long across the flat, two women started a gambling game with bones, one wrapped with leather and one slick. Everyone gathered to watch, to guess which bone was in which hand, take sides, sing to confuse the guesser, tease the loser, egg the winner on. The captain from the fishing day started a speech. A young man matched him gesture for gesture, with slow and counterfeit solemnity. This the speaker manifestly enjoyed. He forbade the young men to laugh, till they were choking on their cider and guffawing it onto the ground. With that, the young speaker stood on his hands and walked, lifted one arm, orating upside down, and fell over.

"*Kaáika,*" Bahé laughed.

She asked for words: "laugh", "cook", "give", "take". *Tabó* was grass. *Dishí,* the black oak. *Duwidá,* evening. She came on well with English, but the strange sounds of her language slipped easily from my mind, and I let them go, taking them as music.

At length, the speaker man came to sit with Bahé, very large and naked, with great scars on his cheeks.

"Man," she said. "*Matuku.*"

Something she told him made him smile at me and nod. "Give meat," she said. "Mellie give."

They got up another game toward evening, pushing a ball with hooped sticks. The play grew fierce, with cries of despair and triumph, the young men outdoing themselves, mothers pulling their children out of the way. Then everyone went into the game in two gangs, striving to push the ball over the enemy line. Men dropped on the sidelines, exhausted. Mothers fell in laughing heaps with sons and daughters. The only one who could still move was the young man, the acrobat, the clown, *Kaáika,* playing he could walk only on his knees, and the children shrieked and climbed over him, toppling him to the ground.

Law would be up the valley overnight, so I didn't hurry, though shadows gathered along the edges of the woods and a bright curve cut the pale west. *Dashuwé,* the new moon. As long as I milked before moonset, my cow would do well. I lingered there with the people happy and the stars coming out. *Tótól*, the stars. The moon was the rim of a wagon wheel above the western ridge when I took Matthew up to go.

It was darker than I'd thought under the trees, and steep going down, but Joe took good care of us. I could see a light at the cabin from a long way off, so I knew Law's plans had changed. I put Joe up and went in. Law was at the table, looking dark, with his chin down, drinking.

"I'm sorry you found no supper, Law."

"Sam never split out his shakes," he said, "and I won't do it for him. Where you been?"

"Up the ridge."

He dropped his head into his hands.

"They're celebrating already," I explained, beginning to unwrap Matthew's cloth. "It will be big, the acorn dance."

"You'd sooner be with Indians than your own family?"

"Tush, I'd half my family with me, and I didn't look for you tonight."

Law wrung the whiskey glass in his two hands. "Won't you stop before it's too late?"

"Stop what? Being neighborly?"

"I turn my back, and you're after the Diggers like a bitch in heat."

He stank of whiskey. I took Matthew and the lantern and made for the shed. Law followed. I laid Matthew squalling in my lap and tried to milk, shaking so it sprayed my skirts.

"You're as bad as your father," Law said behind me. "There's no talking you to earth. They ain't same as us. No pride, no ambition..."

"Generous, kind, cheerful ..."

"You don't know what's doing at the coast."

"You'd better tell me, then."

"Indians killing stock. Good animals destroyed."

"Somebody should have thought of that when they ran stock over their land and drove off the deer."

"What about us then? Do you want to give up our stock? Do you want to work for Sam Brandt all our lives, or starve?"

I dug my head into Jill's flank and stroked her bag. She was bursting, hot and dry, but wouldn't let go her milk.

"Come see the acorn dance," I said. "They're not what people think. Plain folk, if they do dance with feathers."

"We ain't going up there. We're Americans from the States. We didn't come here to be savages."

Matthew was sliding off my lap. I gave up trying to milk. Law stood at the edge of the lantern light, the moon gone and the stars behind his shoulder high and small.

"Sam and Jakob will see the dance," I said.

"I ain't asking you," he said, "I'm telling. It's worse than you think. The settlers at the coast, when they find stock missing, they don't ask why. Men hunt through the rancherias, and they don't care who they kill. Is that the way you want us to go? Indians bring out the worst in whites, I don't know why."

"Will it help to treat them like strangers?" I said. "We meant

75

to do different here." Matthew was screaming. I gave him the breast, and he bit hard, my milk not coming either. "Up here, we said, a man would stand a chance on his own way."

Law shifted in the straw, dangerous, red-eyed.

"There's going to be trouble, Mellie. I can't stop it, and that doesn't make me any less of a man. But it makes you less of a woman, if you expect me to make everything come out some pretty way you thought about in your mind."

I could feel it slipping, then, the hope I'd had. I leaned on my cow and cried. Poor Matthew. Now the milk rushed out and choked him.

"Want to have your heart broke all your life?" Law said. "Do you, Mellie?"

He went back to the house.

I'd never known a man before Law, but I'd always known I'd have to find one. Santiago was only two days' ride from Monterey and flush with men in '51, miners and emigrants and Californios. They tipped their hats to me and my sisters, jostled us accidentally, tripped over each other to apologize.

"All of us men lose our heads when we see a woman," Father said. "Even the good ones."

We laughed, because we had no idea of being women. Even Nannie was only fifteen.

"Don't get drooled over," Father said. "Wait for a man who can hold his spit."

Law Pickett could hold it. He came to load wine at the Mission one spring morning when the glimmer shone over the whole valley from the mountains to the sea. He jumped off the freight wagon where I was hoeing peas by the fence. The Padre's old dog, General, got up to snuff at the muscular, smiling man who hunkered down in big boots. Law ruffled the dog's fur till he lay back down and flapped his thick tail in the dust.

"I thought a mission was all priests and Indians," Law said.

"We shipwrecked at the port. The Padre took us in."

"Don't say."

"Been to the mines?" I asked.

A smile started in his eyes and caught a corner of his mouth. "Reckon the gold is in the land. You Catholic?"

"Protestant. Baptized Episcopal."

"What's that?"

"Something back east."

I showed him the old workshops, the vineyard, the dead olive trees, the cloister with the Padre's yellow roses, the broken waterworks, the well.

"Must have had land in the old days," he said.

"Half a day's ride north and south, and all between the mountains and the sea."

He whistled.

I didn't tell him about Father's spells or how the Padre went purple and dropped dead behind the altar, all our heads down for the *non dignus sum*. I didn't tell how tired I was of sewing in the window, of the adobe crumbling, how I wanted a real home. But I thought of him afterward, a blunt man and ready, easy with animals, and when he came back for grapes and apricots, I asked him to stay to dinner. He stripped off his shirt and scrubbed it in the trough, said it would dry in ten minutes. Bessie put on her blue dress, pulled low in front. Nannie cut flowers. Father suited up handsome in a waistcoat, sat at the end of the Padre's table, and served Law plenty of potatoes. The long blue room was cool and comfortable, windows cut three feet deep in thick adobe, but it would leak, come winter rain.

"I admire a man who can wear a damp shirt in company," Father said. "Are you familiar with the works of Shakespeare?"

"My reading has been McGuffey's and the Bible, and I don't overdo those."

"I wonder how a young man purposes to live without books," Father said. The straw seat creaked in his chair as he reached Law more meat. "By dint of knowing no better, I suppose. You're looking for gold, of course, like every fool in California."

"No, sir, looking to settle."

Father chewed and swallowed. "Why did we come west, I ask you. Was it not to get away from the settlements? Yet here we settle and do all the damage that we did before. We have produced an Indian who smiles, if you can call it smiling, and thieves behind our back. You're not an optimist, I hope."

I stepped on Father's foot. He could go on like this an hour.

"No sir," Law said. "Land's pretty well taken up around Santiago. I'm going north."

"Shouldn't a young man take an interest in the mines? The coming place is bound to be the Colorado."

"I reckon one spot is about as good as another," Law said, "if the land is good."

I began to like a man who could stand up to Father.

ೞ

NOVEMBER 1855
Mellie

We never saw the acorn dance. Law wouldn't have it. And still
I had no kitchen, Law always helping Sam with something.
I didn't like the way Sam told Law what to do and he did it. I
didn't like thinking about Law that way.

"Sam can't leave you alone," I said one morning.

Law flung over in the bed.

"He gave you a cow, girl. He's thinking big. He's thinking
about a store."

"No one to come to a store, only you and me."

"There will be. Sam wants to bring in settlers, get a town
going, and he will. Jakob's the one gives me the itch. Brooding
over something all the time, but don't say what."

"I'd keep quiet too," I said, "if my brother set up for boss of
the creation."

Law slammed out on the floor and kicked his boots on.

"Don't get so mean you can't look ahead, Mellie."

He teamed south again before the big rains. He meant to
sell the wheat Jakob raised while Sam was planning what he
meant for Law to do. He took some of the jerked meat and was
gone for days, and I didn't miss him. The sky let go. I gave up

cooking on the open fire and huddled with Matthew in the cabin eating cold sprout beans till Law came home, soaked as a sailor and cheerful the way the road made him. He'd sold the meat and bought a glass window and a rooster and nine hens, though two drowned in the wagon, a pair of mules to break over winter, and a dandy stove with four holes, an oven, and a shelf above for warming. He split logs and laid a puncheon floor, levered the stove onto it, put up a roof, and filled one end with firewood to block the wind. The smoke went out all right unless the mist hung low, which was frequent. Clouds blanketed the mountains, and bare oak branches stood out in the wet forest, hung with moss. I filled a tin box with coals to put my feet on and work my fingers up to sew, or took Matthew into bed to play. Law threw up a shed for the animals. On fine days, he kept warm building a proper kitchen.

The wheat field came up green. We sometimes saw a party of Indians out hunting, lumpy in rabbit-skin cloaks. How did they stay warm and dry, with the rain coming down their smoke holes? When I was a girl, Grandma had the Negroes up to the gallery at Christmas, to the big punchbowl, and gave them extra cornmeal. She wanted them to say thank you, Ma'am, not just get drunk down the quarters, where the fires flickered around the cabins, where the singing was. I hid behind her skirt, scared by so many gathered faces, worried at their scaly, dark feet, bare in the cold.

"Aren't they perished?" I said.

"Bless your heart, darling," Grandma told me, "they don't feel it as we do."

ಐ

DECEMBER 1855

Jakob

What Jakob liked in Mellie, she was quiet. True, she was a woman, but she didn't fill up all the space with talk. You could still think, around her. He made sugared nuts to take her over for Christmas dinner and set up a little fir tree hung with nuts and cakes, the way they used to do in the old country, and she liked it. She didn't have her kitchen finished, just that walled-in puncheon floor, but she had the wagon bench and the two chairs in the cabin, and she put the meal out on planks laid over the bed.

Sam plunked down his jug of whiskey and set himself to copycat the baby, Matthew, wave his arms and kick and drool. Jakob could almost remember when Sam was that small himself, but he was a big, heavy fella now, bigger than Jakob by a long chalk. After ten minutes of kicking and gurgling, Sam pulled out his handkerchief and swabbed his head and said he hadn't a prayer of equalling that baby.

Mellie served the dinner, and it was good and heartening. Deer meat and biscuits, potatoes, beans, pickles and blackberries.

"If you had a springhouse to keep the sun off," Sam told

Law, "you'd be set. San Francisco's growing, and this is good dairy land. Mellie could do your milking."

"I'm not a dairy man," said Law. "Anyway, how you going to ship it?"

"Put the butter down in fat, team it over to the coast. You'll be a bigger man teaming, maybe, than anything."

"I'm a stockman," Law said.

Mellie brought out a cake baked in her new stove, with a sugar crust that set up nice. She asked Jakob to cut it. Before they ate the cake, Sam read the Bible story about the reign of Caesar Augustus, when all the world went to be taxed, and opened up the whiskey jug.

"Jakob and me are planning to prove up on 160 acres each, then advertise for settlers and sell town lots. Bring in some neighbors. You want to get in on that, Law."

Mellie was rocking her boy in one arm. She looked tired.

"Slow down, Sam," Jakob said.

"Slow down? Going to be big changes around here. You missed the acorn dance this year, Mellie. You want to make that man of yours take you next year. Won't be but so much chance before these rituals are swept away."

"I thought we were giving them a berth," Law said. "Prevent trouble."

"Well, it is a fearsome thing." Sam winked at Mellie. "Very wild. I wonder you didn't hear it. They got a drum makes the whole mountain boom. You might be hiring some of the fellows one day, Law, your business gets big. The ranchers down below, they use them."

"I don't know about that," said Law. He got up and fed the stove.

Jakob wanted to ask Mellie about the Indian woman she knew, but Sam and Law got to dealing about Sam's breed bull, pretty loud, and so deep in whiskey the progress was slow. Sam counted his bull's virtues, how black he was, how wide the shoulders, how long his sheath. Mellie was having a pretty thin time of it.

"Sam," Jakob said, "a lady's present."

"What's your price?" Law asked Sam, "to borrow that bull?"

"What you got? Nineteen cows?"

"Twelve. I'll not breed the heifers."

Sam drew again at the whiskey jug. "He has work at home. You can have him a week."

"He'll never cover all my cows in a week."

"Use your own yearling, then."

"Come, Sam, I can't put him on his own mother! What do you take me for?"

Sam slapped his knees and howled. Mellie gave Jakob the baby and took some plates out. Jakob didn't know really how to hold the little boy. He was soft, and his different parts seemed to go all directions.

"Ten days, then," Sam said. "What are we offered to participate, me and my bad boy?"

"Participate!" cried Law, snorting whiskey till he choked. "What part did you think to play, Sam?"

Mellie came in after more dishes, and Jakob managed to get a hand free to cork the whiskey jug and slide it under the bed.

"I'll steer him home," Sam cried. "You do the honors on the distaff side. Less you want Mellie to hold her. Ha!"

Jakob stood and asked Mellie to show him her chickens and her spring. She wrapped Matthew warmly, and they walked down to the creek and watched the water scud along.

"I wish I could have seen the acorn dance," she said. "Law doesn't favor it."

"Sam favors it now. He's apt to change his mind," Jakob said. "Well, he's Sam."

"I don't mind the way he rubbed it in about the dance."

If he could be partial to any woman, Jakob thought, it would be Mellie.

The sky was clearing off, cloud layers following each other on the wind. The water rushed along with many voices.

"Did you ever find your Indian woman?"

"Yes, but Law doesn't like me to know her. I call her Bahé, but it's not her name. She wouldn't tell her name."

"They don't none of them tell their names. Name's too sacred. They'll call themselves anything, so long as it's not the name."

"Men have so many ways to find things out," Mellie said.

Jakob rejoiced in the cold, clean wind. He watched the water run over the willow roots, pulling along fast, and the leaves toss and dip in the current, seeming to drink gladly of it.

"I got some of their language," he told her, "one way and another. I know they're having harder times. Game scarce. Fish too, where the cattle trample the streams."

"What do they say about the cattle?"

"Say they stink."

"Well, they do," she laughed. The boy fussed in her shawl, and she cupped his head in her hand. "Law thinks they're bound to go."

"Sam too."

Dusk was falling blue, the window from the house lit against it.

"They might not be right about it all," Jakob told her.

He helped her scatter breadcrumbs to the chickens, and she told him about her father. Jakob got the idea the man wasn't much good. This Padre Rafael took them in, her and her sisters, at a Mission down below. He let them stay three years.

"I don't hold much with Catholics," he said.

"You might have liked the Padre. He used to ask us every Christmas what new life was born in our hearts."

"Well that's all right, I guess."

When they went in, Law kissed his wife, took Matthew in the crook of his arm, and brought in a fresh box of coals. They had more cake all around, and Sam said it was tasty enough to fill a person with goodwill toward men, even the nearest and dearest, like Jakob. He got out his fiddle and played *The First Nowell* and *God Rest Ye Merry*, and that sweet old tune about the winter rose. They sang *Lord Lovell* and *Barbara Allen*, and all agreed there were sure to be flowers by February.

2

MAYBE SOMEDAY
SHE'LL KNOW SOMETHING

JANUARY 1856

Mellie

I worried about Law. He couldn't sit still. The rain went on that winter, wet snow sometimes, and he fretted up and down the one room, whittled pegs for a someday barn, and wished for pig, talked of nothing but pig, said he could smell the bacon, till I worried for our little boar. The only thing gave him pleasure was riding through the rain, counting over his stock. Then the wheat washed out, and he cussed himself for planting too low down the slope.

"Don't worry," I said, on my way to feed the chickens, collecting the old bread off the shelf. "We have neighbors."

He looked at me with hot, hurt eyes. "Now Mellie, we already had that fight."

"I don't mean the Indians. We can buy wheat from Sam if we have to."

"I'm damned if I'll pay him two dollars a sack."

"Don't be too proud to eat."

"I guess we can eat bark," he said. "Saw some Indians doing that way on Deer Flat last week. Some say the hungrier they are the quicker they'll go."

"Law!"

"I ain't saying it."

"Nor putting a stop to it either."

He asked why was I so snippy, was I in the family way again, and then I did want to hit him. He stamped around and knocked over the firebox. Some of the coals burned into the floor before we could get them up, and then he started kicking himself for sure.

"I'm no use, Mellie," he said at last. "Best you can do is throw me out. Maybe I can get us a deer."

He took off on foot. I promised to take hay to the cattle if it snowed deep, and that evening a slushstorm blew in, but it was Law I went to bed worried about. Was he the same man I knew, the one who'd courted me at the Mission?

He'd ridden up the wagon track then in the milky autumn sun, come straight to me, where I was digging carrots for dinner, and made me walk with him under the feathery shadows of the acacia trees. It made me breathless, being so near a man.

"I've been and fell in love," he said, and my heart skipped a beat. "With a little valley," he went on, "in the coast range. Pretty and wide. Good water. Couple of brothers settled there already, running stock, fixing to fetch up wives. It's a beautiful country, Mellie, and I know you're a worker."

He took my hand, and his was big and plain. It made me dizzy, the salt good smell of him, and dusk falling. I let him keep my hand awhile, and he came the next evening and the next.

"Indians still around there," he said, "but peaceful. Ain't no way to lose, the land's so fine. A man can work hard, have a chance at his own way. Grazing's good most all year. We'll only have to lay in a little hay, in case it snows deep or dries up early."

"A dull boy," Nannie said in the morning. "He's read nothing. Thinks nothing but green manure."

"He might suit me all the same," I said.

Bessie tossed her coffee dregs into the bougainvillea. "He thinks forty acres is a farm. Once you get tired of teasing him, Mellie, throw him back."

"I don't tease him."

"I could do worse for a son-in-law," Father said, spreading marmalade on his bun. "He could be mean or drunk. He could drool."

Law and I walked in the garden, the last fine days before the rains. The evenings were warm, with roses under the moon. He wanted to build a barn for calving out of the wet. He could run both sheep and cattle if he moved the sheep before they cropped the range too short. Would he never come to the point? He stepped on a border of little carnations, sending up a crush of clove, and jumped back, clumsy and shy. I laughed and looked up at him.

"Are you with me, Mellie?"

I couldn't help asking, "Why not Bessie, Law?"

"I'll take the girl without the frills," he said.

Came a crack in the dark, a tearing, so I knew I wasn't asleep any more or back at the Mission either, but here in bed at Oak Valley, and then something slid, a mule screamed, and I shot out of the bedclothes, caught a foot in the quilt and fell, bit my cheek and drew blood. I left Matthew wailing, got a coal out of the stove, blew up the lantern, and rushed out barefoot in the mud. It was black dark and sleet coming down hard. The shed roof had given out under the weight of ice, cut the mule's shoulder and killed three chickens. The mare panicked at her halter rope, everyone soaked and frozen. I got Joe into the smokehouse, chased the hens in after, all in hysterics, and went to thaw my feet in bed and nurse Matthew back to sleep.

When I could stand and walk, I got my boots and the whiskey jug. Joe had an ugly piece of hide hanging, the flesh raw, oozing blood. I sloshed it with whiskey, cut the flap off, skinned a dead chicken and bound the breast meat to the wound with rags. Fetched him one of my blankets. Matthew was howling. I went and hugged him, told him he'd have to grow up quick and take care of himself, because we couldn't lose all that hay. I piled what I could around into the house. It was a long night, and when I was done I put the mare and the cow under the thickest pepper tree. It poured cold rain, and they had to stand it.

Padre Rafael used to preach on the animals at Christmas, the dark church lit with candles, bare feet brushing the packed earth floor. They knew no evil, he said, so they were worthy to see Christ born, the morning star that knows no setting. That was what I thought about, shivering in bed, my hands like blocks, my boy's breath coming in shudders, his face patchy red, no stars to be seen, and plenty of misery to go around. The animals stood stoic in the rain three days. I fed them some of our barley.

It cleared then, and Law came home with a deer, having

hunted it some way, cached it, and tramped to Kaikitsil for the news. He looked at the hay piled in the house and stared at the mud hole where the shed had been. "Perfect for pigs," I said, but he didn't laugh. He cussed up and down, jacked the shed roof up and double-posted it, threw brush in for the animals to trample, sacrificed the wagon bed for a hay floor. Joe's scrape frightened him, until he saw it was more raw than deep.

"Why Mellie," he said, "how'd you think to doctor him that way? You've likely saved him."

We built up the fire in the stove and feasted on the dead chickens. Some of his news was good. They were starting up a paper in Kaikitsil with dispatches from the City. *The Sentinel.* Some news was bad. Down around Santa Catarina they'd rounded up dozens of Indians, driven them to work on ranches for the harvest, and then turned them loose with nothing but a shirt and blanket in the rain.

"Easy, Mellie, now. I don't defend it. Bound to cause complication in the end. Heard a good story, though. Seems the neighbors were coming the high and mighty over a woman there in Kaikitsil, a Mrs. Perkins, till she had to ask them didn't she smell good or something, and so they rated her for her husband being a squaw man before she come into the country."

"Squaw man?"

"Them that live with an Indian woman. What do you think she answered, Mell? *Mr. Perkins will never take anything but the best.* Don't you reckon that settled it?"

॰ॐ

APRIL 1856
Law

Some of Law's redwood fenceposts slicked up and slimed on him, it was so wet that spring. The oak branches colored up orange, but the rains went on forever, till at last came drying winds and field flowers, and one morning with all the world bright and blowing, Mellie drove Law and Matthew out of the house so she could scrub everything, even get the last straws out of the bed. Law took the plow and bogged down in the field with six-inch mud boots, Joe frowning back at him like he was crazy. Matthew took off crawling that very day.

All through the spring, Mellie fed travelers, prospectors and miners bound for the Trinity country, loggers, tan-bark strippers, travelers to Oregon. Law's was the first place on the road up from Kaikitsil. She always had milk and bread, smoked meat and fish, and root vegetables held over winter. A skinny little miner that bunked a couple of nights in their kitchen took Matthew on his lap and told a tall tale about a valley on the Merced River with rock walls half a mile high and waterfalls all along. Mellie tried to get him to admit it wasn't so, but Law understood the man didn't mean no harm. It made a good story.

The sheriff came up from Kaikitsil to have a look around.

Told how their potatoes got the wire worm and they had an idea to plant tobacco. Law didn't think tobacco would ever make good in this dry a country.

"Why don't you try sheep? Sheep can get by on awful short feed."

"Sheep and cows don't mix," the sheriff said. "Sheep crop the grass too close and destroy the land for stock."

"Not if you run them smart. Sheep take care of you twice, meat and wool."

The sheriff said again, "Sheep and cows don't mix."

Once people get their minds made up, they don't listen. Law had seen it before.

One evening, Sam stopped by to brag how smart he'd been to get Law to bring up an extra stove. He'd been advertising down below for settlers, offering help the first winter.

"New neighbor coming up," he said. "John Riley. I sold him that stove."

"For three times what you paid me for it, Sam?"

"Only twice. Plus freight. By God, it's been a wet spring."

After it dried up a little, Law went over with Sam and Jakob to help John Riley fence. Riley was hairy as Esau, a red, healthy fellow, and a good carpenter. Law offered him the borrow of his plow, and he was to help Law build a barn. His wife had coughed all winter down around Esmeralda, and he hoped she'd improve in the mountains, but it seemed she couldn't stand the trip, not yet. She'd stay a while at her sister's, where it was sunny in the hills.

"I hope you've had no Indian trouble," John said. "I don't

want to bring Hettie into any trouble. I don't think she'll bear it."

"No trouble," Law said. "Not a mite."

"Fellas cut the equipment off this Indian up around Harkin and stuffed it in his mouth," Riley said. "You ain't had no need to punish?"

"Nope," said Sam.

"Leave them alone," Jakob said. "They're all right as they are. I seen them at the coast, fishing and trading." He sank a post in the hole Law made for him and leaned on it. "Got a different language over there," he said.

"Regular Tower of Babel," said Sam. "Another sign their time's near done. You want to get some of their baskets, John. They'll be a curiosity one day."

"Long as we don't have no vigilante justice around here," Riley said. "That only makes more trouble. You need a strong law. Trouble ain't so bad with a strong law."

Law was struck by that. He picked up a shovel and dug another post hole. "That's true," he said. "We saw a man hanged in the city, irregular. Guess he deserved it, but that's a terrible thing."

"We don't aim to let things get out of hand," Sam said. "Aim to get the Indians working one day. Everything can't be done by a woman or a mule."

"How you going to get them to stick around and work?" John Riley said. "Wherever it's tried, they melt away. You can't change that."

"Can't or won't," Jakob said.

96

"Jakob's near Indian himself," Sam said. "He's learning the real way to hunt deer. Creep up beside the flock with antlers on his head and graze and stamp and smell at the females till they think he's a buck and invite him in to dinner."

Law noticed even Jakob laughed at that.

&

APRIL 1856

Father

My beloved child, Vermella,

Your sister and I have been at Nevada City two weeks. It is a weary life. We treat the usual run of venereal and stomach troubles, accidents. The worst of it is the snow and rain, no decent place to dry out, only a saloon that stinks of beer and grease.

The wretched Aborigines have few acorns and less game. They are used as pack mules in the mountains, and starve about the camps, drunken and picking over garbage. More wonder that all do not resort to thieving than that some do. The Superintendant of Indian Affairs proposes a reservation east of the Sierras to rid the state of this class of population, as he says. He might as well come out and advocate for murder.

We hear that Bessie has eight dresses and her little high-heeled husband adores her. However, I think she likes him less well than the clothes.

Nannie is well, but this old world is no friend of mine, and I am disgusted.

The *Queen of the Night* plays at the theatre in red velvet. Ought it not to be blue, Mellie?

With ever fondest wishes for your health and happiness,
Give Matthew a kiss from Grandpa,
Matthew T. Roberts

ॐ

MAY 1856

Law

Two men came in to run stock together in the east valley. Law let them bunk in his shed while they threw up shacks. Bob Meenan had a wife down below. It was her money they'd put up for the stock. What he knew about land could fit on the head of a nail, and he didn't take suggestion. It took him half a day to hoe a row of onions. Jeff Thrush was a younger fellow, knew how to work, but moody and mean. He'd make much of Plato and then kick him out of the way. In Law's opinion, you could tell a lot about a man by how he treats a dog.

Bob went to criticizing Sam one breakfast when Mellie was boiling him an egg.

"He's all right for a Kraut, but we need Americans in the valley."

Law like to have dropped Matthew. "Why, he lived in Wisconsin all his life."

Mellie asked Bob to pull the eggs out of the pot, but he said he didn't aim to start on women's work, so she snatched them herself with her own fingers.

"By God," Bob said, "you got cast iron hands."

"Better had, kind of help I'm getting around here."

"You're not going to get ahead of Mellie," Law said. "Go on. Eat. Didn't Sam give you a good deal on your lumber?"

Bob admitted it. "Still, once we're settled, it's the native born should hold office."

"If you don't like it here," Law said, "you can sell out high in a couple of years, thanks to Sam Brandt."

"I don't know how those two ever paired up," Mellie said after Meenan and Thrush left the place. "All they agree on is they don't like anybody."

It wasn't long before they quarrelled, and both complained to Law. One of them built a cabin next a spring the other wanted. Thrush said Meenan was a baldheaded, greedy hypocrite. Meenan called Thrush a whippersnapper cuss couldn't nobody live with. Law tried to keep out of their way. He had fencing to get to.

In summer came a spell of unsettled weather with lightning high up in the range and a smell of smoke, and one night a glow of flames on the north ridge. The next day, Thrush came up to Law's place. Fire was burning down the draw toward his cabin. He needed help to fight it.

"Where's Bob?" Law said.

"We ain't speaking."

"That's convenient, ain't it."

Law took his buckets and shovel and went along, and they cleared brush to the north and east of Thrush's place, wetted him down from the little branch that ran through there, and watched the fire go by. Thrush thought the Indians set it.

"They do burn grass," Law said, "for the deer and acorns. Not this fire. This is a lightning fire."

101

"Fit to ruin me."

"It ain't up in the trees, won't do no harm," Law said. "Makes better grazing. Did you never live on the prairie?"

"Don't know why we put up with them."

"Indians never set this fire," Law said.

"Sooner they're gone, the better."

Law figured Thrush for scared. "They're going, he said."

"Exterminate, I say. Else they'll be back and back."

It wasn't much of a fire, only the smell and crackle and the ash on your boots. Still, nothing blacker than after a fire, and sad. Exterminate, though, that was a five-dollar word. Whatever the Indians got up to wasn't like to amount to anything so mean as that.

"Spared Thrush's place," Law told Mellie when he got home.

"Thank goodness," she said, "for I couldn't have taken him back in this house another minute."

Law considered Mellie, the way she kept on with few treats and few complaints. Maybe she was right, and it wouldn't hurt to know something about what the Indians were up to, if fools like Thrush were going to take on thataway.

"Maybe we ought to go up this fall," he said, "and see their acorn dance."

AUGUST 1856
Mellie

I lolled with Matthew in a shallow pool of the creek with nothing to do till milking. Law was building us a real kitchen with a milkroom at one end and a glass window, nailing the floor. One, two, three. One, two. All at once, we heard hoofbeats gallop hard along the valley floor, and I got my clothes dragged over my wet skin just before Jakob Brandt tore hell for leather around the big rock.

"Law, Law," he called, and pitched off his horse and ran into the house.

I took Matthew on my hip and hurried after.

"...a long time," Jakob was saying. "I come by chance, looking for a draw knife I lent him. You know doctoring, don't you, Mellie? Riley stuck his foot over a rock and got snake bit."

"We ought to get that Doc Gray at the coast," I said, "if John's bad."

Sam was in Kaikitsil, politicking to be Justice of the Peace. Jakob knew the Indian way over the mountains, and his horse could keep the trail, so he went. He would have to lay up on the downslope till the moon rose, wouldn't make the coast till morning. I milked the cow a lick and a promise, Law got the whiskey, and we rode for John's, feeling pretty bad.

John Riley had a small house, but all he made with his hands was nice. His corn was higher than a man, and he'd cut a second crop of hay. Law made a hammock of my shawl and hung it low in a tree outside the door for Matthew to go on sleeping. He took a long time at it. I was in no hurry to go inside either.

John dozed in a chair, his leg set on a stool, swollen two or three times the size, purple, oozing, full of cracks. He'd ripped off the pants leg and tied it above the knee.

"How are you, John?" I said.

He started awake and waved a shirt at the flies. "It don't hurt too bad."

He'd been cold before. Now he was hot. He'd got pretty deep into his whiskey, and he was ashamed, for he'd wet himself, sitting there. It hurt too much to walk. Tomorrow he'd go for Hettie. If she hadn't forgot him.

"She thinks of you always," I said, and other fool things, to comfort him. Father would judge the leg should come right off.

John's eyes rolled back and he snored.

"More whiskey," I told Law. "A lot more. And I'll need a good knife. Can you hold him?"

"Mellie," he said, white with shock, "you can never."

"It's his only chance."

It would have to be a long knife to get through all that swelling. Go in behind the knee, find the middle of the joint, between the round, slick ends of bone. A long knife hung on a nail by the door. Law flicked his eyes to warn me John was watching.

"Have some whiskey, John," I said. "You'll need it."

He looked at me, sane and despairing, and began to keen and rock himself.

"You'll want to see Hettie again," I said.

"How can I help her with one leg? I can't be a cripple man!"

Law talked to him, while I started a fire to clean the knife and found a blanket to tear in strips. John was gone again, in a half sleep. Law helped me tie him to the chair and bind his thigh to the stool. All this took a terrible time but not long enough for me to be ready. I went out for a look at Matthew, sleeping still. A flock of little brown birds feeding in John's stubble took off and flew chattering to the pine edge. I took that as my time and went in and took up the knife, and now I had to come to it. Law held to the chair. When I looked at him, he nodded, with gaunt eyes. The light ran over the table and the two men swam together. I blinked, brought the knife behind John's knee, and drove in between the bones. The fat knee popped, the water from the swelling flowed over my hand, the knife twisted, Law flinched and let go the chair, and John lunged at me with a roar, bringing the chair and table with him, going for the knife. I flung it out the door. Law stopped John, too late. Too late for John altogether. No use trying to cleave him now. Matthew screamed, and I ran to him, fearing the flying knife, but he'd only waked and spilled out of his hammock. I carried him out to see the mules, smelling his

105

milky hair, remembering that other night when the animals shifted like black holes in the starlight, and life, not death, awaited to begin.

When we went back, they were drinking, cheerful and re-prieved, Law's arm about John's shoulder.

"Is that little Matt?" John said. "Did you hurt your head, young fella? Never mind, for you're going to have a better life than I."

"Keep your heart up, John," Law said.

We got him to bed and kept him full of whiskey. Poor John Riley lay all night with his leg blackening. It was Hettie he talked of, fainting and raving. Hettie and the thirst. We gave him all the water he could take, and told him he would see her soon, which was true enough, since she was not long for this world either. Some people have no luck. At little before dawn he went right off his head, and by sunrise it was over.

Sunlight fell across the crocks and cups. Matthew waked, babbling in the awful quiet. We made wretched playmates, Law and I, drinking John's buttermilk, stunned into silence. Law watered the mules and packed the whiskey in a saddlebag, along with some of John's corn to take home with us. At last he came to the door stoop and sat by me.

"When I saw you with that knife," he said, "I didn't know you."

"It was all for nothing. John's pain. His fear of the knife."

"You couldn't have done it."

"I don't know if I could. You didn't let me know. You let go the chair."

Law picked up a stick and whittled at it. "I don't know where you get your ideas," he said. "You're my wife, but sometimes I think you're nothing to do with me."

"We don't always think alike," I said. "That's all."

"Are you so set on your own way? Will you fight me always?"

"I don't aim to. We mightn't have saved John anyway. It wasn't a good chance."

"You are the dangedest."

"Don't you like me, though?"

"Yes, gal," he said at last, "I guess I do."

We found an address on a slip of paper in John Riley's Bible, and I wrote her a letter. Ruth Harriet. Hettie. I had looked forward to her coming. She would have been another woman in the valley. Jakob and Doc came in toward sunset. We buried John on the rise south of Sam and Jakob's place, first burial in Oak Valley, for the Indians burned theirs, so Jakob said. Doc said a prayer, and Law put up a board to mark the grave.

SEPTEMBER 1856

Father

from Shingle Springs

Beloved daughter Vermella,

I am sorry about the poor snakebit fellow. Even if you had succeeded in taking the leg off, Mellie, it would likely have been too late, if it was suppurating as you said. Do not worry over what you can't do a thing about. This is good advice, as I would find if ever I would follow it myself.

The placer mines are played out, and the swashbuckling days over. Men go with the big companies, so most have steady wages but drink everything they have. A sack of potatoes costs a dollar, a pint of milk at least five, but whiskey comes cheap, half dollar a bottle. Women at the mines come in two kinds, homely old shopkeepers and the other sort, with red curtains. Your sister scolds the latter into what cleanliness she can.

The worst class of whites whore among the Indians, and many of the latter are affected with the venereal. I saw several fellows in one camp so far advanced with ulcers they could hardly walk. I pay their remedies out of my pocket, so I cannot get ahead, and Nannie rates me for it. I am about worn out, and will have to leave this place before long.

With ever best wishes for your health and happiness,
Your devoted and admiring father,
    Matthew T. Roberts

ॐ

SEPTEMBER 1856

Mellie

"Your friend the Indian," Law said. "Go up and see her."

It was my day to be surprised. "Won't be time yet for the acorn feast," I said.

"We better know what's doing. Could be trouble, if some people have their way."

I went up to the ridge that morning, thinking of Father, how he piled up a stack of worries wherever he went, so wherever he was, he couldn't stay.

I was thirteen when Dacey scolded him up the path from the pump in Texas. Brooding, thin, he'd left us for weeks, then ridden up with a brace of partridge as if he'd breakfasted at home that morning.

"You're free to go," he told Dacey, "if you don't like the shape of things. You've been free since Mississippi. Do you want the papers?"

"Free," she said, planting her feet by the prickly pears. "I like that. Free to leave these children to the devil, while you scouting with the so-called Rangers and never say where you been at or is going. Don't talk to me about no papers."

Another time, a neighbor woman drove up and took him

to task for leaving his girl children to grow up wild, nothing but a nigger to mind them.

"Dacey I trust implicitly," he said, "explicitly, licit and illicitly, and any other way you like. And as for you, Madam," – he swept her a low bow – "it is your country I defend."

"You'll get yourself killed," she told him, right in front of Bessie, who was only nine. "Riding as far as the border, and Santa Anna all down there. Who do you think's going to bring up your children?"

"Cowards die many times before their deaths," was his reply.

She was struck by it, I could see, though it was only Shakespeare. She climbed up into her buggy and drove away.

"*Julius Caesar* fetches them every time," Father told me.

The truth was, he didn't believe he could be killed, he so much wanted it.

When I got up to Bahé's camp that morning, it was full of bustle. After the dogs ceased surging around us, I let Matthew crawl on the grass with Bahe's little Rose, and the children took them up and stood them on their little bow legs.

They'd climbed the mountains, she told me, making great use of signs. Up, then down. "Sun going," she said. West. She signed big trees, a stream. They fell on their knees to eat.

"Grass?"

No. She drew three ovals on the ground.

"Clover."

It must have seemed green and good after winter. She swept a big circle with her arms. An enormous flat.

"The beach, the sea? You've been all the way to the coast? The water."

"Go," she said. "*Sha.* Water go."

"Low tide?"

"Hunt." She tumbled her hands. "*Dika-sha.*"

"Fish. Surf fish running?"

"Running?" She lifted her chin toward the children darting in and out of lodges.

"Children run. Fish run."

"Chwil." The word twisted her mouth. "Cut," she said, showing me how they skewered the fish on sticks. "*Tsa.*"

"Cook?"

She shook her head, rippled her hands.

"Fire? Smoke."

"Smoke," she said. "*Tsa.*" She showed me baskets of smoked fish, dried boards of kelp, and made me take some, showed how they gathered the slippery strands of kelp, dried it, packed it in baskets. "Walk little water, going-down water."

"Running water. You walked up the creek?"

"Running?"

I shrugged. "Water runs. Children run. Fish run."

Bahé laughed, got a sudden pain in her back, made a toothless mouth like an old woman. "Trade," she said. "Fish. Milk." Her hands held something hot. She opened it. It smelled good.

"Bread," I guessed. I changed Matthew's cloth, and he sprayed an arc of bright piss.

"Running," Bahé said. "Running water," and we laughed.

But as I was leaving, she turned me by the elbow to face the line of ridges toward the sea.

"Hunt," she said. "*Tschok.*"

"You had good hunting at the coast?"

She shook her head. "*Tschok*. Shoot."

This couldn't be. No one would let an Indian have a gun. I didn't like the thought of armed Indians myself. In the Indian village at the Mission, a woman made a little money selling eggs, and her husband stole it to buy whiskey. She waited inside the door of their hut, and hit him on the head with an iron skillet. Killed him. "We can thank the padres," Father said, "who took the old ways and put whiskey and the paternoster in their stead."

"Shoot. Indian shoot," Bahé said.

"Surely not. The men won't stand for it."

All this talk of shooting. I gathered Matthew and our things. I couldn't make her out. I spoke some Spanish and understood the Latin of the Mass, but Bahé's *tsa's* and *sha's* were too many for me. Not that she wasn't remarkable, what she made me understand. I couldn't have given any account at all of our lean-to falling down, the animals huddled wet and miserable, Law plowing too early. When I told Law her story, I left that out about them eating clover on all fours. I wanted him to like them.

ಬಿ

OCTOBER 1856

Jakob

Jakob had been looking forward to the acorn dance all year. The morning of the day dawned fine and clear, air bright and cool, smelling of resin as the color rose in the woods. Every leaf was shining. No breeze disturbed the spiders' webs drying in the brambles. Jakob saw people coming in from all around the country. Mellie and Law and Sam, of course. And Indian people. A man made for the ridge with a frail old woman swung in a net from a headstrap down his back.

"Not so many as last year," said Sam. "Two, three hundred. I'm looking for baskets."

The people milled in the open space among the lodges, tying on headbands of red and yellow feathers, trying out clapper sticks and rattles. Men in feather kilts cooked meat around a fire. Matuku, the fish chief with scarred cheeks, was one of them, and Kotshim Xaba, who when he wasn't hunting flaked obsidian. They called Jakob over and gave him a taste of venison. Very good.

Bob Meenan and Jeff Thrush showed up, boding no good. What would they be looking for, except trouble?

"Might as well see the show," Meenan said.

Thrush laughed when he saw the meat. "What's that? Coyote?"

"All this talk about how they're hungry," Meenan said. "This could feed a small army."

"They've been fasting all through the dark of the moon," Jakob explained, knowing he might have saved his breath.

A nutty smell rose from the acorn mush bubbling in the baskets. Women heavy with shell necklaces ladled red-hot stones into the baskets, pulled out the cooling ones, and made the children stand back when they crowded too close, eager for the hot acorn that stuck to the cooling stones and came off in crisp flakes. The woman Mellie called Bahé offered a crackling to Matthew, but the little boy whirled his face into his mother's neck, too shy.

The word went around that the leaders were leaving the sweat house. Guards were set upon the meat, and everyone moved along, caught up in the flow down into the roundhouse. Jakob thought to keep close to Thrush and Meenan. He watched over the heads of the crowd while the *tshakale*, a blind old man in canvas pants and a red shirt, with slick, wet hair, climbed to the top of the mound and tottered on the tuft of grass, throwing out meal in four directions, thanking Earth for the gift of Acorn. Kotshim Xaba in the entrance to the roundhouse took up his words. They spoke in solemn alternation for some time. Meal offerings flew on the wind.

"Get on with it," Thrush said.

Within the dancehouse the drum began to sound, a deep, slow boom that seemed faint at first, but grew like a ripe heartbeat, till it was all that could be attended to. The hair stood on the back of Jakob's neck. Everyone moved down the slope, pressing down into the earth, stepping to the boom, boom of the drum. Jakob kept an eye on the two men, who appeared half curious, half bored. Sam, of course, was nowhere to be seen. Once past the fire by the door, everyone sat cross-legged around the circle. The fire made the only light. Singers knelt around it, clapping split sticks in their palms. The lead dancer sounded the drum, a plank laid over a hollow pit, dancing on it, beating it with a club. He wore a crown of fur with beads and feather flags. In ordinary life, he was Haiyú Wínawa, who made cocoon rattles and hunted rabbits and small game. The old and sick were brought in on blankets. There were many of them, and Jakob thought many must have died that year. The sacred place was nowhere near full. Women and children were too few. An old woman circled the roundhouse with a basket of water, sprinkling the floor.

"How long does this go on?" said Thrush, but no one answered him.

Three women danced, facing the drum, beads rattling. Men with striped faces countered them. The songs were short and sung over several times, the singers suddenly changing rhythm all together. Mellie pulled Jakob's elbow, signaling that she recognized the slim dancer who reached out to touch the earth with a skillful foot, twice for each beat. Kaáika. Jakob swayed with the drum, the deep calm at its heart. Of a sudden then the singers let the song dwindle, dropped it with a "Ho!", and talked among themselves. Jakob saw that Law had fallen under the spell. He shook himself, looked sheepish, took Matthew, and went out. Jeff and Bob left too, pulling bottles out of their pockets.

Jakob knew he ought to follow them, but the best was still to come. A sweet, wild melody stirred at the door, and something fluttered and unfolded, fearful and terrific, a magnificent mantle of black feathers that floated in the air of the dancer's movements like a live thing, sailing and rustling. Animal spirits came to life around him. Salmon swam, hawk flew, rabbit and deer with stick legs leaped and grazed. Jakob did not know whether the time was long or short. The music changed again, and the dance led up into the autumn sunset, into creation's dawn, burning green and purple under the new moon, *dashuwé*. The line of people snailed around a fire under the biggest oak. An elder woman circled it, swaying, offering acorn to the earth and sky.

"Look," said Mellie, coming up beside him. "Sam on the outskirts of the crowd. I declare. I think of him always at the center."

Arms full of small baskets, Sam stood by Tcadín Tsuduyín, ever the kindest of women. Her two young children were with her, one dark, one pale almost as Matthew.

Everyone was tired, happy, hungry. The women took wet spoons, dipped acorn mush from the cooking baskets and dropped it hissing into water baskets lined with juniper. The mush crunched like fritters when it hit the cold. They pressed the first food on the strangers. Jakob loved the taste of acorn, mild and sweet, with the tang of evergreen. Then came roast venison, roots and lily bulbs, berries, and more dancing, social now and jolly, the musicians faithfully wielding the clapper sticks.

Sam crossed the dancing space with his baskets, stuffed with beads and rattles.

"Do you aim to rattle," Jakob said, "in the time to come?"

"People will pay well for curios," said Sam. "What's your count, Jakob?"

"Since last year? One in ten people gone."

A shout interrupted the dance circle, and another. A crowd clotted around an angry man in a turkey feather kilt. Jakob saw Jeff Thrush make a dash at him, the way you'd try to scare a bull, but Kotsim Xaba was not the sort to scare easy. He stood and glared, and Thrush had to go back to stand beside Bob Meenan.

"Easy, Jeff," Sam called.

"What's it to him?" shouted Thrush.

"I told you, Jeff," Bob Meenan said.

Two women laughed on the edge of the crowd, hiding their faces.

"He's probably their husband," Jakob called.

"We would have paid them," said Bob.

The women were gathered back into the crowd. The men stood squared off still.

"The squaws didn't mind one bit," Thrush said.

Jakob shouldered in to stand between the two white men and the Indian, facing Jeff.

"They didn't know what you intended," he said.

"They knew all right," Thrush laughed. "They wanted it. This ain't your business."

"*Dishin wínawa chadíl, danek,*" the Indian said. "Get them out of here."

"They could never imagine what a bastard like you wants," Jakob said.

Thrush hit Jakob across the cheekbone and knocked him down. Jakob came around to the rich sound of Indian laughter. Law and Sam were dunking Thrush's head in a basket of cold water.

Mellie and the woman she called Bahé helped Jakob to his feet.

"I'm sorry they made trouble," Mellie said.

"Lotta trouble," Bahé said. She looked at Sam handing Thrush his hat. "Him too."

ૐ

MARCH 1857

Mellie

Law cursed his luck, going through the second winter without a barn. If a cow had trouble calving, he knelt in the open field and came in wet and shivering, and I poured hot water to soak his feet. Still, he took a fever, and one night I birthed a calf myself, feeling for the little hooves in that wet, pressing hotness. When she seized up I thought she'd break my arm. That was the pick calf, that went to Sam. I made mustard plasters, and Law threw the fever off and was weak and sweet a few days, bouncing Matthew on his knee and talking about a pony. Matt could say "Doe" for Joe, and "Papa". As soon as he was able to get out, Law took his broadaxe and climbed the green hills, looking for likely timber. He could taste that barn.

On a spring morning, when the pepperwood was showing light, sweet blossoms, I took Matthew up the ridge. Near the top, we turned Joe into a clearing and went on foot. Matt wanted to walk by himself, but he made slow progress, so I picked him up and turned him upside down and ran with him under the firs. I was with child again, but not yet heavy. The fog drifted away through the tall trees, and the manzanita flowered in white and pink clusters of bells. A few dogs and children played about the lodges. The winter had been bad. Not very cold, but their acorns hadn't lasted. They'd had to give many to their relatives on the North Fork.

"Starve there," Bahé said. "Them little ones."

She too was with child. Her son played skillfully with a cup and ball, seven or eight and well-grown now, the boy who'd brought me water that first time.

"Can they go into the reservation?" I said.

She looked puzzled.

"The reserve? Indian land?"

She laughed. "Hungry land." She had been to the coast herself and had fish. Her man was in the mountains, hunting. Matuku. "Hunt, hunt," she said. "One deer."

The boy made great play with the cup, catching and dropping the ball. Matthew grabbed, behaved badly. She spoke to her son, and he let Matthew have the toy.

"Will you go to the coast again?" I said.

"Bad road," she said. "*Tshók.* Do us that way, maybe."

"Tshók?"

"Shoot."

"Who's shooting on the road?"

"White brother. Shoot. Take." She shrugged.

"Take what?"

"Woman."

Matthew whined and fussed, threw the toy down when he couldn't make it work. I was upset enough to scold him till he cried. Bahé squatted down to him, put her hands both sides of his face, and spoke to him gently.

"Please tell me," I said, embarrassed and distressed. "How can I help?"

She looked at me, almost amused.

"Tell man, not shoot *diwí*."

"Not shoot coyotes?"

"Take a lot, little white brother," she said. "Deer, snake, crow. Shoot Indian. No good, shoot *diwí*. Make earth, Big Man *Diwí*."

I didn't know her. How could anyone take these Coyote tales seriously? How could he be the Creator? According to Francisca, he was always getting it wrong. Quail talked him into taking a ride on a bent sapling to fly up and see the stars, and he came down splat.

"Why Coyote, Bahé? How could a coyote make the earth?"

"Live so long. Think a lot."

"They eat the lambs."

"Twenty lamb. Eat one, *diwí*."

That was true, but it wasn't going to change how men felt about coyotes. You can't run them off. If you don't kill them, they come back. When I got home, I asked Law if he knew an Indian woman had been shot or kidnapped on the road.

"Don't believe everything you hear," he said.

I told him the way people thought, Coyote made the earth and had to be respected.

"That's good," he snorted. "Worship coyotes."

"'Tisn't that, exactly, but maybe it's bad luck to shoot them."

"Our Coyote which art in heaven. Yip, yip."

"Don't make me laugh, Law. He's smart and doesn't quit.

He always comes back. Maybe killing him discourages people too much."

"You ever seen a lamb torn to pieces?"

Certainly Law shot coyotes. Coyotes had to be killed, or they destroyed your lambs.

ℰℭ

JUNE 1857
Mellie

The June grass brushed your knees on muleback, and the Indian women came over the hills wearing long skirts, beating the grass heads, making the seed fly into the wicker scoops.

Three new families took up land that spring to raise stock or plow. One that came was Henry Nott, a carpenter, and his wife, Ella. Henry built Sam a store to stock knives and tools, soap and pans and pins and bolts of cloth and plows and patent medicines and tack and gear for prospectors, timber men and settlers going north to the Trinity Alps, to the Clear Lake country, or over to the Sierras. May Potter was one I liked the look of, a slight, wry, Quaker woman, but she was hard to know. With six children and an unlikely husband, everything fell to her, pretty near. She had books to lend, one by Trollope about a Dr. Harding and his violincello. I helped her with planting, and she came when I put up my peas. Her girls distracted Matthew from hugging our legs and making us spill the scalding water from the jars. It was good to have company.

Henry Nott helped Law measure his barn timbers, drill them for pegs, and put together the end frames, post and brace and beam. But Law hurt his back levelling the foundation timbers and had to lay up a while, so the barn had to wait. When he was better, he took off in the wagon to help Bob Meenan fetch up his wife Arabella and her furniture. A sofa shifted, as it happened, and a carving broke off the back. Law glued it, but we heard Arabella was unhappy, so Matt and I went to make amends and bring her our first peaches. Arabella Meenan had bows on everything and little curtains that went halfway down the window. She gave me to understand that my peaches were not as big as the freestones she was known for in Platte County, Missouri, where she'd put up fruit since she was in pinafores.

"Come sit by me," she said, patting the sofa. "All the way from Philadelphia. Mother had it from a man in Bucks County. It's a blessing she never lived to see it chipped."

I sipped my tea, not knowing how to answer this.

"And I have no children to leave it to," Arabella said. "Now don't feel sorry for me. I'll be your Auntie Bella, won't I, Nat?"

"Matt," I said.

"Would you like to eat a peach, Nat? I'll give you half a one."

"His name is Matthew."

"Forgive me, I'm a little hard of hearing. I'll just fetch a knife. Don't kick the sofa, Matthew."

She bustled into the kitchen, and I got his feet away from the sofa before she came back.

"I've had to work so over my kitchen," Arabella said. She peeled a peach and gave a piece to Matthew. "Mr. M. kept things just terrible. All he cares for is acres and rates of return. That's why we're up here anyway."

"Nobody thinks the less of you," I said, "for your kitchen being unfinished. It took me a whole year to get mine."

She lowered her voice. "Last Tuesday some Indians came around near the house. Close as that tree."

"They want the grass seed. They won't hurt you."

"Let them keep to the hills, I say."

"They're not hill people. They've always lived in the valley."

"There, Matthew, another piece of peach."

He reached up sticky hands.

"Say thank you, Matt," I said.

"At my sister's," Arabella said, "near Sacramento, they came right in the house. She had to get her dogs to chase them out. And now the Army has to go on the reserve to keep the peace. I don't like the sound of that."

"If the settlers left them alone," I said, "they'd be all right."

"Dirty things. Do you take their part?"

"Not very dirty. They're always bathing in the creeks."

"Sonny, I'll thank you to eat that peach right away from the furniture," Arabella said. "Go sit in the doorway, now."

Matthew pouted at her, but went.

"What's wrong with that baby? Are his nerves all right?" She plumped down again on the sofa. "This country's meant for Christians, not Indians. You'll find I don't mince words. I call them pests."

§

JUNE 1857
Bahé

Bahé wondered what the Spirit was up to. Two came that time, three summers before, two white men. Two of them came, piled stones to live inside. How strange it was. Who were those men? She didn't know. She watched. Listened. White people came a long time ago to the coast, the old people said. They wanted skins. They killed the otters that stick their heads up in the water like the bulbs of kelp, killed them till there were almost none. Those went away. Then came the ones that built hard houses on the cliffs and cut into trees so the trees screamed. They left the woods shattered. They knew nothing, how to let life go on, how to help it. The earth was sore wherever the white brothers touched it. And they were many. The people on the coast hungered now, their medicine no good and poison everywhere.

For a long time, no strangers came to the valley, but then those two came. Piled stones into a house. Two men. Gave food, traded a nice tobacco, acted friendly, had good blankets. Where was their family? "How well disposed he is," Tcadín Tsuduyín said, "the fat one, how good looking. He makes me laugh." She adopted him. She fell in love and had a child.

Pretty soon, spotted deer ran all over, white and brown elk. Called them *cow*. Called them *horse, mule*. They made a stink, made mud in all the streams. Fish didn't find the water to swim up. Did they come to poison? What did they do in their own country?

Two more came to the Big Egg Rock place. What for? What did they come for, always in twos? A woman that time, ready for a child. Throw up this, throw up that, running all day. It didn't look like they knew themselves. Still, everything might never be the same.

"Wait and see how it turns out," the Spirit said. "You're going to be all right."

So Bahé watched. Two came, then four, then twenty. Came like rabbits. White people ran boats around the valley. Called them *waton*. Ran all around, shot guns. Shot deer, snake, crow. Made a big, hard house, too many, cut up the earth. Everything hurting. Some of them acted like they had no relatives. Shot people. Stole people. And this Mellie, she didn't know much about it. Got to be grown and still didn't know how the earth gives and takes, how a child comes, how the year goes around. How evil comes.

"What are you doing?" Bahé asked the Spirit.

"Watch," the Spirit said. So Bahé watched. Listened to Mellie's questions, showed her everything. Didn't know how to tell her, we do this way so we know who we are. Mellie was like a girl, little eleven-year girl with no mother. Still, she didn't seem a stranger. Looked a little, listened. She could learn a little, maybe. Maybe someday she'd know something.

๛

JUNE 1857

Sam

It killed Sam that Law would have the first barn in the valley. Beat him to it, fair and square. So when Law set the day for the raising, Sam made sure to talk it up, like he was in on the whole thing from the start, which in a way he was. He tuned his fiddle and got everybody to bring their food and dancing shoes. He was there by dawn himself. Couldn't sleep. Mellie gave him coffee. She'd killed half her chickens, been up since three, rolling drumsticks in flour and frying them in hot lard. Neighbors began coming in about seven o'clock, in wagons or on horseback, bringing tools and ropes and ladders, turning their animals in to the corral. Mellie's little dog lost its head barking, so she had to shut him in the smokehouse.

The women spread out blankets in the shade and piled food on the tables. Sam milled with the men around the foundation timbers, kicking at the beams, whittling a few more pegs, in case. Law already had his twenty-four and thirty-six-foot timbers laid out on the ground, posts and beams pegged together. Henry Nott knew what he was doing, what the action was going to be. He got started tying four ropes to the top of one of the end frames, thought about that, then fixed them a little different. At last, he whistled and rubbed his hands together, and Sam ordered the children up on the fence out of the way. Henry wanted a man on each of the ropes. He was smart enough he didn't have to say much. Sam took up one. Henry counted a "one-two-hey", and they slid the end frame snug against the foundation. Then Henry had the men on two of the ropes walk forward and the others back, till all the ropes were taut.

"You fellas pull," he said to Sam and Bob, "and the others slack off."

Sam and Bob hauled on their ropes so the frame hinged on the foundation timber and swung up, while the others counterbalanced, and so the west end stood up. Law and Henry ran in and pegged the bottom. Henry shinnied up the frame with a line around his waist. The women spelled the men on the balance ropes, and Sam helped pass a beam end up to Henry.

"Give me another foot, Sam. A little more. Too much. Let her down six inches."

Henry roped through the auger hole to hold the beam in place. He walked along the frame to the other end. Law and Jakob angled another beam up there, so they had the frame braced. It was something to see how fast it went. One minute, nothing, and the next, a piece of barn.

Sam was hot and winded. Now he'd helped them get started, he left them to it, clapped Law on the back, told the children on the fence to watch so they could tell *their* children, and had another cup of coffee. By the time he turned around, the east end was up and Henry was scaling it, roping up a long beam end with the pegs ready in it, and when it was square, hammering the pegs home. Henry was everywhere, walking the beams, roping, driving the pegs. Law climbed up too, arms out for balance, but Henry looked to have been born up there. Sam admitted to a little jealousy, but it was a pleasure to watch anybody good at his job.

Once the frame was up, people took breaks and visited. The children rode the mules, swam in the creek. May and Ella quilted in the shade of the young orchard. The boys shouted and sang the rafters up and clung to the slope to nail shakes. The siding took the best part of the afternoon and into evening. The women kept food coming all day. Most everything was done by dark, and they nailed the floor by lamplight, ready for dancing. Law felt pretty good, Sam saw, and he didn't begrudge him. Not a big barn, but the first. Of course Law couldn't have done anything without Sam, and Sam's barn would be bigger. Darned if Oak Valley wasn't coming along pretty much the way he'd planned. But when he saw Law with Mellie, he couldn't help wondering why he'd gone so long without an honest-to-God wife.

ॐ

Mellie

On the day of the barn raising, the children got into the smoke-house to play hide and seek, and let the dog out. He ran off with a piece of fried chicken, full of sharp bones, and I had to take it away from him. Poor Plato.

Toward the end, after the floor was done, I got up there with the men to nail siding, and when we finished, I thought I was too tired to climb down, let alone stand up, but the music persuaded me to shake a leg, and we danced the new floor down. *The Foggy Dew, Arkansas Traveler.* Sam wasn't bad on the fiddle. Not bad at all.

When I went out to clear my head, feeling luckier than I thought could last, the old moon was climbing the eastern ridge. Jakob leaned on the corral fence, smoking. Light spilled out the barn door with the music of the fiddle, Jeff Thrush's harmonica, and the stomping and clapping.

"All this noise," I said. "Can they hear us now, you reckon, the Indians?"

"Oh, they're listening," Jakob said.

"Bahé talks like people have been taken at gunpoint on the coast road. Women."

"Yep."

"I'm tired of not knowing what to do. They're trying to feed the North Fork people and don't have enough themselves. How will they hold out?"

"They're breaking up now over rights to acorn trees. Quarreling. It's what they call poison." Jakob scraped his foot on the fence. "I guess trouble's hard to stand."

A couple of May's children tore in between us, young savages chasing a ball, and then Law came for me to dance. Nobody thought of being tired. Sam played till he'd used every drop of sweat he had in stock, he said, and then Jeff Thrush, with a whiskey jug down by his right leg, carried on with the mouth organ, *Old Folks at Home*, sweet and sad. Jeff, who never let a sweet word pass his lips. People sang and danced until children sprawled against the walls asleep, and women in blue skirts and red began to lug their baskets toward the wagons. Law looked the happiest I'd seen him ever, and he thanked the people, and I fell in love with him again. Then Jeff Thrush slipped his mouth organ into his jeans and raised his hand for a toast.

"To willing hearts and hands for one in need," he said.

Law had his arm around my waist, and I felt him bristle.

"First barn in the valley," Jeff said, "but you wouldn't be nothing without neighbors willing to help make you what you are."

"Don't preach to me in my own barn, Jeff." Law said it easy.

"It's a proud man won't admit his need."

Law let me go and said he wasn't in no need at all, Jeff

didn't understand a goddamn thing. People came in between and swept them both up in the leaving.

"Don't let him spoil the day," I said to Law. "He means well. Got the feeling wrong. He has no family, only Bob."

"He don't mean well at all," Law said. "Neither him nor Bob."

So I told Law the truth, another child was coming, and that did cheer and please him. Nothing could spoil my happiness. It kept me skimming along shallow in my sleep, and I was up again before dawn with the stars still sharp and the barn black and trim against the hills. Quiet welled out of the earth like water. I wanted to fill my ears with it before what was left of the chickens got up gabbling. Stillness like that pours strength into your bones. To think I was ever afraid of it.

ॐ

JULY 1857

Mellie

Bahé came to harvest grass seed on the hill with three or four
other women, and I went out to her in the afternoon, as they
were coming down to the creek with full baskets to sit in the
shade, letting the water run over their feet and unstrapping
the babies from their cradles. Bahé was pleased with the harvest, running her fingers through the smooth and tight, light
seed. Among the children playing with sticks, I noticed a little
girl picking her way behind the others, limbs soft as a kitten's,
her face turned sideways behind tangled hair. By a lost gesture
I guessed she was blind. I caught her up and held her on my
knee. The eyelids were stuck shut. I made her lick my handkerchief and worked at the dirty, gluey stuff until it loosened
and the lids came apart and the little black nuggets shone clear.
She wriggled away and ran off.

"Look, Bahé. She sees!"

"Poison," Bahé said. "Come again sick."

"It's only a discharge from the eye. It can be washed away."

"Poison woman done that. Come again sick. Maybe die."

There was a medicine, I told her. I would seek it out. She
looked at me patiently, tolerantly. The poisoner had fled to the

North Fork already, and everyone knew there would continue to be trouble.

When I mentioned this to Law at dinner, he put down his spoon.

"What are you getting into, Mellie? This ain't no sick cat."

"Looks like an ordinary inflammation."

"We don't know what it is. And you with child again?"

I passed him the bread and butter, but he pushed his plate away.

"Did Matthew play with the blind girl?"

"They were good friends all the afternoon."

"My God, Mellie. The eyes running? And you, supposed to know so much about doctoring."

I got up to cut the pie. "Why, what do you think it is?"

"Do I have to spell it out for you, how they get these vile diseases? Where's Matt?"

"In bed. Where do you think?"

"I don't want him near any sick Indians. Mellie, do you hear?"

I had a flash of terror about how things could go wrong. I turned, a tin plate in my hand, and went to sting him.

"Whose fault is it they're sick? Abuse them and throw the blame on them. You men are better to your beasts."

"Who cares what happens to the damn Indians. Look after your own, Mellie."

"Jakob doesn't talk like this."

"Jakob? Why, he's no Christ Almighty," Law said. "He fucks squaws."

My plate clanged on the floor.

"Didn't you know? Been going up to the North Fork, getting the edge off twice a week for years. Did you think it was pure goodness? Got brats up there, for Christ's sake."

"Law," I said. "Law? We've gone too far. If there's a way back, I don't know it."

I sat and dried my hands and folded them in my lap. "Law? You've hardly eaten anything. I believe Matthew's all right."

He dropped his shoulders and set his head in his hands. "I hope so. But you push a man too far."

I miscarried of my second child that night, in a few hours of pain and ache. I held the little snail in my two hands, shaking with loss of blood, memorizing the closed almond eyes that would never open. Law said little, but he cried, it hurt him so. If he thought the Indian sickness might have been to blame, he didn't throw it up to me. May Potter was all buck up and cheer, told me it happened all the time and she'd miscarried twice. "Never look back," she said. But Law and I were lost to each other again. I had a bad conscience about him. I defended the coyotes, the Indians, everyone but him. I knew it.

Why had I ever come to California?

We'd sailed from Mazatlan in Mexico, Father and my sisters and me, lost the rudder in a storm and drifted for days, until a new wind drove us on shore some distance north of Monterey, at Santiago. A brave man struggled through the surf with a line, and the sailors tied us in rope slings and brought us down to the beach, hand over hand, like spiders. I was ecstatic, and as soon as my feet touched the sand I wanted to do it all again.

Father carried Bessie up the beach, and that was when we first saw the Padre, come down in a broad-brimmed hat in all that wind inquiring if we might be travelers from the ill-fated ship. He himself, he said, as the last priest at the Mission, was in the category of survivor.

He brought us, shivering and bedraggled, to still, white-washed rooms with beds and blankets and a flowery breeze coming in the windows. In the morning, we discovered Joaquín's wrinkled Indian face, the well beside the ruined wall, the gravel paths, the cool white doorways deep in shade, and Francisca's bowls of apricots and peaches, avocados, grapes and artichokes and melons. The Padre was an ugly man, so bitten with smallpox scars that no one could feel ashamed in front of him. As he pruned the grape vines on the rough poles, Father stopped him with a hand on his sleeve.

"I do not know how to thank you."

Padre Rafael said there was need to cover the melons from the sun, and we could help if we would like to stay.

"Tell me, then," said Father, "whom to thank."

The Padre studied Father's face, the twisting lines that drove him across Texas into Mexico and up to California. "This is the place," he said, "of Nuestra Señora de la Paz."

Father turned away into the squash vines so no one could see his face, until Nannie and I tugged on his thumbs to come cover the melons. Later, the Padre told him of Indians who were sick, and Father sent for medicines and began doctoring in the valley and the Mexican towns.

Mis tesoritos, the Padre called us, and me he called "the little

Protestant" because I wanted to know why Indians lived in brush houses with bugs in the roof, and why he said Mass every day when only three Indians came and the two señoras from the town, and why he crossed his hands over the cup. And because I loved the psalms. We said them out of Mother's book, walking the rows of grapes, the Padre practicing his English and I watching where he made the cuts and holding the basket for the prunings. "Then shall the earth bring forth her increase." InCREEZ was how he said it. "And God, even our own God, shall give us his blessing." The Indians lived like that, the Padre said, so they could hear God breathing in the wind all night. As for the Mass, two or three was enough to ensure Christ's presence, and he crossed his hands to show that Jesus was both God and man.

"How can he be both?"

"Is a man," the Padre said, and thought a bit. "And full with God up to the brim."

I understood that I could never marry Padre Rafael, but I prayed for a lace mantilla, because I'd promised God to go to Mass every day, so I would need it. The Padre took my chin in his hand and made me look at him. He told me to open the eyes of my heart to all God's world and watch always for miracles.

In the nights after I miscarried, Padre Rafael came to me in dreams, his face pebbled with scars, his fingers matter-of-fact among the roots and cuttings.

"Cut out the weak shoots," he said. "Open the hearts of the trees. *Coraje.*"

139

"*Treze melocotones* last year, *Padre.*"

"*Prodigioso. Vamonos. Corte aquí.*"

So I pruned my fruit trees, and because the Padre had loved the wildflowers of the country, I brought some close to the house. Mustard, lupine, and the yellow poppy Bahé dug to cure toothache. Law brought me bare-root roses from Sonoma, white in the shape of stars and red, like blood.

ဢ

OCTOBER 1857
Bessie

Dear Sister Mellie,

I have meant to write to you, but I have forgot, and how can I tell you now about our trip to Mexico? It is too long ago. It was heaven, and I am the most fortunate creature alive.

I am sorry to think of you in the wilderness. I wonder how you eat. How do you get your dresses? If it is I that luck smiled on, I am surprised, having been the least and youngest, and the most ignored of all of you.

We have come to live at the rancho of my father-in-law east of Aquilero by the river. My white mare Luna is up to her knees in clover. We have Indian servants in plenty and the best of everything. My husband brings me every day a present, and I am hardly allowed to raise a finger. Everyone wishes to drive here and talk to him. Even if it is for the sake of his father, the most important man in the region, they will soon discover how far-seeing *mi querido* is.

Indians are the drovers here. They rumble in from the beach in big carts with the wheels hacked out of a tree round and unload at the market, dumping sacks of onions. The Americanos all say the Diggers are dirty and low and will not hire them, and indeed the Indian men look foolish in serge pants and a stuff shirt. The women wring their rags out in the fountain where they drink. Our dusky vaqueros call to the mares and colts and hang about the fence, as like to step on one another's toes in play as to work. *Mi querido* is forward-thinking and says they will never have the get up and go. Everyone knows it takes three Indians to do the work of one white man.

Father rode down here on his black to irritate everyone and embarrass me. He will defend the Indians against all sense. I could not move him to the least admission of difference, except it were in the Indians' favor. He said the wetched Irish in the cities at the North are filthier still. They are not our kind either, I said, and he said there is only one kind, as if I were still a child. Just the human kind. He is old-fashioned.

The country slopes down to the river, deep in grass. Along the track up to our house are locust trees both sides, masses of blue agapanthus, pomegranates, lemon trees, honeysuckle, beds of mint. *Mi querido* is planting wine grapes and means to have everything the finest. I have sewn him a handsome waistcoat of red silk. Our Mayor Domo is a Mexican, but we wish to hire American workers so soon as new blood comes into the country.

I cannot imagine you are happy. I suppose you are poor and must do your own work. I am sorry.

Ever your affectionate
Bessie

JULY 1858
Mellie

A Methodist preacher began coming to May Potter's parlor once a month. Quaker though she was, May set her chairs around, sat the children on the floor, and stood the men behind, to shift from foot to foot. The preaching was thin, hopeful stuff that made me homesick for the Padre, who called us "my dear children" and told us how much we were loved by God. I never doubted he talked with God often, but Mr. Lawrence seemed never to have met Him. He spoke of God as if he were President Buchanan, or a professor at Harvard College.

Sam built a house near the store. "In town," he called it. It had a porch with posts and a round tower on the sitting room. When it was done, he took the coast steamer down to San Francisco, had himself sworn in as Justice of the Peace, applied for a post office, and got a brocade vest and a bride named Myra, all in the same week. On the Fourth of July he set trestle tables out in front of the store so we could all meet her, a widow from Georgia with corsets and feathers. You'd have thought a woman like that wouldn't leave the city, but Sam must have sweet-talked her as he did the rest of us.

Everybody brought food. It was a feast. Sam read out the Declaration of Independence and made a speech. He intended to bring in a surveyor and lay out a street in front of the store and divide his claim in lots, and that wasn't all. He was going to build a tannery and a grist mill on the creek. Brandt Creek, he called it.

"Twenty-two souls in the valley," he said, "and we're just getting started."

Pete Waps, a New England man, had some of the newspapers. "This Lincoln in Illinois," he said, "claims the government can't last half slave, half free."

"Why not?" Sam said, making his way through a plate of ribs. "It's lasted that way eighty years."

"The slavers broke the Compromise, going for Kansas."

Sam reared back. "People in the territories should have a free choice, Pete, same as you or me. That's equality."

I was afraid at what I would think of Jakob, after the things Law said about him, but he passed the cornbread just like himself, and everybody reached for some.

"The slave owners don't want freedom," Pete said. "They want to get rich."

"Equality ain't the half of it," said Jeff Thrush. "Lincoln claims the nigger's his brother. Hell, he ain't no kin of mine, no more'n a dirty Indian."

"He is of mine," Jakob said,,

"Why Jakob," Sam said, "I'm pure surprised. I thought you were white." He laughed and squeezed Myra around the shoulders.

144

"And I thought they was kin of yours, Jeff," Jakob went on, "but then, I thought you was human."

Jeff spat behind his chair.

I guessed Jakob wasn't the only one with a wife among the Indians, but I couldn't feel the same about him as I had before. And here he was, talking so bitter. He might be lonesome out on the old place, with Sam and Myra settling in town.

"The Declaration was meant to apply to *us*," Myra said. "Our people."

Sam's face was a picture. A woman standing up for him. He didn't know whether to sing or pray, but he got a thumb under his braces and hitched up his belly. He was getting prosperous.

"No need to study over this," he said. "We settled it when we came to Calfornia. We're not abolition and we're not secesh. We're for the Union."

We all drank to that and passed the fried chicken and cole slaw. Tired, thin Ella Nott sang *Silver Threads Among the Gold*, apologizing that it wasn't patriotic, but all said no apology was needed, they liked it fine. Jeff took out his mouth organ, and we sang *My Country Tis of Thee* and *Aura Leigh*, rather thoughtful, and then *Old Folks At Home* till there wasn't a dry eye and Sam had to fiddle up *Oh, Susanna* and *Betsy from Pike* to send all away cheerful.

"We ought to have a tannery," Law said in the wagon going home. "Such a waste, burying hides."

I was thinking about what Sam said. Twenty-two souls in the valley. Something was wrong with it, but I couldn't put my finger on what.

"When we jerked the meat to sell to the lumber camps," Law said, "all that good leather went for nothing."

Then I thought what it was.

"Don't Indians have souls, Law?"

He was blurry with whiskey.

"What?" he said.

ॐ

AUGUST 1858

Law

Luke Potter wasn't up to running stock. He had no idea of a bull, and half his cows were never bred. Law felt sorry for those that were, for Luke could never get up in the night to help any of them, couldn't stand to be miserable or wet. It was the same way with his children, May told Mellie. He'd been ill, and wasn't up to much. May, on the other hand, had enterprise. She kept a little dairy herd, made cheese, put butter down in kegs, poured lard around to save it going off, and shipped it through Kaikitsil to the coast.

One day when Law was freighting to Kaikitsil, Mellie and Matthew came along as far as May's, where he was picking up her butter. May gave them biscuits, and they sat a little. Law enjoyed keeping Matthew on his knee another minute.

"I see Myra stole your preacher," Mellie said to May.

"Oh well." She pulled out her mending, always busy. "Her parlor's bigger, and that kind of woman will demand her due."

"It'll save you making coffee," Mellie laughed, "but we'll all have to admire her needlework."

"I wonder if thee'd keep an eye out, Law," May said. "Luke's

147

having trouble with the calves. Three gone without a trace, so it's not coyotes. He thinks it's Indians."

"If it was Indians," Law said, "they would have taken cows. They could have gone down a gully. I'll have a look now, if you like."

"Nonsense. Be on thy way," May said. "But if thee sees anything…"

"Stay, Papa," Matthew said.

But time was short. Law unwound the boy's arms from his neck and gave him to his mother. May offered to have one of her boys hitch up and drive Matthew and Mellie back, but Mellie wanted the walk and set off with their son on her shoulders. No one could look more cheerful and strong, going across the pasture with the hills behind. Law didn't know why he got so mad at her sometimes, why he said the things he did. It was one of those days that bid fair to stand off winter rain forever.

ಙ

Mellie

Matthew took sick that night, his head on his little neck drooping like a cut flower. He worked up a fever and a croupy cough. A little one can go down so fast, it takes your breath away. I sponged him and read to him and got out the ipecac, and prayed. He breathed well, though, all night, so I let him sleep, and in the morning he was well enough that I didn't worry when I had to go out to milk and feed the chickens.

By afternoon, he was hot again and miserable, his hair stuck to his head in wet curls. I tried to remember the songs Mother sang, but they didn't somehow come to me, and when I remembered *Bist du bei mir*, it caught in my throat. The poor cow lowed to be milked, but I daren't leave Matthew and with Law at Kaikitsil had no way to get word to anyone. Changing the sponging water, I broke the blue bowl I'd carried all the way from Santiago, and I cried.

The second night, I couldn't stay awake. I dozed and woke. Matthew was hot and weak. Toward dawn, sponging behind his neck, I felt lumps, and saw he was coming out in a rash. Thank God. Measles. Not the croup. I ran out and stopped May Potter's Seth, going along in their wagon to sell milk. His mother sent her girls. They'd had the measles, and they set the cow to rights and did the outside chores.

Next day, Law clattered in and jumped off the wagon in his dusty boots.

"Boy," he said, "your face looks like the map of no man's land."

He whipped up armsful of soapsuds and washed everything. He'd brought lemons from down below and made the lemonade himself, which Matthew was well able to enjoy. That man could work. I gave thanks for the red hen stepping over the evening grass, for lemons and big freckled girls and dusty boots. Everything ordinary.

හ

Father

My dearest child, Vermella,

It is not surprising that your Indian woman should speak English if she trades, for I believe their intelligence is much like other men's. I never thought their ignorance of our ways, or their reluctance for a fight, spoke much against them.

I am disappointed in Bessie. She has married a fool and despite occasional spats is in perfect awe of him. On his father's death, he has taken over the best ranch in the Aquilero valley, and he will be the ruin of it. When I went there lately, he carried on in the most abysmal ignorance about hiring American workers from the mines.

"Let me persuade you," I said, "of the excellence of your Indian help. The influence of a man like you (up to his eyes in gold, I meant, but he thought I referred to his sterling qualities) can change the course of events."

"What is this to me, my friend," he said, his fine hand dangling from the arm of his chair.

I am not his friend, but never mind. "In their native state," I told him, "they are peaceable, domestic, fond of dancing and singing, have plenty and share it, make no slaves of women,

151

were never drunk or murderous till we set them an example, gambled but not to any harm, were licentious but knew no prostitution or venereal disease."

In short, Mellie, I raved on as usual. Can you guess what he said? "I favor blue eyes."

Well, let them go to hell in their own way, these trivial idiots. You ask whether it be possible to protect your valley from the disintegration that has overtaken the Indians at the mines. Gold attracts men without wives or mothers, footloose and violent, and brings out the worst in them. But among families, away from the gold fever, if Law and others truly understand that the wealth of California is her land, perhaps you can avoid that kind of trouble.

It is not the way of the human race, however, to do a thing the right way from the start. The Indians' star is declining. Think of Coyote, who made all this, the sun, the planets, man in all his glory, and still never picked up a bow and arrow but to shoot himself in some one of his vitals. Should we take comfort in the fact that he always comes back to life?

With ever best wishes for your health, peace, prosperity and happiness,

Your devoted father,

Matthew T. Roberts

☙

OCTOBER 1858

Mellie

Whenever I saw Jakob, I tried to think how we could be friends again. He lived alone out on the old place. He and Myra didn't get along, and he wasn't in the store much any more, except on Saturdays, when he stocked or otherwise lent a hand. That was the day Sam made coffee, which turned into whiskey in the afternoon, when the men talked things over.

One dusty Saturday when Law was plowing for winter wheat, I went down to the store for sugar and coffee and a few other things. Myra sat perched on a high stool at the counter, knitting. Sam straddled a barrel, going over his accounts.

"I go by Douglas of Illinois," Bob Meenan was saying. "Let the Negro or the Indian have all the rights they are capable of, but this is a white nation."

"Let's not worry about the Negro," said Henry Nott. He was sorting through a stack of handles, looking to replace a broken plow haft. "We don't have none of them."

"They have them in San Francisco," Bob told him. "Bound to come up here someday."

May Potter, slipping in to see the new dress cloth, caught my eye. "Evil of the day not sufficient?" she said.

"I wish they'd send a softer color calico," said Arabella Meenan. "This green doesn't agree with anybody."

Jakob was slinging sacks on the shelf. I could smell the puff of coffee.

"Say now," Bob asked Sam, "if a black come in the store, would you serve him?"

"I would if he had money."

"Would you sell him land?"

Sam thought a minute. "No. I would not."

Jakob slid a hundred pounds of sugar off his shoulder, thump. "You'd have to, Sam. You're Justice of the Peace."

"I could do as I please, like any American."

"Cut out the Negro or the Indian, and it does not stop with him."

"Why Jakob," Sam said, "you talk like a Black Republican."

"Do you like the way these Indian Agents talk? Government buys cattle for the reservation. Superintendant gets the Indians to mind them and sells them back to the government for meat. The Indian gets a thin blanket and a handful of grain."

Bob Meenan laughed. Everyone had seen those blankets turning up in other places.

"That was unfortunate," said Sam, glaring at his brother, "but it was stopped."

Jakob came up to the front of the store, and Myra moved to the back side of the counter.

"Superintendent's been investigated, maybe," Jakob said, "but ain't gone yet. Fellows with all that practice being sharp will do in you or me if they get a chance."

I wanted to speak up for Jakob, if I'd known how.

"You may call the blankets thin," said Myra, "but nobody said we had to give them anything."

"They deserve something, surely," I said.

"Everybody's so damn careful of the Indians," Bob said. "Fat lot of good that garrison of soldiers does. Won't punish without sufficient evidence."

Jakob jacked his knife open and ripped the top off another sugar sack.

"All these cattle they're supposed to steal," he said. "If they got all those, I wonder why they're starving."

"I'll be damned if they're starving," Meenan said.

"Your language, sir," said Myra, knitting fast on her sock.

"Ain't this a public place?" Bob said. "You're not going to shut me up, are you, Sam?"

Sam thumbed his order book. "Mind the ladies, Bob. Let's try to get along."

"You all seen the meat at that acorn dance. Now they're running off Potter's calves."

"Potter lost those calves himself," Sam said. "Law found them down a gully, starved."

May looked up sudden from her calico. I felt her hurt.

"Anyone can make a mistake," I said.

"If we starve the Indians any more," Jakob said, "we'll drive them to kill cows, and then we can murder them."

"What are you talking of?" said Sam.

"Don't you read the papers?"

Jakob elbowed by me, his sleeves rolled, stinking with sweat

155

and labor. He snatched a newspaper off the counter and shoved it at Sam, who didn't take it.

"All right, I'll read it to you," Jakob said. "*To punish the savages in the vicinity of the Mendocino Reservation for killing the cattle of nearby ranchers, a party of 30 has been organized to wage an indiscriminate war upon all who can be found in the valley or the mountains.*"

"That ain't here," Sam said.

"Thirty-five miles. Near enough."

"What Jakob can never understand," Sam said, "is the necessity that the Indians should disappear, given the advance of civilization. The country never will be satisfied till they are gone."

"The country," Jakob said. "Who is the country?"

He pulled off his apron. No one said anything.

"Well," Jakob snarled, "you can unload your wheat and whiskey by yourself."

On his way out, he put a fist through the glass window by the door.

"My God," Arabella cried.

"Nothing you could have done, Sam," Henry Nott said. "We all know how it is. An Indian is an Indian, and sooner or later he has got to go."

"Got to and is going to." Sam stood and stretched. "Let's pitch us some horseshoes, Henry. Why did we come to California anyhow? Next time Law goes to Esmeralda, Mellie, he can bring some glass. Folks around here are going to need windows.

3

THE COUNTRY NEVER WILL BE SATISFIED

∞

APRIL 1859
Mellie

The Indians had a sickness in the fall, and a hard winter. Bahé's band was badly used up. There should have been fifty or sixty in the village, and they were down to forty. Lodges were falling apart. Kotshim Xaba was among the dead, and many children. Skilled men had died, men who made fish traps and bows, who flaked obsidian for arrowheads and tools. Bahé's smallest child was dead. She'd cut her hair like a widow and smeared tar around her head, with ashes, awful to look at. The older boy survived and the girl Matthew's age. Rose. Bahé did not know what the sickness was. It was a thing of bad tongues and skins the color of the lupine flower. They had coughed and vomited. It was not the first bad sickness she remembered or the first where their medicine did not work.

"Come whitesick that time," she said. "Die mother, brother. Die little my sister. Just girl that time."

Others had the eye trouble, the lids red and sticky.

"Can you trade for things you need?" I said.

Trade was going badly, she told me. The people quarreled, not knowing whether to be friendly with the whites or withdraw. Some were getting white man's whiskey. Some at the lower coast had gone up into their mountains and barred the way.

"What will you do?" I said.

"Die." She said. She didn't laugh.

"Bahé?"

"You come, we die."

I conceived a horror of her fate and her acceptance, and in the night I wept for her. I had not found her the eye medicine I'd promised. Not even that. I was with child again, ill many of the mornings, but I persuaded Law to take me with him to the coast, now that the wagon road went through, my first journey in four years. I wanted to see Doc Grey.

We climbed the western hills into the belts of fir. At the crest, a thumbprint of blue ocean showed, miles away on the horizon, and we chased Matthew through the grass, thick with blue flags and poppies. Along the river further down we camped under huge, still trees, frilled at their feet with ferns as high as houses, and in the morning passed the stage stop among brambles thick with dust, and farms and narrow pleasant valleys lit by the westward sun, and by late afternoon were on the cliffs. We put up at a farm with clean Scandinavian people. The hotels, Law said, were too rough for the likes of us. We played in the bright wind on the beach till Matthew's feet were blue with dancing into the surf.

In the morning, a sawyer Law was acquainted with showed us over the mill, very proud of a new saw that screeched into the logs. Indians worked in the lumber yard, thin but not starving. The wind blew off the sea, and Law wanted to take

Matthew to see the fishing boats. This was my opportunity, and I walked up to Doctor Gray's, where the wild roses straggled down the cliff. A hard-looking man in black came out, straightened himself and put his hat on, and I went in. The room was bright with windows on the sea. I explained the Indians' sickness in our valley and asked Doc if he would come and look at them.

"Can't take it on," he said. "Sorry, Mellie. Pressure of work. How's the boy? How's Matt?"

"Had measles in the fall, but well and strong."

Doc sat with his back to a wall of ingenious little drawers, one above the other.

"They've been hit hard," I said. "Their eyes plague them. The lids stick together. If we could just do something about the eyes."

"Now, Mellie," Doc said, "why did you really come to see me? There's another one on the way, isn't there. Are you going along all right? No bleeding? Pain? You look well enough. Get plenty of meat and milk? How's Law? Traveling agree with him?"

"Seems to."

"I'll need to have a look and listen."

I loosened my clothes, and Doc cupped his ear to my belly and felt around with cold hands.

"He has a nice strong heart," he said. "You're well along. I'd say about September. That what you reckon?"

The westward sun pierced the window, striking fire in a brass balance on Doc's table.

"Would you see an Indian," I said, "if she came to you?"

"I'd see her at the reservation at the request of the Agent." He looked at me. "You can't take this on, you know. It will break you."

"I hear they don't get much to eat there."

"Yes. Well." He washed his hands in a little bowl. "Poverty is a terrible thing." He shook the drops off and reached for a towel. "Now then, Mellie, all appears as it should." He went to one of his little drawers. "This child, now, may come too fast for me, but you'll know how to do. Let me know right away, so I can get over to see him." He dropped a paper packet in my lap. "A powder for the eyes. Wash it in as best you can. No, you don't owe me anything."

Clutching my packet on my way through town, I passed a clapboard building with a carved angel and a notice board. A chapel, shared by all the churches. The Methodists met on Friday. Catholic Mass on Wednesday. In all these years, I'd had none of that bread, but by Wednesday I'd be on my way again. I went in and sat a while with my packet of powder for the eyes, for Bahé.

It was strange to see a town. Impossible to imagine where all the people were coming from, or going. I stocked up on pans and calico and breathed the bustle of it and read the papers, full of complaints that too much land was given to the Indians. Jakob claimed the Indians feared going in to the reservation, feared death from freezing or starvation, and dozens were leaving. Sam counted on Law to find out how much of this was true. At the harbor, Law met a correspondent for a San Francisco paper, likewise interested in the reservation. He hired a trap and offered to take us to the cliffs to see lumber loaded into the schooners.

The cliffs stood eighty or a hundred feet high. Chutes sloped over the water to the anchored ships heaving in the swells. The planks slid smartly down the chute and flew off, eight or ten feet long, each caught by a man on deck who ran with it and stacked it forward. While we watched, a plank came too fast, struck a man, and clattered on deck. A brakeman hauled up the seaward end of the chute to stop it.

"Don't look, Matthew," I said.

"Is he dead?"

"I hope not."

The struck man lay awhile, then got up and limped away, and the planks flew again. How frequent injury must be in heavy seas, for it passed for a calm day on that shore.

In the morning, the correspondent, Mr. Borland, drove us to the reservation in a soaking fog. Outside the gate, on desolate dunes above the surf, a poor Army post occupied a cedar brake with a few men employed about the horses. Inside, a handful of Indians lounged about a gritty flat. A low building crouched among shacks. Inside, Mr. Borland introduced himself to an officer with a letter from his newspaper. The only furnishing was a deal table and a window so low we could see nothing unless we had sat down. The officer, fresh-faced and earnest in the uniform of the Indian Agency, informed us of his mission to protect the Indians and raise them to a steady way of life. Law asked him if they farmed.

"Just getting started. Cattle is their best crop, as you would expect, given native custom."

"Animal husbandry forms no part of their custom," Mr. Borland said.

The officer shrugged cheerfully and assured us we were welcome to go up to inspect the farms, but as they were five miles in, there was no road, and we had no mounts, this was not practicable.

"We hear of settlers encroaching on the land," Law said.

"If they do, they meet the Army."

"How many Indians have you on the reservation?"

"Two or three thousand."

As we'd seen only eight or ten outside, this was hard to credit.

"Most of them are in the mountains gathering nuts and berries," said the officer.

"I wonder," I couldn't help saying, "what nuts and berries they'll get in April."

Law gave me a stern look, and the officer called upon the Agent from an inner office, a large man in civilian clothes, who shook hands all around, even with Matthew, and offered that he would be honored to make all clear to us.

"The Indians employed at the sawmill," Mr. Borland began, "what is their pay?"

"One meal a day, sufficient to their wants. Blankets are distributed to them here."

"How often does the doctor visit?" I asked.

"There has been small occasion for a doctor."

"How many deaths of women of childbearing years?" Mr. Borland kept on. "How many live births this year?"

"The rate of death is no greater than in the wild. If anything, it is less. My assistant, who keeps such records, is just now at the city. If you would return in two weeks or more, I could accommodate you with particulars of all you wish to know."

Thereafter, all we asked was met with like answers. We walked out into the dust and wind and blowing fog, Mr. Borland struggling with the papers on which he'd made his notes. As we neared the Army post, a junior officer hailed us and introduced himself, Corporal Jakes. A wiry man with eyes blue as his uniform. Were we writing for the papers?

"Why do you ask?" Mr. Borland said.

"I could tell you a thing or two, depending what you want to know."

"My readers want to know anything worth knowing. My paper wants to know why the settlers oppose the reservation and whether they are succeeding in driving the Indians out of the country. We've just been told that two or three thousand Indians are happily employed and provisioned here."

The corporal laughed. "The provisions go in, wagonloads of them, but they don't go to the Indians."

It was so windy on that bluff, Matthew buried his head in my shoulder, and I turned sideways so he could breathe.

"A band of Indians camped right here last month," the corporal said, "in this cedar brake. Eating their pet dogs. Infants wailing all night. The agent said he could do nothing for them unless they came in. Yet they would not go in. I tell you, none of us could sleep. One morning I assembled the company at the supply depot and requisitioned beef and blankets."

"On whose authority?" said Law.

"My own."

"By God," said Mr. Borland. "You're done for, son."

"The Agent has requested my removal, but these things take time."

"What does he do with the beef," Law said, "if the Indians ain't getting it?"

"Sells it in town."

"Glory, Mellie, don't some people know how to feather their nests."

"How does he sleep at night, Corporal Jakes?" I said.

"He sleeps sound, I'll wager. Once the Indians get the taste of beef, he told me, there's no stopping them. They'll go after cattle. Likely he believes it."

We left town that same evening, after Law loaded his lumber and my pans and things, climbing up river to camp in the trees. Matthew and I played that we lived on one of the little green flats down there, so close to a real town.

"Lied to our faces, Mellie," Law said, marveling still. "A man's word ought to be his bond. How can you get along, otherwise?"

Mr. Borland would write about the reservation in his newspaper, Law told me, and these bad practices would be sanitized, once exposed to the light of day. But I wondered what the next excuse would be. Matthew chattered about boats, and Law promised him his feet would grow enough some day to wear big fisherman's boots. The mules were rested and drew steady. We pulled up on the height in time to see the sun go down in the clean spray. Late the next day we overlooked our own valley, bright with lupine and poppies, and were home by moonrise, and all well.

I mixed Doc's powder with spring water, put it in a stoppered bottle, and took it to Bahé with half a quarter beef. I promised Law I wouldn't stay, with my child coming. I would have liked her to be with me at the birthing, but Law would never have put up with that.

AUGUST 1859
Father

My dearest child Vermella,

I do not think Law right to worry so about the sickness of the Indians. There is an element of contagion, but I have been among them constantly and believe I have never yet taken ill from them. They are enfeebled by their fate, and often suffer gravely over what passes easily with us. But I am sorry. If a single person dies, it is a tragedy to the remainder. A husband without a wife, a child without a mother, are terrible things, as you and I both know. If ten die, each of whom played a part in the whole, what is to be done? Who will make baskets, now the old craftswoman is no more? Who will fletch the arrows or hunt the deer? If twenty die, or a few twenties, the young cannot learn, for the accustomed ways cannot be gone about. I have left the mountains, where many have lost heart and wander about the camps, picking garbage. Their life is gone. I cannot bear to see it.

We are at home in Santiago, but there is little of the old life here. Bessie is unhappy. She has left her husband through some dispute with his mother and come to me. I do not ask the details. I hope she will go back again when his mother travels to Mexico in the fall. You will be sad to know Francisca died last winter. A sudden infection, so no long suffering. Joaquín is in a poor state, very low and not long for this world.

With ever most heartfelt blessings on you and yours,

Your loving father,

Matthew T. Roberts

✃

SEPTEMBER 1859

Mellie

I asked May Potter to be by me for the birthing, but the labor
was hard and sudden, and I nearly lost my balance before ever
Law fetched her. May was doing better since Sam had the idea
to make Luke Potter barkeep. Luke was handier at bottles than
he was with stock. But I found May too mild to boss me as a
woman should at such a time. The little girl looked around
wide-eyed, singing from the first. We called her Jane. Matthew
pinched her hand, only to see, he said, if she was big enough
to play with.

இ

OCTOBER 1859

Bahé

Bahé carried her burden basket down the ridge between the two forks of the river into the deep earth of the east side of the valley, pushing past manzanita scrub, through evergreen bush chamise. Above the rolling fir-green ridges loomed the blue rocky shoulder of Kenaktai, Old Woman Mountain.

She had food for winter. Tar-weed seed, wild oats, chestnuts, acorns, lily root, kelp, smoked salmon, clams, abalone, dried berries. Many would need help this winter. She passed the spring where yesterday she had got water and came to the grove where she had gathered buckeye nuts, the place where she had dug a large hole, lined it with stones, burned a fire down to coals, put in the buckeyes together with the water, and covered the whole with earth. The poison would be gone from the nuts now. She began to dig them up. She had not slept well. She had dreamed.

In the dream, she walked in a dark forest. Mellie traveled with her, eager, in a red hat, a spirit cap with a long red feather such as no one had ever seen. They passed a man drooping, head down. Many boats raced around the forest, very swift. They flew with the speed of the hummingbird, crashing into

171

trees. The noise and smoke were terrifying, and Bahé woke crying. This was the troubling dream of a Dreamer. But she was not a Dreamer. If she was going to Dream, she should have been a man, and she should have been training all her life. But everything was changing. There was no one to ask about it, only the old man.

The earth was still warm and the nuts very black and open, ready to eat. Bahé scooped them into her basket. She asked the Spirit if the dream came from him and sat back on her heels.

From the edge of the trees a bird sang over and over, a little brown and black bird that looked right at her, so she knew what the song said. "Don't worry. I'm going to use you."

Bahé carried the buckeyes up the ridge and spread them in the sun outside her lodge. Mellie's powder had made her eyes less red. Mellie's meat was soft and tasteless, but much. Inside the lodge, at the back, she got three shell necklaces out of a basket, looped them over her head, and went to the old man's place, waiting outside his door.

"Is that you?" he said, inside.

She went in and sat without a word. He handed her a small basket of dried meat, and she ate in silence.

"I've been following you," he said at last. "Spirit told me to watch until you were ready. "I sent word in the night for you to come."

"But I am not a child. I'm not a man."

"No. You've been cut out different."

He threw dried leaves on the fire. They made curious

smells. Clean smells. She took off her shell necklaces and laid them on his side of the fire, making sure he heard them, for he couldn't see. He burned some manzanita twigs, which crackled, and held his hands toward the flames.

"Great-Uncle," he said. "This Dreamer you have chosen, she's sitting beside me now. She's going to be a good doctor. That's what I'm praying about now as I bless this fire."

"I don't know how to pray," Bahé said.

"Say what you think."

"Grandfather," Bahé began, her heart in her mouth. "Thank you for the bird. I know you want to help us. But I'm worried. I'm afraid."

The old man nodded. Said nothing.

৪৩

OCTOBER 1859
Mellie

I was sweeping the yard when Sam rode up, wanting Law. Wouldn't take coffee.

"Indian shot a deer in the north valley," he said. "Had a shotgun and come near the house. Meenan ran him off with dogs."

"Be right with you," Law said.

"Fellas are looking for trouble."

All I could do was wash the pots, sweep out, scrub the floor, pull a row of carrots, milk, feed the chickens, bathe the children, put them to bed, sew by the lantern till I couldn't see, and all the while waiting. Past midnight, I was watching the moon go down, when Law slipped in the bed beside me, shivering. They'd gathered at the saloon, Meenan, Thrush, a new rancher in the north valley called Powell, and two or three men paid off from the lumber camps who had taken to hanging around the store.

"How they talk, Mellie. 'Wives and children in danger. Whose side is the Army on? Time the Indians learned a lesson.'"

"Ouch, Law, your feet are cold."

"The weather's turned. I can't get warm. 'Cringing, half-starved creatures,' Meenan says. 'Law-and-order men organized at the coast, we can do the same,' says Thrush. 'They look damned fat. Ten to one they're killing cattle.'"

"Those two still at it, then."

"'Didn't take any cattle,' I told Jeff. 'Had a gun, though,' Bob says. 'Where'd he get it? I want him looking down the other end of it.' And Jeff says, 'I'm going to get me a few, get me a squaw.'"

"God bless us." I rubbed Law's toes and heels and ankles, thinner than I expected.

"'Indians probably learned their lesson,' Sam said. 'Anyhow, Bob got the deer.' All laughed at that. Sam got Potter to hold the drink till it looked like some of the men wanted an excuse to quit making fools of themselves, and after that he opened up two three bottles on the house. So now you can breathe a sigh, Mellie, and we all can."

Arabella Meenan wasn't through, though. She camped out in the store for a week to tell how that Indian walked around with a shotgun large as life.

"Large as life," she told me, sitting on an apple crate.

"Maybe he could try to be a little smaller next time," May Potter whispered, bringing in a can of her cream to sell to Myra.

"What are they to eat?" I asked Arabella.

"If we remove them," said Myra, "to some place where their wants might be supplied, the memory of their old homes would fade in time."

Arabella fanned herself with a cigar company flyer. "Who will enforce the law? That's what I want to know. Indians are not to have firearms. Otherwise, they'll shoot your cattle without so much as a by-your-leave."

"Please, Ma'am, may I shoot your cow today?" May murmured. She was a treasure.

OCTOBER 1859
Mellie

Doc Gray opened the back of his nickel watch, big as a turnip, and let Matthew see the little wheels tip this way and that.

"What is it for?" the boy said.

"It tells the time."

Doc was staying the night. In the chill evening, I rocked, nursing Jane.

"Why does it have two sticks?"

"They're called hands. This one tells the hour. Seven. And this the minute. Half past."

"Bed time," I said.

"No," said Matthew.

"Very soon," Doc told him. "When the little hand comes to the eight and the big one to the twelve." He clicked the watch closed, got to his feet, knees cracking, and reached to the mantel for a candle. "Bed time for me. I'm saddle sore. Well, Mellie, he's healthy and curious. Been well since the measles?"

"Very well."

"Good thing you're not a little Indian boy, Matthew. The measles might have done for you."

"I had a rash."

"You're lucky that was all. Many Indians died, and not the boys only. Ask your mother."

"Measles?" The word slipped in my mind, came loose and slid. I stood up, holding Jane close. "It can't have been measles, Doc. Bahé said they turned purple and choked."

"That's it, all right. They take it hard. Saw it on the coast in '55."

The house was suddenly too small. My dress bound at the waist, the neck.

"We carried it to them?"

"No, no, don't blame yourself. The local air, their unwholesome way of life..."

I had thought to help. I looked to my shelves of plates for reason, order. I had done nothing. Worse than nothing.

"Now Mellie, buck up. Contagion's just a theory. They could have taken it anywhere. You have Law to think of, children to take care of. It'll all come out in the wash."

I thought a night's sleep would set me right, but after Doc left in the morning and Law rode up to the cattle, I had to get Matthew to watch the baby so I could lie down and cry, sobs that wrenched up like vomiting. I saw Bahé with her head cropped and smeared with ash, saw the thin children, the listless men. I had done evil. What had evil to do with meaning or intention? The world closed down around me. Why had I ever come up here? What excuse could there ever be for me?

Law pled with me. All did not depend on that one thing.

"You cared too much," he said, bewildered. "Now you don't care at all."

This was a ray of hope in the darkness, that he knew me a little, that he understood. I sleepwalked through the days, dreaming, walking the uneven stone passages at the Mission, visiting the stable with the stiffening leather tack, the huge black pots shipwrecked beside the fire holes in the old kitchen, the tallow-scented alcoves, touching the great books lettered with square notes all in colors and the bright faded vestments, smelling the pink Castillian roses and the prickly yellow kind the Padre said were Scottish, losing myself in the flicker of bats at night, the bees, the books with crackling white leather bindings we softened with tallow and the twittering of the linnets under the eaves, drowning with the catfish in the river and the slow carp.

Once, on the day I turned fourteen, the gate beyond the church was open. Just that once. It was a spring afternoon of jewel-green grass and a cutting wind from the sea. Below the yew trees, white crosses went on down the hill, grave upon grave, painted with single names, Paulo, Rosa, the names they gave to Indians. Dozens of them. Hundreds. Padre Rafael sat at the bottom on the grass, looking off to the mountains where the eagles flew.

"Two thousands, four hundreds fifty-nine," he said.

The buildings of the town rose against the green hill. The hotel balconies, the high, whitewashed walls of the jail.

"It was a great work, saving souls for God," he said. "That the soul comes already from God, that it lives in a body, some forget." He shook his head. "Padre Mora locked the men up here, the women there, all night without air. Some ran away. If captured, beaten. If they came back, beaten. He beat himself before the altar every day. Poor Mora."

The Padre gathered his gray robe, eyes fixed upon the eagle mountains, and folded his legs another way, for his knee joints pained him.

"Sometimes," he said, "there is little you can do." He shrugged. "But always something. Do that. For the rest, it does not depend on you."

Now in Oak Valley I tried to rouse myself. I had trouble in the mornings getting out of bed, even for Matthew, wandering in the cold with nothing but a shirt. May Potter came or sent her girls, to help me. I missed Jakob. I wanted to ask him how he bore it, being to blame, being imperfect in a bad world.

ಙಒ

NOVEMBER 1859
Bahé

Bahé watched for a time when Mellie's man left the valley in his boat. There was a word for it, *waton* or *wakon*. Once that man had run his elk at her while she was getting acorn. Stink elk. *Cows.* She fled, with the other women and children. Now she went for acorns on the hill behind the Big Egg Rock. She was working alone. It was late for acorns, but a good acorn place, and dry. She filled half her basket and Mellie did not come out. Mellie's house had a thin wall in places now, like ice on a pool in winter. You could see through. Bahé came down near the house and leaned her acorn basket on a tree, rattling, half full. She was inside, Mellie, making the things she used as sleeping covers. Bahé could see her through the ice wall, but she didn't see Bahé. She wouldn't. Bahé waited.

"Go away," Mellie said.

Bahé waited a long time, a cold feeling in her stomach, until Mellie came out.

"Go," Mellie said. "It's not safe. You must not trust us."

Bahé did not know this word, *trust*. Mellie looked bad.

"That sickness," she said. "We took it to you, Matthew and I."

"Took it?"

"Poisoned you."

"Poison? You?" Bahé laughed the hurt out of her belly. It had long been known that sickness followed the whites, but this woman was no witch. Could she be ignorant that sickness does not come without evil spirits?

"We don't mean to," Mellie said, "but we do poison you."

Bahé did not know how to explain about poisoning, that it cannot be an accident. Anyway, Mellie was the poisoned one. Anyone could see it.

"You do not know us," Mellie said.

This was funny too. "Know you," Bahé said. "White brother run all over, everywhere. How forget? Come in dream too. Big wakon fast like falling star."

"I have nightmares too," Mellie said. "And some are true. A grand jury is demanding to be rid of the 'miserable half-starved creatures infesting every neighborhood.'"

Bahé did not understand this, but she saw Mellie's anger, like a fire, and that was good. She would live. Bahé stooped to pick up her basket.

"Wait," Mellie said. She had things to give from her plants. Corn was good if you boiled it up, so Bahé said yes. Mellie got her mule. This animal worked for her. They carried a lot of food to the ridge that way.

"Where are the men?" Mellie said.

"Work. Coast ranch. Get horse, guns."

"Why guns," Mellie said. "Why do they want guns?"

This was not honest. She said this, though she knew why.

"Arrow you follow all day," Bahé said. "Gun kills quick."

"Not guns, Bahé. Don't let them get guns. People will never stand for it."

Mellie understood little. Maybe if she were wiser, she could change something. But perhaps not. Of course, extremely powerful, unknown poisoners might be sending her and all the whites. In that case, it was possible the whole people might be destroyed.

%

Law

Law knew Bahé was taking acorns. Mellie had told him, though she never mentioned the carrots and turnips and beets and beans and corn. Maybe she thought he hadn't noticed.

"How many Indians am I feeding?" he asked one evening. "What about my hogs?"

She made a movement of despair.

"Hold it. I'm not a bad fella. Not one of the mean ones."

He was reading the Kaikitsil *Sentinel,* Jane nestled in his lap sucking her thumb. A man shot in Long Valley in a dispute about a fence. A courthouse going up in Kaikitsil, everyone to be taxed $1.65.

"That's a lot of money," he said, "and I still have to work my stint on the road."

"You'll be glad of the road."

"But what'll we feed the hogs? I thought the Indians knew not to come in by the house."

"You never chased them away, did you?"

"I might have discouraged them a little."

"Law!" She clanked the plates together and started to the pump. "Kill the hogs when cold weather comes."

"We'd get a better price in spring."

"Aren't you lucky to expect to be alive, come spring."

So that was left unsettled, as usual. Law went out and down to the saloon. He enjoyed the saloon of an evening, customarily, but this evening Jeff Thrush hung at the bar, breathing all over everyone, skunk drunk.

"Killed three of the vermin coming over from the coast," he said.

Vermin. Nobody spoke along the bar. Tom Carter, the blacksmith, was there, and Henry Nott, and some others. Everybody kept their mouths shut, angled over their whiskey.

"Bagged me a squaw," Thrush said. "Now do I have your attention?"

Carter shifted to one elbow. "Did you?" he said, rolling his eyes up Thrush's face. "So's we all can be jealous? If you bagged her, where is she, then?"

"Use her and lose her, boys. Use her and lose her."

"Go on home, Jeff, and sleep it off," Law said.

Thrush turned to stagger out in that fool hat with the two hawk feathers, aiming to climb up on that paint of his. "At least I know what to do with a squaw," he said. "Your pretty friend Jakob Brandt wouldn't know what hole to put it in."

That stung. Law had wondered about Jakob, but that was no way to put it. And he didn't know, did Jeff kill somebody or bag himself a squaw or not? It worked on him. He told some of it to Mellie later. They were hanging meat in the smokehouse, Mellie up the ladder, Law tying loops in the string and boosting the cuts up to her.

185

"Ten to one," he said, "it's brag."

"I wonder if his mother knows what a bad man Jeff is. I hope he breaks her heart."

"You ain't heard the worst," Law said, and found himself explaining about Jakob, which he never should have. Anyway, she couldn't understand.

"You know," he said. "Doesn't hold with women. Wants another man."

She gasped, like he knew she would, but he didn't expect the look that came into her face, hadn't seen it coming. Now he was in trouble.

"Is that true?" she said. "Is he that way?"

Law lit a pipe. Sucking on it bought him a little time.

"Or what you told me before," Mellie said, "that he went with squaws up at the North Fork, was that true?" She came down the ladder and sat on a lower rung, eye to eye with him. "You said Jakob had a woman up there. Women."

"I thought he did." Law played with his fingers in a loop of string. "Well, I thought he might." He looked at her. He was going to have to come clean. "Here's what it is, Mellie. Sam had an Indian woman before Myra. She lived with them at their cabin they had first, the one Jakob has still, and she had a child. When Myra come, Jakob took care of the woman and her child, and I thought…"

"Not if he's…."

"No.

"You lied to me."

"I didn't know for sure. I was mad. You thought Jakob was God Almighty."

"You thought Sam was."

"I didn't like to think what Sam was doing, so I put it on Jakob and I guess I half took it for true. But you didn't listen to me. I thought Matthew would get sick if you kept going up there."

"What else didn't I listen to?" Mellie said.

"The races won't get along. If they won't, it ain't right to try. You never believed it, but it tears people up to buck the way things are. I saw it back in Illinois, when the Fugitive Slave Act come in. Aunt Maisie hiding them in the barn, Uncle Fred digging them out at gunpoint."

Law didn't like the disappointed way she looked.

"Don't, Mellie. I ain't the worst by a long shot."

"No," she said. "It's me." She slid down the ladder and sat in the ashes. "I didn't find out what you believed in. I just thought you were wrong."

"Well," Law said, going back to tying up meat, "that's the whole truth of it. I don't know about Jakob except he helps that Indian woman out with food and such. Some men will do what's right." He wanted to cheer Mellie up and get her back up the ladder. "You might a been right all along to be friendly with the Indians. Them that go the other way, like Thrush, they just turn mean."

ॐ

Mellie

I loved watching May Potter move about her kitchen, her strong, small hands working the butter in the wooden trough, squeezing out the buttermilk, pouring it off into the crock.

"They say he's mad," May said, "but it appears to me John Brown only did as he would do, were he a slave himself."

"I thought you didn't hold with force of arms."

"My land, no. But he did, and he lived up to the Golden Rule."

Outside, a slanting rain scourged the edge of the pine wood.

"How do you suppose they're doing, with the cold coming on?" I said.

"Who?"

"The Indian children. Women molested on the road. What of the children?"

May dried her hands and turned the bread for the second rising. "Are they always on thy mind, Mellie? Thee can't know everything. Goodness gracious!"

I wished I knew less than I did. I wished I could be always safe with May Potter in her kitchen.

Law was making a weekly run to Kaikitsil for mail and sup-
plies. He stayed overnight, came back late the next day soaked
in sweat, only to heave out of bed and go to work double hard
on all there was to do at home. Sometimes he fell asleep on
the road, but the mules were good and took care of him. Just
before Christmas, he brought a book I'd seen talked about in
the *Sentinel*, a poem by Longfellow, much admired for its wis-
dom. It came packed in straw, a thick, handsome volume, very
expensive. After everyone was asleep, I opened it on the blue-
checked tablecloth in the candle light. *Hiawatha.*

I walked the floor with Jane, reading. She'd had a spell of
teething and sore gums, and I couldn't put her down. There
was beauty in the birds and animals, the snow, the little boy,
sweet like all boys.

> *Ye whose hearts are fresh and simple.*
> *Who have faith in God and Nature,*
> *Who believe that in all ages*
> *Every human heart is human...*

Here, I thought, may be a truth that will set the world to
rights. But then I came upon an Indian maiden, blue-eyed,
with hair as the corn silk. What kind of Indian could she be?
The famine and fever were a wholly Indian business, nothing
to do with whites. And Hiawatha, dreaming his people scattered, driven west like leaves before the storm, yet welcomed
the white man with joy, as only a fool would do. All eastern,
wrong, and far away. Some bearded white man's dream. I threw

the book on the fire, then pulled it out again, for Law had gone to some trouble and expense for it. I read him some of the verses. He liked the sound of the Islands of the Blessed, the Land of the Hereafter.

"They're not real Indians, though, are they, Law."

"Course they ain't real. Better than real. Who'd write a poem about a regular dirty old Indian?"

He ducked the pin-cushion I shied at him, but was good enough to go down on hands and knees to gather the pins and needles from the corners of the room.

ॐ

NOVEMBER 1859

Sam

Sam encouraged people to put in winter wheat as soon as it rained, and then worried when clear mornings succeeded one another and the hills grew pale and no more rain fell. He thought to get up a picnic while it held fine. He set up plank tables in a sunny spot behind the store, and got Doc and Tillie Gray over from the coast.

Sam looked down the table where Pete Waps was studying the *Sentinel* and Mellie and May forked fried chicken onto plates. He stood and cleared his throat and joked they'd have to build a hall to hold everyone next year. He gave thanks to the Almighty for the good oats and corn, the pretty good wheat, the fine stock, and the game such as it was.

"The way he goes on," Bob Meenan grumbled. "I don't know why he thanks God for it. Who done the work?"

"Hush up, honey," Arabella said, and stuck Bob in the elbow with her fork.

Sam made as if he didn't hear. He drank a glass of Arabella's blackberry wine, plenty strong, and waited for May to get to him with the cornbread.

Jeff Thrush offered a toast to John Brown. "A swift passage out of this world, and fire and brimstone in the next."

Sam kept an eye on Thrush. He'd made a lot of money on cattle and pissed it away. Anyhow, he was mean.

"Amen!" cried Bob. "Brown is insane."

"Madman," Thrush said. "Thought the slaves would rise."

"Crazy," Bob said. In spite of his bickering with Thrush, he liked to think he was in with the wild young fellows.

"All settled, then," Sam said. "Mad or insane or crazy, one of the three. When do you suppose they'll put the railroad through to Kaikitsil, May? You can keep your dress clean all the way to San Francisco."

Pete Waps got up, wiped his face with a blue bandana, and said he would read John Brown's final address to the court.

"*I see a book kissed here which I suppose to be the Bible. It teaches me to remember them that are in bonds, as bound with them. I endeavoured to act up to that instruction.*"

"Acted up, all right," Bob said.

Sam heard scattered laughter, but Pete went on, slight and bald. The bones in his head stood out.

"*Now, if it is deemed necessary that I should forfeit my life for the furtherance of the ends of justice, and mingle my blood ...*"

Thrush banged his knife and Meenan joined in.

"Wait a minute," Sam called out. "This here is history. They're going to hang him. Meantime, he's had his say. Let's hear it."

Pete went on. "*...and mingle my blood further with the blood of*

192

my children and with the blood of millions in this slave country whose rights are disregarded by wicked, cruel..."

"Blood!" cried Arabella. "All this talk of blood!"

"Oh, my dear," Myra said. "People will be murdered in their beds."

"At least Brown dies game." That was Doc. "I'm no abolitionist, but..."

They drowned Pete out. Tillie had brought her frosted angel cake, God bless her, but how was he going to keep the peace, Sam wondered. And this Lincoln, saying it had to come to a decision.

ॐ

APRIL 1860
Bahé

Winter was hard. Bahé learned the new songs. She slept badly, dreamed painful dreams. Her friend Tsu Daiyan was jumped on in the road, dragged into the bushes, forced and hurt. Her husband tried to blind her in one eye, the old way, but she escaped and came to Bahé, hair torn and streaming. The people chased away the husband when he appeared, because this was not adultery, and so Tsu Daiyan lost everything except her eye and one sorry little girl. Many shell beads and deerskins had been given at her marriage. Bahé gave food to her.

Then the child fell sick. Bahé sang and shook the rattles, and for some time the girl seemed better. Then she went down and down and Bahé could not stop it. She was trying to learn doctoring, but all she could do was not enough, it was too ordinary, and her friend was not happy. Drowsing in the morning after singing all one night, Bahé felt even the roots of the trees pulling her down.

"Grandfather," she prayed. "I can't live this way. You've got to let me go."

"All right," the Spirit said. "You can sleep tonight, but I'm not through with you."

The old man could not save the child either. When she died, the mother would take no comfort. Everyone knows doctors understand the ways of poison, so she made accusations.

With her daughter's body waiting to be burned, she went to Bahé's lodge and took her soapweed brushes, knives and nets, and seven of her baskets. Took them and went off to the North Fork people, who were not friendly any more. Bahé let her go. She was too tired to do otherwise, and too sad.

Sam

Come spring, Sam had sold all his land in town except the home place and the store. He was surprised how fast it went. The valley was filling up with settlers and looked like a real town. Always the smell of smoke, sounds of ax and hammer, a grist mill going up.

Ezra Haskell, a widower with grown sons, claimed the last big tract of bottomland, 160 acres for each man. Coming behind him, the Tooms family had to take hill land, though they wanted more to farm than run stock. The Haskells fenced along the hills so the Toomses had to go around to get to their place. They were mad enough to run Brush Creek into an irrigation ditch and dry up the Haskells. Sam had a job keeping the peace.

The new settlers didn't want wild Indians underfoot. It might be an idea to get the Indians working, Sam thought, living steady, with something to eat. Course they were going out, but meantime the ranches were short-handed. A white man could do better tanbarking or even at the mines. What about training a few Indians to work? Sam went around to Law's place to discuss it, but Law was down the valley working a new team, so it was Mellie he talked to.

"Down below and over to the coast they use them on the ranches, men for the heavy work, women to wash and fetch water. Thanks for the coffee, Mellie. They say it takes two or three to equal a white, and that's how they pay them. Don't you think they could do all right?"

"I guess you know Indian women," Mellie said. "And so I guess you know they're not afraid of work."

She picked up her baby and put a little dress on her and soft shoes. Sam wondered how much she knew about certain things. Mellie was a handsome woman, and she had spirit.

"It all depends," he said. "When they're having their monthlies, they won't even feed themselves. Their fingernails are poison."

"What stuff," Mellie said, tucking her head into Jane's tummy. What *stuff!*" The child giggled and grabbed at her breast. Sam could almost feel it himself. Mellie put him in mind of a certain slim Indian woman, not upholstered like Myra. Too bad a man had to marry. But he was getting distracted.

"Would the men work?" he asked Mellie. "They ain't used to a regular life. When the salmon run, they take off. I'd work like that if I could. Send Myra digging roots."

"With those fingernails? That would be poison."

"Glad to see you got your kick back, Mellie. Would people take to Indians working, at the town?"

"They'd be for it and against it."

Sam laughed. A sturdy little fellow came in, tracking mud across the floor and climbed on a chair to reach the old bread on a shelf.

"That damn rooster'll peck me to death if I don't feed him right now, Ma," he said.

"You better hurry up, then. Greet Mr. Brandt, Matthew."

"Hello there, Matt," Sam said.

The boy obliged his mother and went out.

"Speak to Law," Sam said. "We'll give it a trial with the leading citizens. We'd only have to pay seventy-five cents a day. For men. Wouldn't things go better here with some help? Who's going to kill your hogs? Does he think you're going to do it?"

A few days later, though he hadn't heard from Law, Sam rode up to the Indian village and hired a big, handsome Indian to help out in the store. Called him Jake. Jake had scarred cheeks, little parallel designs, like a comb. He wanted money for a horse, and he looked a sight sweeping up inside a store. He couldn't serve customers, since he spoke no English, but he was willing. Sam liked showing Jake what to do. He gave him plenty to eat, till he looked good. Some people didn't like finding an Indian in the store, but not many. Sam talked Jake up, and the Potters hired an Indian, and the Haskells, and the Smiths up in the west hills.

Mellie came into the store one day as Jake was cracking a sugar hogshead.

"What's Law say?" Sam asked.

"He's busy," she said, "with the fencing and the stock and crops. He's on the road more all the time, hardly ever light-hearted with the children. Always a springhouse or a chicken-house to build. The more we do, the more we have to do. But he won't hire. Prefers to take care of ourselves."

Sam sighed and slid her packet of coffee across the shelf.

"You're the trouble, Mellie. You're too good. You even mark the cows. You should have stayed indoors like Myra. Once you're known, you're lost, girl."

❧

Mellie

"I beseech you, brethren, by the mercy of God that you present your bodies, a living sacrifice." That was the text Mr. Lawrence preached in Myra's parlor one dazzling summer Sunday. The heathen were not to blame, he said, for their ignorance of Christ. We were to blame if we left them in darkness. After service, when everyone made for the pepperwood shade to picnic, I sent the children out with Law and asked Mr. Lawrence for a word in private. We stepped out of the bright day back into the parlor, and he took wine from Myra's sideboard and made a show of sniffing it. I asked him how he thought we could help our Indians.

He looked startled. "Any number of ways."

"They are hungry and sick. Their way of life is breaking down."

"Disorder is to be expected among heathens."

"They are losing heart, Mr. Lawrence. At the end of winter, they wail over the corpses of little children."

I couldn't help it. The tears came. He waited kindly, giving me a handkerchief with A.L. stitched in red in the corner, begging me not to be distressed, or to trouble myself. It seemed to comfort him to find the phrase, "trouble yourself."

"Are we not to trouble ourselves to be neighbors?"

"Reason must be our guide. God who fed the young ravens...."

"To speak plainly," I said, "we have taken their land and livelihood."

He set down his glass. "The land was free and open for settlement."

"If they come to their hills for grain or game, they are driven away."

"Their time is come, I fear, in the great providence of God." He seemed to struggle with a temptation to stare at my bodice. My milk was leaking, making a spot. "Why can they not go to a reserve where they can be educated and taught true religion?"

I willed him to look me in the face. "They work without pay at the reserve, they shiver under thin blankets."

"Surely not. I fear you have been imposed upon. The Indians are not lacking in trickery, though their intelligence is known to be low."

The house was dark, with too many curtains, too much upon the walls. How did Myra come to have so much needlework? She must be older than she made out.

I tried again. "Women are seized upon the roads."

He came and took my hands.

"Ask Doctor Gray or Jakob Brandt," I said. "They won't deny it."

Where was Jakob? I missed him.

Mr. Lawrence sat down suddenly, took another glass of wine, and acknowledged that the state of affairs was overwhelming. He hated California. The white-gold hills looked brown to him. "Few care here for religion, short of the deathbed. Thistles stick to my stockings, everywhere I go. It is impossible to find out the truth of anything." For a moment he seemed a human being, though a sad one. But he soon became polite again and offered to be of counsel at any time. He was most eager to influence people to prepare their souls while good might still be done. Presently we walked out to the picnic.

Sam was boosting someone to be judge in Kaikitsil, and the talk was all who would whup who in the election. I left Matthew watching Law pitch horsehoes and wishing he could do the same, took Jane and walked up the shallow creek, barefoot on the bright pebbles. We sat still in a shady blue gentian place, near a stand of redwood trees whose tops stirred the sky far up, and she nursed and slept. Time poured slow as water. We sat so long, a doe came down with pretty big ears, stretched her neck at the soft ripples, drank, and leapt away, clearing the chapparal at a light bound. Shots and shouts came over the hill, then peace. I watched a chip float and circle, hang on a stone's edge, then go on down.

When I got back to the picnic, I found the bleeding doe. The men had bagged her when she wandered into the clearing.

❧

AUGUST 1860

Mellie

News flew to us across the country when the express came in, the stage and then the ponies. New York to San Francisco in two weeks. Another two to us. If Lincoln got elected, people said, abolition would destroy the south. They'd have to secede. That would mean war. Myra said Lincoln was an ape who would marry a coon if one would have him. Everyone teased her in the store one Saturday about how Lincoln would put his feet up on the furniture when he got into the White House.

"Don't you just hate that man, Mellie?" Myra said. "You're from Mississippi. I should think you'd defend our way of life."

"You can hate him," Pete Waps said, "but Lincoln's upholding the Declaration."

I was hunting a pair of shoes for Matthew, watching Sam big-belly around the store and wondering whether he'd hire his own halfbreed child and pay him a third of what he'd pay a white, when Jakob walked in, looking like death. He hadn't spoken to his brother in two years, or me either. I'd had the wrong story about him and done him wrong in my heart, and I felt the lack of him. He and Sam took a long look at each other, but it was me he wanted. I had my children with me, so we all went out, stepping around a pile of whiskey barrels on the sidewalk, past the smithy and the church abuilding on the corner. Jakob turned down the east valley road between corn fields with his face set like a stone, and Matthew ran ahead of us to the creek.

"What is it, Jakob? In God's name…"

"I can't say it." He hunkered on the creek bank, hugging himself, squeezing, holding in place some great agony. The day went suddenly cold, harder than winter, as the alders leaned their pale bark over the creek, and Matthew called for me to watch him splash between pools.

"I should have been there," Jakob said. He hugged and rocked. "You're not supposed to know this, Mellie, but Sam had a wife and child up at the North Fork. I've been looking after them. It would have been safer for them on the homestead, but she wouldn't come down." His eyes hunted the fir crests of the hills. "Oh God, the country's full of wild men with no one to hold them to anything."

"What's happened? Tell me."

"I went out to Split Rock Valley yesterday, where that bear was seen, and when I rode back, it was late. Where I thought to see their firelight, nothing. Where I'd left Tcadín, both her children, the old woman, the others, the four lodges, nothing. I had to wonder, had I been pulling too much on that whiskey bottle? But there was the shoulder of mountain, the skinny oak just so. I hunted around and found a warm rock, a fire stone. Then the moonlight showed me the lodgepoles piled back in the brush. They'd gone into hiding. I should have been there."

"You couldn't be there always."

"I knew where to find them, in a thicket over the ridge. They had a small fire, baffled, boiling herbs, all crying and screaming silently over the girl, her hand a bloody stew, Mellie, blood welling. The old woman sopped it away and I caught a gleam of bone. They'd gagged her. But the sounds."

"Go on."

"The Yahai-Tshakale, fish-spear chief, sat against a log with his stomach open, a hash of blood and cloth."

Jakob shook steadily. I gave him Jane to hold and rubbed his knees.

"Look, Mother," cried Matthew from the creek. "I found a stick."

I waved back. Matt whacked the water to a fine froth, a little warrior.

"Sweat stood on his face in lumps," Jakob said, "and poured down his chest. They gave herb drinks to calm him. He could not help clawing at his guts, till we tied his hands back to the log. I shook so when I gave the Yahai my whiskey, the bottle rattled against his teeth."

"Were others hurt?"

"Tcadín was dead. Sam loved her once, a good woman and a friend of mine. I saw her wounded foot, but after the great burst of blood from her mouth, she could not have been in pain. Her other child, the light one, one eye had come out on his cheek, a handful of brains piled on his chest. Sam's son. But Sam's forgot about all that since Myra."

I smelled the hot straw on the bank, the dusty bramble, the

water of the creek among the stones, the leaves of the *bahé* tree, the wild tar scent beyond the corn.

"The Yahai died quick after the whiskey," Jakob said, "and the girl lay quiet. They took the gag off. The herbs got a grip on her, and anyhow she had no voice left for screaming."

"How did this happen?"

"They came at suppertime, the old woman said. Tcadín was cooking, waiting for the mush to boil. Three men rode up the draw. They wanted her to go with them. They offered money. She answered in English. No. One man raised his voice, demanding. The Yahai-Tshakale came out. The dog barked. The man pulled out a pistol and shot the dog. Let's go, another man said, and they started away, but the one shot Tcadín in the foot. She fell down, screaming, and the children ran to her and the men shot at them all. Then they shot the Yahai and shot into the lodges, wounding two boys."

"Who were these people?"

"Two were tree cutters from the lumber camp, the old woman said, but the one who shot first was from the valley. One who wears two hawk feathers in his hat."

"May I take off my shoes, Mother?" Matthew called.

"All right. No deeper than your knees."

"That south valley woman," Jakob said, "who is crazy, who stole from Bahé, after the girl died, she lay down in the fire, put her face in it. We pulled her out, but she lost all her hair and the lips melted together." He shivered like a man with ague. "I'm sorry Mellie. I didn't know who else to tell it to. They were afraid to burn the bodies, to show a fire. They fled over the mountain, and I stayed to do the burying. I've just rode in."

"We must talk to Sam," I said, "ask him what the law is going to do. He can't close his eyes to this."

Jakob shook his head. "I could have protected her, if she'd just been willing to come down."

To lie down in a fire. That woman's despair haunted me. I almost could understand it. I could have wished this horror to be over sooner, rather than later, *in the glory of the sunset, in the the land of the hereafter.* It's what that *Hiawatha* nonsense is good for. When you want to draw the curtain.

ॐ

Thrush

Jeff laughed. There were no witnesses. Indian testimony wouldn't count.

"I want to know why you did it," Jakob Brandt said.

"What are you up to?" said Bob Meenan. "Come right in the saloon and accuse a man of murder?"

"Was it for fun?" Brandt said.

"Ain't my fault it went bad," Thrush said, offended. "I told some of the boys I knew where they could get women. There's squaws up there can't get enough white dick. What would you know about that?"

"You lost your head?"

"Hell no. I didn't shoot nobody."

"That ain't what I heard."

"Well, a dog."

"That ain't all I heard, either."

"Didn't kill nobody. I tried to get the boys out of there. Those boys been in the woods a few months, they don't have no patience."

"Leave the man alone," Bob said.

"I don't see a man here," said Brandt. "I see a coward and a worm."

"Listen, ass fuck," Thrush said, pretty warm by now. "Here's the story. There's only three things you can do. First thing, mix races. That don't work, they won't learn our ways. Number two, drive them out, then they go somewhere else and the country's filling up, so they'll be back. Number three, kill them. That's the right way. Some of you ladies don't like to think of it like that, but that's what it amounts to. You have to exterminate. Everything else is just talk and comes to the same thing in the end."

"Why do you shoot children, Jeff? Odds not good enough with men?"

"It wasn't me, but a nit will make a louse."

"You don't even do it clean."

"I agree with you. Those fellas from the lumber camp, they use too big a calibre. A .44 blows their head apart. Tears the kids up something awful."

ॐ

AUGUST 1860

Bahé

Bahé was pounding acorns when they came in, ten people from the North Fork. Where they came from, blood, blood, blood. They had a boy with the knee-pan shot off, had to carry him. A young man shot through the thigh, heavy to carry. The quarrelling with the North Fork, nobody thought of that now, but Bahé was thin herself. She did not know how she would feed them.

The old woman told how they had come, circling the valley. They'd waited till sundown, traveled all night, walked in the creek. They had a little dry meat and found hazelnuts. Next evening they came out in open country, saw two elk feeding by an alder spring. One raised up his big, horned head and ran. Brush cracked. They heard a whistle, dropped down in the fern, and saw hats go by. When real dark came they moved again. Something rustled behind them, maybe dogs, but it was a skunk family following, a mother and five little ones. They got two of them to eat, and at daybreak found a little flat way down a gulch in heavy timber, and slept. They had nothing more to eat, just water. On the third day they came on, still hungry.

One old man, an old woman, a young man, three men, these wounded, and two children. No snare, no deerskin, flint knife, nothing.

"What about the others?" Bahé asked.

"No others."

"Where are they?"

"All gone where people go at last."

ॐ

SEPTEMBER 1860
Sam

To the Editor, Kaikitsil *Sentinel.*

Allow me to inform you of an outrage that took place here last Wednesday evening. A party of Indians living north of this town were peacefully cooking their evening meal when they were interrupted by three men who demanded squaws to go with them. Upon being refused, they shot a dog, wheeled their horses, seemed to go back, then returned and shot one of the women in the foot. She fell down screaming until they shot her dead. Upon her children rushing to her, those were shot also. The men then fired into the lodges, killing or wounding some four or five others. These men are perfectly well-known to the Indians and to several in the community, but I have doubt of finding a jury that will convict a man for killing an Indian up here.

Respectfully yours,
Samuel S. Brandt, Justice of the Peace, Oak Valley

ॐ

Mellie

After I got Jakob's story, I took a 100-pound sack of flour out of the barn and shoved it up over Joe. I got the two best hams out of the smokehouse and tied the baby in my shawl and rode to Bahé with questions I should have asked long ago. The color was fading on the hillsides, the sun losing its bite. I was watched coming in. Bahé sat by her lodge, thin and wintry looking, her head turned northeast, toward Kenaktai. She looked at me as though I were a stranger. I asked her why I hadn't seen her lately, why she hadn't come for acorns. She had no answer. I put the hams and the flour sack beside her. She did not move or look at me.

"Acorns are good around my place," I said.

She laughed. "Send dogs, maybe, bite us, say we steal."

"Take all you want," I said.

"Ask the man."

"I have not asked. I have told him."

I saw not another soul in the village except the watchers. Not even a dog.

"Could you work?" I said. "For money?"

"Peck on bright thing, like crow? Turn white?" She looked

213

at the food I'd brought. "Eat strange, medicine no good." She looked toward the mountain as though she saw death coming. Then her glance caught a corner of my eye. "Starve," she said, "medicine no good also."

Once, we would have laughed.

The next week, Bahé and two others came for acorns. They filled their baskets, and I made sure no one stopped them.

From time to time all winter I took food to her. It was a hard winter, with a lot of rain. Matthew played alone till my heart hurt and I vowed I must keep him better company. When anything came by on the road, he was on the fence. He wanted to work a team when he grew up, with big bare arms and lots of shouting. He was keen to see what lay behind the mountains, and I promised to take him one day when the work was done.

I waited a long time for a dry afternoon to go down to the store and see if Sam had any quilt batting. I left Jane with Law and took Matthew. Food was low everywhere, and Indians were coming in town to trade for meat and flour, offering bows or baskets, clapper sticks and skins. Curiosities. An Indian woman tried to sell me a rabbit skin, with a rough-neck from the lumber camps clawing at her. I told him to be off and bought the skin, and she went on down the road, but after I found the goods I wanted in the store and got Matthew some rock candy, there she was again, hair wild, skirts disarranged, staggering drunk.

I'd never been in a saloon before, but I made up my mind to go. The place smelled of new pine behind the whiskey and the smoke. I strove to ignore the men looking me over.

214

"Isn't there a law," I asked Luke Potter, "against selling liquor to Indians?"

"Yes, Ma'am. I never do it."

"But you sell to men who do."

"Can't help that, Mellie."

"The minute they're outside your door."

"Truth to tell, anyone can do what they like outside my door."

Luke's impatience barely showed. May would have never married any but a courteous man.

"Luke Potter," I said, "are we to have a decent town to live in, or are we not? You have girls. A woman here needs food. She can hardly stand."

"It's a free country, Mellie."

"Pish tush. Free for those who can defend themselves."

I heard a snort behind my back. "Pish tush!"

"You'd never let a white man drink like that," I said.

"I couldn't stop him, unless he was here in the saloon, and ain't no Indians coming in here."

Sam was Justice of the Peace. Sam owned the saloon. Might as well talk to a gang of coyotes about the lambs. I walked out, burning with shame. I couldn't do a damn thing. I was a fool. The Indian woman weaved toward me, stinking, chattering. I pushed her off, yanking Joe's bridle around toward home.

"Doesn't Mr. Potter like us any more?" Matthew said.

"He's a good man by his lights, son, but we favor Grandpa, so we take our knocks, like him."

"What knocks did Grandpa take?"

"He worried about the swamp in Mississippi. The damp brought ague fever and the babies died. He wanted to drain the swamp."

"Did all the babies die?"

"No. But many of the black ones did. I was Grandpa's little girl, and he carried me before him on his horse, same way I'm carrying you now. He got a gang ready with shovels, to ditch, but Great-Grandpa didn't like it. The old veterinary medicine was good enough for his slaves. "I'll whip any nigger ain't in that cotton field in ten minutes," he said, and rode off, didn't even wait to see them go, because he knew they would. No one would cross Old Massa."

"How did Grandpa drain the swamp, then?"

"He didn't. That was the end of it."

Matthew was silent a minute, thinking it over. "Great-grandpa was mean."

"No, son. That's just the way things were."

We found Law at the house. I gave Joe a rubdown and made haste with supper. I told Law about the laughter in the saloon, expecting he'd laugh at me too.

"Sorry, Mell," he said. "There's things you can't do nothing about."

I turned away, wiping the shallow bowl we'd had potatoes in, surprised into tears.

ॐ

JUNE 1861
Law

Fort Sumter had been fired on, and the country was at war. Law worried about divisions in the valley. Everybody thought the North-South conflict would soon be over, but Law wondered what would ever settle the Toomses and Haskells? The Haskells were Free Soil men, and the Tooms pure Sesech. To celebrate the battle of Manassas, the Tooms boys got drunk and shot out a string of windows in town. The Haskells scared up a broken-down horse, painted "Old Jeff Davis" on the side of him, and tied him outside the saloon. Then the Toomses whitewashed a donkey with "Old Abe." The thing went on all summer.

Law was at home, reading one of the papers, when an item struck him. "Listen to this, Mell."

"Stand still, child," Mellie said. She had a piece of calico, pinning a dress for Jane.

"*In the whole of California are no more Indians now than in a single county before the Americans came. Many people are inclined to put on a sentimental air and charge that the white man is the cause of decimation among their ranks.* That's bad, ain't it."

"Much worse," Mellie said. "Decimation's only one in ten."

217

"The truth is, they have served their purpose in the great economy of God."

The pins twitched between Mellie's lips.

"The great economy of God," Law said. "If that ain't some swell with his head in the clouds and his arse in a chair in San Francisco. *Of course, this does not give the white man license to help rid the country of the aborigines. The great law of Christian charity demands that they should receive just and honorable usage.*" He dropped the paper and flung out of his chair. "They talk the worst kind of hog slop."

Mellie was staring at him. He shoved his hands in his pockets.

"Well, it gets my back up, the way people talk. They never think what a practical man has to reckon with. *They're* not going to have the grief and trouble. How can you treat them honorable when you're turning them off their land?"

Mellie stared at him. Just stared.

That same week, Sam came over, sat with Law awhile, showed him the Shasta *Herald,* where they told how some Indians raided animals off the farms. The men made up a party and killed four Indians, and one fella recovered his horse.

"No need to get Mellie involved in this," Sam said.

Law agreed.

"So far, ours ain't struck back, but they won't starve forever, peaceful."

What do you mean to do?"

"Get the Indians settled down and working, living on ranches. Jake's working out well in the store. You can't desert me on this, Law. Look here, where it says they got scalps of Diggers hanging to fence posts. Do you want your children to see that?"

꩜

Bahé

The air was clear and light, a good day to start a basket. Bahé had a new song from her Dream. *It Goes On.* She fasted and prayed that morning, then went down to the trees. You could see Kenaktai, Old Woman mountain, from there. Tomacaak came with her and Kaicai, still a girl, really. Not many girls, now, or babies. The young man from the North Fork, though, with the hurt thigh, was better. Perhaps he noticed Kaicai. Bahé sang the new song. *It Goes On.*

They moved among the cows. Behind the cows all over the earth was shit, round and thick, like puddles. In spite of this, the sky was blue, the grass burned gold, the smell of the *bahé* trees came to them on the wind. It was good to sit on the earth together. It is a solemn thing, starting a basket. Silence fell first, and then a song.

Kaicai dug lily bulbs. Tomacaak and Bahé wove and told stories. In the afternoon, Mellie came up with her children. Matthew helped Kaicai dig and played the shell game with Dashuwé, whom Mellie liked to call *Rose.* Mellie wanted to make a basket. Bahé gave her a pointed piece of horn and made the start for her, a tight disc. She showed her how to coil, snailing out around the rim. She knew the rules about fasting before making baskets, but many things were changing and it was good if Mellie learned something. The Dream had told her so.

"Okay, tell story now," she said. "Snakes not listening."

"Wait," Mellie said. "I'm in a pickle."

Tomacaak took the work up and showed her again. Straighten the wet sedge root between the teeth, stick the little horn in to widen the hole, let the root follow, wrap to the left, pull tight around the willow stick.

"Talk a lot, that Wren," Bahé began. "Talk how smart he is, not working, go around, say, feed me. Talk and talk. Okay, people feed him, feed him, feeding but getting tired. One day don't feed him no more."

"I'm no good at this," Mellie said.

"Hard," said Bahé. "Why we fast, get help from the Spirit." She straightened out Mellie with her reed, then went on with the story. "Get mad, Wren, don't feed him. Say he shoot out Sun. Say like that. All them people laughing. Okay. Okay, shoot."

"I'm all thumbs," Mellie said. "It was the same when I was learning to knit. Grandma didn't know what to do with me."

Bahé laughed. Mellie was so serious. She straightened her out again. "Shoot then, that Wren. Hit Sun. Get dark, whole world. Sun, Moon go out, stars go, fire. Can't see nobody. Can't find food. Starving then, everybody. Coyote think, what he do? See light a long way off, send hummingbird steal little piece, fly fast, no one see which way he go, carry like that, fire under chin. Then people see again." She turned to Mellie's reeds. "How you going?"

"Pretty bad," Mellie said, "but you just laugh at me, so I don't mind being all thumbs."

Kaicai came back with many lily bulbs. Now the boy appeared, looking in through the bushes, pushing his face between branches. Kaicai pretended to count her lily bulbs. He entertained the women. Flapped his arms like wings, turned his head side to side, blinked his eyes. Owl. He hopped, lapping out his tongue. Frog. Truly, his leg was much better. He trotted on all fours, looking over his shoulder. The women praised, they barked and howled. *Diwí*. Bahé hummed the new song.

"Look out," she told the boy. "Coyote got his thing caught in a crack."

There was laughter.

"How big are you where it matters?" Tomacaak asked the boy. "Pretty small. Tell me, Kaicai, what will you do to make it bigger?"

The girl turned red. She arched herself and went with him. This was good. This was life in the world.

හි

NOVEMBER 1861

Mellie

Jakob Brandt stood at my door, rain sliding down his hat.

"Evening, Mellie, Law at home?"

"He's in Kaikitsil overnight."

"We've got trouble. Indians ran off some cattle last night on the Red Hill, killed three. Thrush and Meenan caught them this morning feasting and killed three Indians." There was a stillness to him. "I ain't been to town, but some are going to think that ain't near enough of a lesson."

I picked the baby out of bed, heavy, two years old, and tied her in my shawl. She gave me a sleepy smile. She liked going for walks and riding.

"Stay, Jakob, in case Matthew wakes."

He moved to protest.

"I'm the one to go. Thrush hates you. He'd kill you. They won't hurt me."

I wore my coat loose so Jane could breathe. Going up the ridge, the wind was fierce. The smell of rain-wrung trees, the muddy, stony road struck by hooves, running with water, made me think of men in rain gear, horses rearing, lanterns hurrying at home in Mississippi, everyone piling sandbags at the levee on the Big Black. *Bridge out? Not yet. Can we cross? I wouldn't try it.*

I realized when I felt branches in my face that I'd lost the road, and had to beat up through the chaparral to find the Indians' fires. They had a lookout posted, two women with smeared-tar headbands. Bahé sat by the firelight inside a lodge with the bodies of the three young men. She told me one made fish traps, one was a shell-polisher, one fletched arrows.

"Hungry," she said. "Not no more. Hunt cow, hunt trouble, old men say. Young men say eat, live. Say that."

"Where are the old men? Matuku?"

She was not saying where.

"You must go. They are coming."

"Sick, them children."

"Go. They will kill you all. I know them."

She dropped everything then but what she had to do. At her signal, everyone went to work packing, dressing in layers of clothing. Fish nets and spears went into baskets, dried fish and acorn meal, dried berries, *bahé* nuts, pine nuts, pinole, bone awls for making baskets, obsidian arrowheads traded from the Clear Lake people, small baskets, skins, knives, rabbit-skin blankets, shell money, ceremonial capes, feather headdresses.

I tried to help. Jane got in the way every time I bent over, fussing good-naturedly when the shawl came loose and she got wet, her little voice chattering on. I watched always behind my back for something in the trees. It was a foul night of mist and drizzle and at times hard rain. We worked in a frenzy, in silence almost, in the dark, only the firelight from the lodges catching the wet leaves, the dark hump of the roundhouse more felt than seen. I judged there were two or three dozen of us. It was less than an hour before we saw torches coming up the ridge, far down, ten bends of the trail away, at least. I dressed Rose warm, her big eyes full of all the things she didn't dare to ask.

Bahé began to move the people out, children and lame old people. The sick had to be carried. Two young men appeared from the trees, lifted gargantuan loads, and started down the coast side of the ridge. There was no way to take the acorns stored in tall baskets built on legs and tarred to keep dry through winter. The young woman, Kaicai, swept almost more than she could carry into a burden basket. We hung it to her head strap, and she moved off. Horses crashed in the brush six bends, five bends away.

Some of Bahé's best baskets sat on the ground.

"I will keep them for you," I said. "Go. Take Rose."

The people moved into the woods, into the rain and dark. I stood back from the fire, with Jane. We could hear the vigilantes shouting before they burst through the chapparal. One or two young men, including the lame boy from the North fork, stayed as decoys and were chased and shot at. Bolts and bullets zinged into the trees. I bent my body around Jane. The riders were upon us, brandishing pine torches, lighting the clearing, but the people were away.

The men circled the clearing, rode off in the wrong direction, then came back, hunting the edges of the camp. I was not surprised to recognize Thrush and Meenan at the head of the pack. I picked out Abner Haskell and Ezra Tooms as well. On this at least, Haskells and Tooms could agree. They began to vent their fury lest the Indians had got away.

"What hole have they gone down?"

"Teach them to kill stock."

"They'll die over winter anyway," someone said, and I sickened to recognize Sam's voice.

"Follow them," Jeff Thrush said. "They can't be far. Put them out of their misery, boys."

Then they began to notice me, and I stepped forward.

"How come you here, Mellie?" Bob Meenan bellowed from horseback, edging me toward the fire.

"I've come for the baskets I'm owed, and bought and paid for."

"She knows where they are," Thrush said.

My back prickled where I knew the Indians were moving off in the dark. "I don't know where they are," I said. "They're gone."

"In a pig's ass." He brandished a shotgun, ready on the trigger.

"Why in hell you come up here on a rainy night?" Bob said.

"I don't know. I had nothing particular to do. I ought to know better, I suppose. Why did you?"

Jane reached out to pat Bob's horse's mane, and on an impulse I passed her up to him just as though he'd asked for her, as though he did not mean to do what he came for. "Oh my gosh," he said, and ran his shotgun under the saddlebags to steady her with both hands. I took Bahé's biggest basket and put in the flared one with the lightning marks, a round water basket and a cone-shaped one for acorns, and I put in a feather mantle left behind, wet feather crowns, whistles, clapper sticks and game hoops, balls. The things of peace. I chattered about prospects of snow and winter wheat, ignoring the men sweeping the edge of the woods for tracks and bending to hunt through the lodges. Better they thought I was crazy. Something about Jeff Thrush, the slim way he sat the horse and rose up, trotting at the edge of the woods, told of too much excitement. Somebody shot into one of the lodges.

"Hey," someone yelled, "there's dead skunks in here."

"Burn 'em down."

I stood back while they torched the camp, watched the caches flare when the fire hit their tar tops and scorched up into the trees, and the acorns popped thick and fast. In the excitement over the burning, Sam rode up and spoke to me privately.

"I'm here to prevent the worst excesses, Mellie. I beg you to recognize the political necessity. Where are they headed?"

"They're gone," I said, never looking around in any direction. "Now the country can be satisfied."

Men who had started down the different roads were coming back baffled and angry. I hung the big basket down my back the way Bahé did, by the forehead strap.

"She must have warned them," Jeff Thrush said. Raw fear went up my back. The roundhouse caught and billowed smoke.

I picked out a young Haskell boy, asked him for a hand up to mount Joe, basket and all – it was light enough – and took Jane back from Bob.

"You want to go on home, Mellie," Bob said.

"Out the way," Jeff told me. "Git."

I sat Joe watching. Witnessing.

The lodge with the bodies of the dead men was a heap of coals. With a gush of sparks the roundhouse roof caved in. The men shouted around in the woods while the flames burned down, but in the end they had to make do with their disappointment.

"I've got to go," Sam said. "Are you all right, Mellie?"

"Of course I'm not. You idiot."

He rode away. Desolate and dripping, I huddled over Jane, trying to keep her dry. She chattered to me in a language of her own, till all were gone. As Joe picked our way down the ridge, I heard an unfamiliar sound in the gusts of wind and rain and the clattering of wet stones. It was me, whimpering and crying. My child smelled warm and sweet in the rain. After that night, I called her Grace.

4

POISON

જી

DECEMBER 1861

Mellie

Law didn't scold me for helping the Indians get away, though my behavior didn't win him any friends in town, where Jeff Thrush and Ezra Haskell openly boasted of how they killed the three Indians that stole the cattle, and it was generally considered I had lost my mind. One cold day, Jakob and I went up to look at the village. The roundhouse had been too wet to catch right. Most of its timbers were still sound. Everything else was gone. We wanted to go to law about it. That meant Sam, and Jakob hadn't talked to his brother in three years, so I had to be the one.

Sam didn't seem surprised to see me. He asked me into the stockroom, where he had a little office, showed me a seat and sat on the edge of the desk.

"What about the property?" I said. "There must be something the law can do."

"Now Mellie, you don't want to do nothing hasty." He crooked one finger in his waistcoat pocket, the others playing with his watch chain. "God knows I didn't want this to happen. I went with the party to keep order as far as possible. I hate to think what might have ensued otherwise. But there was no damage to life and limb."

I let that go. "Their food was destroyed, their shelter. That's theft, or mayhem, in the law."

"You have no standing, Mellie, if you want to talk law. It wasn't your acorns."

"My word can be taken in court. I'm white."

He shook his head, circled the desk. "You don't want bad feeling with the neighbors."

"The Indians have more than a bad feeling. They're starving somewhere in the woods, or dead."

"You want to think about your reputation. A lot of people wonder what you were doing up there alone in the dark and an infant with you. If you do bring suit it will never come to trial. Judge Meecher in Kaikitsil won't stand for it."

"What about the killing? Three men dead for cattle rustling. That's not the right punishment. You could swear out a warrant against Thrush and Haskell. Everybody knows what they did."

Sam sat down and leaned his chair back, creaking.

"Very difficult to do to Jeff and Ezra. I'm not saying what they done was a good thing, but the Indians know the rules by now, and taken all in all, there's peace in the valley. That can't be said everywhere." He sat up straight, and his chair came forward with a thump. "Be a shame for you to be known as a discontented woman, Mellie. I never thought I'd have to say this to Law Pickett's wife."

"Law's nothing to do with this," I said.

He stood and opened the door, and I went out, unsurprised. I was getting used to losing.

After a few days, Sam came out to the ranch and nosed around the barn, admired a couple of new horses Law was breaking, watched me split a little wood, came in the kitchen and talked about how long we'd all known each other. After the third cup of coffee he came out and proposed a school.

"I'll build it, furnish it, pay a teacher, start a subscription for books. How's that? Will that make you happy, Mellie?"

That was something.

Where was Bahé? I thought of her in the winter storms and dug deep into my quilts. It rained and rained.

୫

MARCH 1862

Mellie

In the spring, a few Indians came back to the valley and settled
on Jakob's place. They had split up at the coast, and no one
knew where Bahé was. We heard New Orleans had been attacked and occupied, and I wondered if Dacey ever found her
Bert. Law was still a Union man, but after the battle of Shiloh,
with the boys falling and peach blossoms dropping on them, I
had no heart to take sides.

May Potter remained my friend, and she and I went to town
one day together when she had bread to sell at the store and
apples she'd held over winter. Coming around the corner by
the church, we saw a group of Indian children, nothing but
shirts on, tied together in a string. Tied to a hitching post,
seven or eight of them, tangled black hair in their faces. May
put her basket down and tried to talk to them.

"Where are your parents, dears?"

They looked sorrowful and solemn, the biggest maybe ten
years old.

"What is thy name?" she asked a little girl.

The child looked at the fruit, the bread.

"Would thee like some?" May pushed the basket closer.

All the hands reached for it, swarmed over the apples, tore the bread, crammed the food into their mouths. In seconds it was gone, cores, stems and all.

"Why, you're starved!" May breathed.

A man in spurred boots came out of the store and spoke curtly to them. They stood up obediently on their bare feet. He gave us a look as if to say, this is none of your affair, untied the children from the post, mounted, and wrapped the rope around his pommel. I found my throat too dry to speak. Nor could I imagine what to say. The man kicked his horse into a walk, and the children followed, running or stumbling.

May burst into tears and collapsed on the sidewalk. "Where are the men?" she begged me, trembling. "Are there men in this town?"

"You're ill," I said. "Come in the store."

We sat in the back, on bolts of yard goods. May pressed her fingers to the corners of her eyes.

"Someone could catch them up on the road," she said. "Sam? There's still time."

There was a stir at the front. Myra and Sam came out of the office.

"Man by the name of Garrett W. Peters," Sam said. "Stopped in for coffee. He's taking a string of Indian children to Kaikitsil. Apprentices, he calls them."

May seized my skirt in white fingers. "Why did I not untie them?"

"Shh, shh," I said. "Someone get Luke from the saloon."

"Apprentices," Sam said. "Thinks he can get fifty to a hundred dollars apiece for them in the lower valleys."

"We could have helped them run away," May insisted.

"Too sad," I said. "Nowhere to go."

"It's all right, May," Sam said. "All was done, he told me, with the consent and at the request of their relatives."

"Do the poor parents think," said Myra, "the babies will be better off with us?"

"Better than letting them starve," Sam said, "as they must, unless they steal cattle."

"How convenient it would be," May cried, "to carry on a farm where apprentices perform the most part of the work!"

Luke came in then, to comfort her. "Maybe they'll be better off," he said.

"Would thee stand by while I gave away some of *our* children?"

"There's nothing can be done. It's legal, by the Indian Indenture act."

"Is there no bottom?" May burst out, and buried her face in my skirt.

&

Jakob

The oak trees put out a big crop of acorns that year. Jakob noticed how they lay thick under the trees most places, with no Indians to get them.

He was farming the old homestead, trying to feed a remnant band for the sake of his brother's dead wife, Tcadín, and his dead nephew. The Indians were good people, and they suited him. But it seemed none of the children could get past five years old, and too many of the women died. This little band had only fifteen left of what used to be a hundred, not enough to keep their life going. They broke up, didn't take to farming, didn't know what to do. A group drank and gambled behind the store. He was sick himself. Diarrhea. He'd quit eating much of anything. Even oatmeal was no good. He'd thought about seeing the doctor, but he didn't want to hear the news.

Sitting in the outhouse one day, it came to him how to settle the Indian problem, the whole business. The Indians were citizens under the Treaty of Guadalupe Hidalgo. A lawyer in Kaikitsil had told him that. Why not put in a claim for them under this new Homestead Act? Settle them on their own land. Then they could find their feet and go their own way. Jakob hadn't talked to Sam in a long time, but he'd have to get a grip on his temper and do it.

The store looked strange to him, with all the water under the bridge. Myra led the way to the back, where Sam sat at a desk surrounded by bales of tow, harness leather, sacks of seed. A bulkier Sam than Jakob remembered. There was an empty chair between a pile of saddles and an open nail keg, so Jakob sat and explained his idea.

"It won't stand up," Sam said. He fumbled in a drawer.

"Why not? They can hunt and get acorns, maybe learn to farm."

"No one will recognize Indian claims."

"You're the law. You can see that they do."

"I'm not a miracle worker." Sam brought out a knife and pared under his thumbnail. "What's to stop anyone taking the land away from them? They can't testify against a white man."

"I'd testify," Jakob said.

"It would only happen again. You're wasting your time."

The carelessness was what made Jakob want to choke his brother. "Can't the law..."

"Understand this, Jakob. Indians don't exist in law."

Jakob seized the nail keg and sloshed it at Sam. A tangle of nails flew out. Sam closed his eyes, and they spattered on the wall behind him.

"I hope that made you feel better," Sam said. He picked nails out of the folds of his waistcoat. He had a spot of blood on one cheek. "Why hate me about it? You don't look well, Jakob. You ought to eat more and sleep better."

"I don't know how you can sleep at all. When I think how it used to be between you and her and how you let her be treated."

"That's an old story."

"You broke her heart."

"No other way, Jakob." Sam shook his head. "No other way."

"You must have broke your own heart, too, cause I don't see no sign that you've still got one. You had a son."

"Shut up." Sam stood and walked heavily to the window. "That was a simple life, a good life, just you and me in the whole country. But you can't go back."

"Why not?"

"You have to move with the times. You have to grow up. I've done it, and you haven't."

"You had a son didn't get to grow up. You left him to die. What would Mother have said to that?"

Sam sat, elbows on his desk. "I don't pretend I done everything right. But can't you forget nothing?"

"This slave trader comes through town and what do you do?"

"You don't know the pressures I'm under, in my position."

"Who cares about your position? Why can't you do right, for once? Could a been your own son took by that trader, if he hadn't already got his eye blown out with a .44."

"Shut up, Jakob."

"You broke that woman's heart. Now it's all Myra, but Tcadín never forgot you till she died with her heart's blood soaked all down her dress, and all you done was that sorry little letter to the *Sentinel*."

Sam had his eyes down, standing nails on their heads along his desktop, one by one.

"Myra," he said, his voice husky. "Myra ain't nothing to do with it."

ᐯᐠ

SEPTEMBER 1862
Father

Fiddletown

My dearest, best beloved child, Vermella,

What do you say, Mellie, is it worse to be killed or be a killer? I am sorry for the poor dead, but they are out of their misery. As for us, our knowledge of our own savagery is just begun.

I am trying for the legislature from Santiago and the valley. I could hardly get in as an Independent, so am running for the American Party, though I don't agree much with them. The session is January to April, a terrible long time, but I must do something against the Act of 1850. I believed in freeing my own slaves, not forcing my neighbors to do so, but standing by while another race of poor souls is chained up under Indian Indenture is too steep for me.

The Superintendent of Indian Affairs has been brought up by his own clerk for mismanagement of funds. He has Indians tend his cattle on government land and makes a tidy profit. This is the same stamp-licking postmaster who once proposed to move the tribes across the Sierras. There is talk of throwing him out and getting a new fellow, but where there is money to be made, the result may be the same. Many are foolish enough to admire any man who gets what he wants.

Kiss the little children for me and tell them Grandpa hopes they will remember him in their prayers. Cross your fingers, Mellie, that we lick the sons of bitches.

Your loving and admiring Father,

Matthew T. Roberts

p.s. I enclose a letter from Bessie. I have not read it, as she says it is private.

My dear sister Mellie,

If I neglect you, it is that I am always busy. We have moved south along the Andalá and seldom see Father and Nannie any more. We have delicious grapes and melons, but the apples have a sickening sweet taste and very tough. It is always warm here, with occasionally a sprinkle to settle the dust.

My husband is gone to Mexico half the time, he says it is business, or to Monterey, about the land grant trouble. When he is home he plays cards and drinks a great deal. I don't know that I have ever done any one in the world an injury, but I cannot stay where I am badly treated, and so have come to his sister's, where I am bored half to death. I try to pass away the hours in reading, but you know I have never liked books. There is no music, no fandangoes, only talking and cooking. *Carne asado, carne cocida, chile verde.* I am sick of it all.

I suppose you have to care for your little ones yourself. I have two girls and a darling boy. My terror is that they may meet with some accident. As to any more, I have told Sancho it is impossible.

A gentleman has made himself agreeable to me, very awkward when my husband is away, but he is everywhere in society here. He is diverting and plays faro very well, but I am determined not to give him a word of encouragement. Yet it is sweet in him to prefer me over all the ladies. He took my hand the other day and held it so long I had to withdraw it. Gently, of course, but I fear he has gone away with sorely wounded feelings.

I sleep very badly, troubled with nightmares. Usually it is Mother, screaming, tearing her face with her nails, and I wake sick with dread. I recall little of her and nothing of her death. I only remember Dacey boiling the black kettle with the wooden handle, her sprigged dress and worried face, the room above hot and dim, darkened with shutters, smelling like wasps. You are older and must recollect. If I could remember Mother, or understand the manner of her death, I am sure she would not frighten me so. I cannot ask Father. He has never got over it.

Your loving sister,
Bessie

ॐ

OCTOBER 1862

Thrush

Jeff Thrush had a spell of bad digestion, his dinner coming back on him, but he had to go down to the store to give Sam an earful about the big stockmen. They were buying up everything. That skunk, Preston Burgess, had his cronies in the land office backdating claims. What kind of Justice of the Peace was Sam? Didn't want to muscle up on the land office, because they were in cozy with the big men. Burgess stole a little piece of land in the east valley, backdated to crowd out some settler, and ran a big herd in there next to Thrush's place. Jeff counted sixty head.

"Nobody be able to live here if them peckerstiffs screw our ass," he told Sam, just as Mellie Pickett came in the door. She gave him a look would freeze mustard.

"Begging your pardon," he said.

"I've heard the words before," Mellie said, "and I don't disapprove of the sentiment."

"Tired of hating me, Mellie?"

"Not yet."

"Then I won't ask if you know enough doctoring to fix my gut."

"Better quit drinking, Jeff, and eat regular."

Thrush was still amazed when he thought of her huddled by the fire that night when they cleared out that nest of Indians, looking like she would have been a squaw if she could have got God to make her that way. Law ought to keep her at home. And what a shame, to bring that little baby out in the rain.

Mellie paid for her coffee and left the store, and Thrush went back to explaining it all to Sam, the big stockmen spreading up from Kaikitsil, men like Preston Burgess, born with their ass in striped pants.

"The way I figure it, the big men mean to get hold of the springs. This Burgess will go into a saloon, find a stiff from the lumber camp, and pay him five dollars to file on a 160, build a shack, hunt on it for a day, and clear out. Then nobody else can go in there. Down in Walker Valley and Two Tree Valley, the big men have the water, and then they have it all, you see."

Thrush had a couple of springs on his place, filed on, legal. They'd probably try to scare him off. That was the way they worked. He was damned, but he was going to stick.

Sam said there was another side to the story. Burgess was grumbling about Law, that he was running sheep and cattle, ruining the range. "Sheep crop the grass too close, where it's no good for cattle and won't grow back."

"That's hog drool," Thrush told him. "Law makes too much of his fine stock, and he lets Mellie run wild, but he manages his range, watches the grass and moves his sheep."

"You and I know it, but feeling runs strong among the cattlemen. I've got to keep the peace."

So Sam aimed to keep sitting on his ass, like he had from the start. Thrush figured he'd have to look out for himself.

Sure enough, it wasn't long before Burgess ran his stock across Thrush's land to eat him out. Thrush had a few head, but he was also gambling in town, fleecing the greenhorns from the lumber camp, and he could always fish. He penned up five or six Burgess cows, shot a couple of them, and salted down the meat. When Burgess's men came looking, he asked if them bone-bags were theirs, in which case he'd charge them for feed, and if they took anything without paying, he'd shoot them.

"You ain't been paid enough to get killed," he said. "Am I wrong?"

They didn't argue. Rode away. Of course Burgess never paid Thrush anything, and Thrush didn't feed either. He just let the cows starve along. He had all the meat he wanted. Burgess had him to court in Kaikitsil. Told the judge Thrush rustled his stock off the range.

"It's free range there, is it?" the judge said.

Thrush pulled out his patent. "Not my land ain't."

"Your cows weren't on his land, were they?" the judge asked Burgess.

"Why no," Burgess lied, crossing his shiny boots. He pulled out a gold watch like he ruined a man every day and could hardly spare five minutes to do it. "Of course not. If they were, I know nothing about it."

"Funny," Thrush said. "They came close enough to my house to shit down my well."

"Nothing much I can do about it," said the judge to Thrush. "Even if I wanted to. Even if you were a man who could keep a civil tongue in his head. On the other hand," he told Burgess, "there's nothing much I can do if your cattle stray."

Thrush used to cross Burgess's bit of land coming and going from town. It was his best way, and Burgess hadn't got it fair and square. Stole it away from some honest citizen. One day Burgess saw him and threatened to shoot him for trespassing. After that, Thrush laid for him, and one morning he saw him, hunched up in a big, long coat, poking around in the brush with a shotgun, likely working out how to get his hands on something that belonged to somebody else. Thrush took a couple of shots at him, nothing too close, and went on to Meenan's for Arabella to give him breakfast. He was just telling his story when she jumped up, pointed out the window and cried out, "There he is!" Thrush and Meenan grabbed their guns, laid the barrels in their elbows and squeezed off a few shots. Burgess took off. Got the sheriff up from Kaikitsil to arrest Thrush, but when the case came to trial, Burgess never appeared. Never had the guts.

"Who's the big man," Thrush asked the boys in the saloon. "The one who steps in his own shit, or the one who don't? That Burgess was just rolling along, till I put a stick in his spokes."

❧

OCTOBER 1862
Law

Law was riding up Pine Mountain, watching an eagle sail in to a nest in a tall fir on the Red Hill, when he noticed a mess in the grass in front of him, red and pale. He got down to it, but he already knew what it was. He hated to see that, smelling like a fish. The slippery, dead fetus of a calf, still in its caul. He rode around till he found Mossy with blood trailed down her legs. A beauty, if he'd ever seen one. He made sure she was all right and rode for a shovel to bury her calf that should have been born in January, but on the rise above the barn, darned if Daisy didn't stand groaning and straining into her hind legs, with a trickle of blood and then a rush of it and the little grey thin calf slipping out with never a chance, its muzzle laid on its feet. Another one. What the dang? Law was in a sweat. It hurt his heart to see it.

One by one, over the next ten days, a third cow and then five of them, ten, twenty-five slinked their calves. It should have been his best year. Instead, he dug graves for his hopes, trying to go deep enough to discourage coyotes. A year's work gone. He couldn't think it out. The grass was good. The rain started early, and it rained a flood, but that wouldn't do it. He racked his brains down to the last cow, and she held on to her calf. Hepsi. What was different with her?

Some of the other fellas down at the saloon had the same trouble, none as bad except for Cal Tooms. Enough to make a man sick to be in a class with Cal Tooms. Law pondered about it and had to admit he'd no idea. One night he took out some of Mellie's paper and wrote down all his cows and where they grazed, along the creek bank, up the mountain. Bessie and Bran, the two empties who hadn't been settled with a calf, liked the high pasture, up at the edge of the firs. Hepsi grazed with them, usually. Most of the others stayed down under the oak trees. Big crop of acorns that year. And now Law wondered if he had it. He rode down to Kaikitsil and checked around with the stockmen, struck a fella with a herd on the west side who knew what he was talking about.

"Oh yeah," he said, "they're bitter. Too many acorns can make a cow slink her calf."

Nothing to do but count your blessings, that's what Mellie said. She was expecting another child, got past the early part. Everyone was well, didn't need clothes for a while, and wouldn't go hungry. Law could feel happy about the sheep, and he still had good stock. Matthew tried to help out in the barn. He'd slip a hand in Law's coming in for dinner, so the ache wasn't so bad. Gracie piped up one evening with something that made everybody laugh.

"Papa, don't be sad about your 'tock."

Then Law found a pony, just the right size, and that cheered them all up. He would make up the loss with teaming. He was all right once he decided that.

ॐ

OCTOBER 1862
Mellie

The first that took sick was Matthew, flushed one evening with a sore throat. I made lemonade with fruit Law'd brought from down below, but Matt couldn't finish it. In the morning, it hurt him to swallow. I gave him the book of fairy tales, for he could read a little, and kept him in bed. On the second day, he was better. Law and I agreed there was nothing to worry about, and on the third morning he went up the mountain with the sheep.

Matthew woke late, feverish and coughing. I brought him to the window to look down his throat. If it were the croup, the airway would have to be kept open. Deep down, I saw a patch of gray. I spoke cheerfully to Matthew, tucking him back in bed. I would catch my breath and read to him in a minute. I found the ipecac and set it on a shelf to hand and held Grace in the door to wave to her brother and willed Law to come down. I must keep her away from Matt. I set her to play in the dooryard with tins, and talked myself through a job of skimming cream. Nothing would happen that bright, crisp morning because I would be busy with the cream. Maybe the sun dimmed a little about noon. Maybe a shred of fog crept over the surface of the light. When Law rode in for dinner, I ran out.

"Better go for Doc Gray. It's the croup."

Law dug in his heels, and Joe stretched his neck for town.

Matthew wouldn't eat. He sagged in bed. He whined. He breathed rough, wouldn't open his mouth. Doc would come on the morrow at the soonest. When I went out for firewood, Law was back already.

"Jeff Thrush went for Doc."

"Jeff Thrush!"

"He ain't all bad, you know."

Matthew must take nourishment. But he wouldn't open his mouth. We talked to him, argued with him, held him, struggled with him. Sleeves rolled, driven by terror, Law at last pinned the boy, pried his jaw open, and we saw the membrane thick across the throat and smelled the stink. Law held Matt's head against his chest and found my eyes over the rucked-up hair. I gave the ipecac and held the basin while Matt gagged up flecks of gray.

If we could just keep the throat open. If we could get through till the doctor came. Law spent the afternoon on chores at home. He read to Matthew from a picture book and carried Grace to the corral to pet the mules. I fed the chickens at the set of sun. Sometimes you feel, when it slips below the horizon, you might still call it back, so warm you feel it in your flesh and bones still. The evenings were closing down now. Toward dark, Matthew took a little broth. I calmed myself to sing *Jesus Tender Shepherd.* We tucked the babies in and ate in silence, in the lamplight. Tried to eat.

In the night, Matthew woke struggling, hot and limp, scraping his breath in, sucking great holes by his collar bone. We sat him up, called him to come alert, wrapped his neck in cloths, hot and cold. He coughed up clotted stuff and seemed to breathe better. I warmed broth, but he wouldn't take it.

"You must keep up your strength," I told him.

He shook his head. "Can't breathe," he squeaked.

My heart was in my mouth. I took a spoon and went after the sticky gray stuff, the foul stuff choking my boy. Blood followed the spoon. Matt coughed up. Breathed.

"Better," he croaked, brave tears in his eyes, and took some broth, to please us. "I like it," he said.

We felt so cheerful. All he needed was the strength to fight it off, and he was strong, my boy. I was going to look back when all was safe again and wonder why I had feared so. Only he was so young. Just seven.

We dozed a while. Soon after dawn, I felt May Potter's hand on my arm. She brought coffee, and she dressed Grace and fed her and milked the cow. Then Myra came, and Arabella, and moved quietly about the house. Luke Potter fed the animals. Law and I were working over Matthew when May brought in the hot baby, spots coming on her cheeks. Terror struck me at the speed of it. We tried to sit her up, but she was weak and soft. We held and rocked, scraped throats, spooned broth, coaxed, crooned. Grace grew less alert, her breath rough. Trying to breathe, she arched her back so I almost dropped her. She curled her sticky hands in fists, hacking, wearing herself out. She was little. Only three.

Doc Gray arrived by noon, plain and grave. With diphtheria, all depended on the constitution. If we could keep the airways open, keep their strength up, the affection would run its course. He tried to rally the children with tricks and teases, pulled silver dollars from behind their ears, got a little faint smile from Matt. They were strong, my children. They fought for each breath. The sticky broth ran down their chins. Matthew's pulse stayed firm. We couldn't talk to the baby the same way. The scraping hurt her so. She curled up, limp and soft, too weak to cry. She choked, flung her limbs for breath, and we had to rouse her for the cruel scraping. I washed up in the basin, the water pink with her blood, and turned away from the mirror. I didn't want to see how I looked. A heartless moon burned over the corral.

By morning, the scraping hardly seemed to do Grace any good, the stuff so thick it didn't peel away. Her pulse went quick and light, her skin blue. We couldn't rouse her. Law knelt with her in his arms and sobbed aloud, but she was gone. Still at last. It tore out of Arabella, as she laid out the little body on the kitchen table, "Thank God I never had a child to die!" I couldn't hold it against her. I almost wished the same.

Matthew was stronger altogether. Doc thought a little brandy might do him good, but he gagged on everything. When he flailed for air and choked, bewildered, it took two of us to hold him, turn him a better way. I held my good, brave son, watching the twist come in his eyes, willing him through it. He slid into a calmer state, further away, breathing hardly at all, but easier. We said nothing to him of his sister, but he opened his eyes and asked me, in a whisper,

"Will I die, Mother?"

I held him too close to see my tears. I had promised to take him beyond the mountain. Doc had long since stripped to his shirt, unbuttoned, rolled and soaked, like a laborer at sheep-shearing. He squeezed my shoulder and went out. Past exhaustion, Law dozed on the floor, sprawled in a chaos of bottles, cups, rolled towels, pools of liquid, rags.

The boy lay in my arms, breath coming in thin squeaks. I saw he could do no more.

"Go, darling," I whispered, hard. "Pa loves you, darling. Go!"

A sweet, obedient child, he sighed and went.

ॐ

OCTOBER 1862
Mellie

Down the long corridors of the Mission, trailing my hand over the brown stripe of paint along the wall, pink above and green below, padding in bare feet over the packed earthen floor, I lost myself in memory, and the mystery walked with me. Sung Latin filled the space between thick adobe walls, under the *vigas* of the roof: *qui per crucem et sanguinem redemisti.* I climbed the pulpit steps, scabby-kneed under my short white skirt, my alb. On tiptoe, I gripped the carved wooden *fleurs de lys,* two of them, one on each side of the lectern, and looking over the railing, shivered. Faces turned up to me in the dimness, in the flat light, in the calm. *Per crucem et sanguinem.*

I fled to the bird house in Mexico, where Father ducked fresh from a gallop under the *portal,* dismounted, and washed his hands in the trough, the water flying from his fingers into the lemon trees. The lady there was sick with fever. In the court were many birds both in and out of cages. The sun shone through the feathery acacias onto the white walls, a cuckoo bird went out and in on the clock, the peaches tasted like incense, and my cheeks loomed up fat in the silver buttons of the gentleman with the parrot, the sick lady's husband. She sat pale in the canvas swing and laughed, and looked at Father.

The cook's boy was slow and pigeon-toed. Nannie and Bessie and I teased him with a pitchfork, and he backed into the cactus fence. He cried. We thought him such a baby. But Father ran and carried him to his own room and took care of him a long time and then stormed out and took us by our sashes and marched us to the woodshed.

"I didn't bring three daughters all the way from Mississippi to become savages." he cried. "Don't you know what pain is?"

Bessie wept because he'd crushed our sashes. On the trail, he washed our dresses and laid them on a rock to dry, but here a señora pressed them, spitting on irons by the fire, and made real bows, the nicest we'd ever had.

Later, I saw a mule caught in the cactus, kicking, a red wound torn in his hide, and was sorry for the boy.

NOVEMBER 1862

Mellie

We buried them together in one grave. I couldn't bear for either one of them to be alone.

Law dwarfed the low, dark, empty rooms. His step made the floor boom and drove me out to walk the hills. He tried to forbid me going at sunset to the grave, to watch the clear light linger behind the pines and let myself ache.

I was afraid I would not want my other child, the one that was coming. May was my only comfort. Several in the valley had lost children, and she lost her Charlie, the one most like herself, the one who made her laugh. But she went about her business, slim and brisk. In her spring house, the butter crocks sat on shelves inside the well rim and the milk in rows above. She envied me, she said, that I was young enough to have lots more children. I envied her that she'd lost only one. So we understood each other. She helped with the birthing. A little girl came. Sarah, after my grandmother.

Law worked hard, and harder. It eased him to be caught up in new things. He teamed to Kaikitsil for goods people needed. He started breeding mules. He went all the way to Sonoma for some mares and randy little donkeys.

When the light was such a way that the single rocks along Kenaktai's saddle ridge stood out clear, I remembered how I'd promised Matthew he would see the other side, and the way I'd kept my promise tore my heart. Songs rose in my head that Mother sang, narrow-waisted in crisp blue stripes when I had the fever, her cool hands opening the blinds, and I wondered why could I not have died then? Though there were chickens to feed and cows to milk, butter to make, and biscuits in the oven, I sat and stared at my leftover child. The potatoes burned, the jelly bag dripped on the floor. The sun poured down, and then the rain. Fences wandered to nowhere. Even the barn stood fragile.

God willing, Father wrote, *we will have more children.* I loved him for the *we*, but my heart went down and down, like bodies slipped over the side into the water of the ocean. One on our ship from Mazatlan went weighted with his miner's pick, one with a clock. It would have taken so little to weigh my babies down. A book, tied on with ribbon, or one of Bahé's cooking stones. The doctor's pocket watch, even. They would have made light little splashes.

Came a proclamation in the winter, freeing the slaves. Garrett Peters went through town again with a string of twenty Indian children, and this time, Sam swore out a warrant for his arrest. But I cared for nothing. Not in this world. People said the Indians brought the croup. They said it was a judgment. They urged me to pray, but there wasn't much needed to be said between God and me. We both knew how it was.

൹

FEBRUARY 1863
Sam

They were splitting off a new county with Kaikitsil as the seat, and three new Supervisors were to be elected. Sam saw his opportunity. Someone with his experience ought to run. First white man in the valley.

"Got to do something about the big cattlemen," he told Myra, who poured him a comfortable cup of coffee in the kitchen he'd had built for her, with the blue and red glass in the window. She'd embroidered a cushion for his chair.

"The big men have a lot of money to spread around," she said.

"I have a few friends myself. Another thing. Some Indians make workers, but not all. They'll have to go in to government land for their own protection."

"You'll never clean that Big River outfit up," Myra said.

"No. You're right. Got to close that down. Open another reservation up north in the mountains. Round Valley, maybe."

"That's a lot of land to give away," said Myra. She put out the ginger biscuits, brought her own cup of coffee and the sugar bowl and sat down beside him. "Now Sam," she said. "The accounts. You make mistakes whenever you subtract. You've got to check your work, add it up the other way."

"Takes too long a time," he said. "Can't be bothered."

"I'm sorry, but you've got to do it. I won't have it."

"All right, then, I'll try." He looked for something more cheerful to discuss.

"What would you say to a hotel, Myra? The traveling men can't all stay with us forever."

"Why, I don't begrudge a meal or two. A traveler's always got a tale to tell."

"I thought you'd jump at it. It would be elegant, and we need a place for meetings."

"There's the school."

She didn't have his vision. That was the truth.

"Sweetheart," he said, "you have no idea how this town is going to grow."

"Where there's hotels, there's gambling and whores."

"We'll get a decent woman to take charge."

Myra stood up and collected the cups for washing. "What would a decent woman have to do with a hotel?"

But Sam was set on it. He went to work on every gal that came into the store, describing the fine new hotel to them till they could see it standing on the corner opposite, with a gallery where friends could meet and a handsome ladies' lounge with a piano.

"We like travelers stopping at the ranches," Mellie said. Poor Mellie wasn't herself after that sad business with her children. "It makes for news and company."

"This time next year," Sam said, "you'll be sitting in a rocker on the hotel porch with a cup of tea."

"Where are the rooms for the ladies of easy virtue going to be?" May said.

May didn't like the price of the green gingham, she had so many to sew for. Sam knocked it down, but for all his efforts, he couldn't get the women excited about the hotel. Myra teased him something awful.

"Don't you want this town called after you one day?" she asked him right out in the store. "Brandtville. Best whoretown in California."

"Hell, Myra, where you been, gal? There's plenty in ahead of us for that."

"You never underestimated this town before," she said. "You old sinner."

A wonderful woman, Myra, but she had a tongue, and her first husband spoiled her.

Still, it wasn't hard to get the backing. The men were all in favor. They helped Silas Stokes, new come from Maine, build a 40-foot overshot wheel on West Creek for a muley saw that could do three thousand board feet a day. Sam promised the girls wicker chairs for the porch and space for a lending library. Hell, a man just feels better in a town with a hotel.

ॐ

MARCH 1863

Mellie

Dear Bessie,

It is a long time that I have not answered your letter. Father will have told you why. I too feel the loss of Mother. Loss is what we're born to, so it seems.

You were four when she died. Don't you recall a little? She used to blow her cheeks up and let you poke the air out with your fingers. She whacked her riding boots with her whip and sang us to sleep with *As A Blackbird.*

When we saw her in that room that smelled like wasps, she tore her nightdress with the pain. Father hurried us to the door and shouted, "Somebody take these children!" We were hustled to a neighbor's garden and served lemonade. Would we like to play ball? We could take down the china doll if we wished. It was horrible that the people *knew.* You lay on the grass and turned in to my lap the same way Mother buried herself in the bed.

We saw her once again, in a white dress and collar, her silver brushes laid straight on the dresser. It looked something like Mother, a little dead baby next her with a closed gray face. Then the minister came in black and white and closed her up in a box, said she was not really in the box, and put her in a pit with water in it.

"Is this the best this country can do?" Father cried, and packed up and took us to the driest place he could find, West Texas.

You were too young to lose a mother, Bess. I hope you will sleep better and be happy.

Ever your sister,
     Mellie

€ŭ

APRIL 1863

Mellie

Jakob found me where they were building the school one day.
Bahé was back. He'd seen her with a few others, but they were
frightened and went back in the woods.

My heart lifted. When I got home, I went out to the barn to
speak to Law, oiling harness for his Kaikitsil run, and told him
I wanted to hire Bahé, if I could find her.

"We need help here," I said. "You've been going too hard.
If she does laundry and such, I could spell you."

He took out his handkerchief and swabbed his face. His
eyes were webbed with blue and red, the bridge of his nose
thin. He'd lost his fight, carrying on, exhausted.

"All right," he said. "Give her three dollars a week."

"Four."

"All right. She better have clothes."

"She's been wearing a dress these three years, Law Pickett.
What do you think?"

I turned toward the house, still afraid of hearing childrens'
voices every time I went in. Or not hearing them.

When two starving Indian dogs came to my ranch, I took it
as the sign I was waiting for. I got her baskets and hung them

264

down my back, put meat and flour in my saddlebags, took the baby in my shawl and rode up through the manzanita, under the big pines along the ridge, past the burned roundhouse. I found her lashing lodge poles, a pile of bark slabs beside her. She looked up, her face pitted and scabby. Very thin. I began to be frightened at how she looked. And this child staring at me with distrustful eyes, was this the pretty baby who'd been at Matthew's birth? Was this Rose?

"Bahé," I said. "I have food."

She went on lashing poles. Said nothing. I unstrapped her baskets and lowered them to the ground. She looked and turned away, old boils and crusty patches on her arms.

"We have work," I told her.

She spat on the ground. "Work? Turn white? White woman?"

She kicked the big basket and the others spilled out. She turned over a small one with her foot, tipping out a cocoon rattle. She picked it up and shook it in my face.

"Dollar?" she jeered.

Her trouble was worse than I understood, than I could imagine.

"Come to us," I dared say. "You've got nothing here."

"Got nothing?" she said. "Got more than you. White rabbit take land, take trees, grass, water, take fish, deer, still don't got enough."

"Let us help your children."

"Take chwilen, make like you?" She turned her back. "White people make trouble every time."

"But what will you do? Bahé?"

"Live here, long time. Die here."

I emptied my saddlebags, left everything. She was the only one who knew what Matthew meant to me. I couldn't even tell her he was dead.

ԁ

APRIL 1863
Father

My dearest Vermella, my beloved Child,

I have been at China Camp and snowed in, and then hurried to Sacramento, and so your last letter was delayed. I hope you keep well through your great sorrow. It will do no good to lose your strength. I think of you every moment and love you more than I can say.

The fortunes of war shift this way and that, but for those who favor the Confederacy, it is an anxious time. How do they make out at Bracken, I wonder. Samuel and Eliza and the farm? I hate the slave system, but Mississippi is my country. Whatever the outcome of the war, we are condemned to live among bigots. The Confederacy is founded upon race bigotry, and it is righteous, bigoted superiority that holds the Union together.

I am elected to the legislature from Santiago. My time is taken up with water rights, but my purpose is to work against the Act by which an Indian can be arrested on complaint of any citizen and hired out to the highest bidder. I argue everywhere that Indians are citizens. It is a fool's errand, but what is a legislature but a great gathering of fools? God has made plenty of ignorant fools and has no law against educated ones either, and there is a plenty of both at Sacramento. Better fool than bigot, I say, but why worry? We can all thrive on the one principle or the other.

Oh, Mellie, my old heart aches for you. It aches. I never could see your beautiful little children. I am afraid this trouble of yours and Law's has embittered me and I take it out upon mankind. You always had a good heart. If it fails you at any time, use your head. It is a strong one, and will help you to trip up the Devil. Trip him up, Mellie, trip him up.

Ever and forever your loving father,

Matthew T. Roberts

ॐ

OCTOBER 16, 1863

Mellie

Sam wasn't the worst of the candidates for Supervisor, and he was the only one from Oak Valley. Law thought he might get in. All down toward Kaikitsil there were people who knew him. I said I'd talk him up to the wives.

"Tell them he wants to get the big men off our backs," Law said. "Don't go on about the reservation."

"I won't talk about Indians," I said, for I'd come to feel talk wouldn't help them.

Arabella Meenan was one I didn't look forward to, afraid she might insist upon comforting me. She gave me coffee and told me she didn't think Sam was a big enough man.

"People have different ideas about who's big," I said. "Where I come from, a man was big if he sent twenty slaves with sandbags when the Big Black was flooding."

"You're a long way from home," she said, and sure enough she started in on me. "Just a year ago, isn't it. I recollect the hills were pale and brown, just that bit of frost on the roof the night they.... But I won't talk about it. It must break your heart."

She got up to kick a spider into her fireplace.

"Here's what I'm worried about," she said. "Some horses got

loose and broke fences on the Tooms place. They say Wes Haskell let them go on purpose. Those people never forget a grudge, and Sam Brandt pays no attention. He's too busy giving Round Valley to the Indians. Thousands of acres of the best land in the state."

"Maybe we owe them something," I said.

"I don't know why you think it's up to us."

"We've caused them trouble," I couldn't help saying. "Half the Indians on the reservation are ill every year, many with our diseases, and a lot of those die."

"Mellie," she said, "I'm sick of it." She got up and dumped her coffee grounds in a pail. "You talk Indians this way. My husband talks Indians on the other side. I don't know what to think. I'd like it to be over. What use is all this nice furniture if I'm scared to get an arrow in my back?"

As I made ready to go, she plucked a long paper from the table.

"Since you're going around, you can take this with you."

"What is it?"

"A petition."

"About what?"

"Why, to remove the Indians." But she cried out suddenly and clutched the paper back to her breast. "Oh dear, I wasn't supposed to mention it to you. You won't tell on me, will you?"

I was about to argue how useful Jake was in the store, but decided to save my breath. I felt a little sympathy for Bob Meenan. If he couldn't strangle his wife, it must come as a relief to shoot an Indian occasionally.

270

ॐ

SEPTEMBER 1864

Mellie

Sam was elected Supervisor, and nothing came of the petition to remove the Indians. Now they were few, there was more sympathy, and Indians were working on several of the ranches. That suited Sam. I put up my fruit for winter, laid the jars away, straightened the quilts on the beds, folded the clothes. I lined up a little row of books with Law's watch on a shelf, following the orderly ways I'd learned at the Mission, where the linens and vestments were hemmed and pressed in lavender, and the rich-smelling cognac stacked on wooden shelves with jars of jelly and preserves and cakes of tallow soap. A year went by. A melancholy song came out from the East: *Hard Times, Come Again No More.*

I came quietly into the barn one morning after soap that was drying and caught sight of Law sitting with the pony tack that hadn't been used since Grace and Matthew, stroking the harness across his cheek, such a terrible look on his face. I went out without speaking, for he never would have wanted me to see that.

Late one night soon after, coming back from Esmeralda, he fell asleep on the Kaikitsil grade and wrecked the wagon. Splintered a leg. Had to lay up and keep still. Doc said he'd recover, but would always be lame. Meantime he was sick and feverish, really unwell. Along with the break, he had an inflammation. Doc gave him mercury, and he salivated something terrible, teeth loosening.

"Take care of him as you would a child," Doc said.

I hadn't taken care of Law, hadn't thought near enough about him. You don't know a man you live with, sometimes. He wanted more children, while I didn't know what to do with the one I had, who wouldn't sleep alone, who came crying into the bed at night, past two years old. Law had been down to the saloon too much. I hadn't considered that enough. I was grateful when he gave in and slept.

I sat Sarah in front of me on the saddle, and we rode the range. Law called her "Sally," and it seemed to suit. We took salt to the stock, forded the low streams, climbed the high, rocky pastures where the hawks circled beneath us. One afternoon, we watched two rattlesnakes fight on a great rock, lashing one another for an hour, rattling and raised up, wrapped together till one struck so hard we heard a pop, and they flowed down opposite sides of the rock, one to live, one to die, for sure.

The spirit of revenge was loose in the land. Grant had Lee in a corner in Virginia, while Sherman burned the country from Atlanta to the sea, and the *Sentinel* guessed at an attack any day on Richmond.

"Nonsense," Sam said. "They won't attack till spring."

ॐ

SEPTEMBER 1864
Father

My dearest child, Vermella,

I have received a letter from your Uncle Samuel. I copy the most part out for you here.

The Northern Army burned the church, the schoolhouse, all the barns. Cousin Fred lost wagons, harness, plows, corn crib, gin house, wheat in the shock. Themselves escaped unhurt, but so broken up they are gone to live with Alma's father. Young Robert is wounded, Brother Andrew gone to Texas early in the war, not heard from. Sister Nancy's husband dead of cholera, her family badly used up. Cousin Mary lived near the main road and suffered much.

The Yankee soldiers stole our stock, wore spurs into the house, smashed china, mirrors, broke Eliza's 'cello. She lost all her clothes, but recovered one trunk. Let the things go, we can live without them, but many families must suffer. The only comfort is, the war will soon be over.

The Negroes I once owned are still with me. Their idea of freedom is no work and plenty to eat. I shall not let them stay longer than Christmas unless they will support themselves. If we could be rid of them the country would be satisfied.

We have lost all but our honor and may have lost that too. Those who were most clamorous for war were the first to shrink from duty, while those who favored milder councils had the fighting to do.

Can you recognize your uncle, Mellie, in this sober, disappointed man? Do you remember how he kept lemon balls in his pocket for children, white and black?

With the dearest, best wishes of your sadder, wiser, ever loving father,

Matthew T. Roberts

OCTOBER 1864
Mellie

Kneading bread one autumn afternoon, looking out at the warm air and bright chaff and the grapes ripening on the vines, I thought of the black grapes of Mississippi and how Aunt Eliza had recovered one trunk. One trunk! A whole trunk full of clothes would be the talk of Oak Valley. Sally beside me braided snakes of dough for little loaves. When I looked up again, a woman was coming around the rock, with a child in arms. I had too much work for gossipping, but I rinsed my hands, reminded Sally not to go near the stove, and went out. The woman turned back a moment, seeming to struggle with the weight of the child. She wore a dusty dress, torn and pieced out with patches. An Indian woman. Behind her came a girl, scuffing along, and far back an old man, very slow. Yes, it was. She had lost her beauty, but it was Bahé, her face lumpy and pitted and scarred. I took the child out of her arms, very pale with flaky skin, no hair, no eyebrows. White eyes. Blind.

"Bad times," she said. "Broke us up."

"Come and rest. Talk later."

The old man sank down in the thick grass on the sunny side of an oak, and the girl, eight or nine, dropped with her head on his knee, her bare feet cracked, black with blood and dirt. I brought milk and bread. Sally managed a blanket by herself, boosting and dragging it with arms held high, stepping on it, tugging it free again.

"For you," she told the little boy in her husky, small voice.

They were near the end, almost too exhausted to take nourishment. Only the baby looked cheerful, calm, not unhappy with me, a stranger. He might have been one age with Sally. Two. They all slept, and I punched the bread down and set the loaves to rise. I had a big basket of beans I was putting up, and began snapping them at the outside table. I didn't want to let Bahé out of my sight. She waked and watched me awhile, then struggled to her feet and began to pick up beans and pull the strings, the skin on her hands discolored with old scars and ulcers. She did not look at me.

"Work?" she said.

"I could use help. Yes."

"Hunt us. Nowhere to go."

"You can stay here, if you like."

"Starving along."

I couldn't say anything. I was crying.

She let go the beans, staggered away, dropped and slept again.

I said nothing to Law yet, still in bed sweating and sleeping. I was thinking of a pretty flat up the creek where mariposa lilies grew. Anyone going into that corner of the hills would have to come by Law and me.

The girl woke up and took some milk. It was *Dashuwé*. Rose.

The name I'd have given Matt if he'd been a girl. Almost too huddled, thin, afraid, for me to know her. But she was alive, and hungry.

"The roses are back in her cheeks," I told Bahé.

"Not quit, this one."

"Lotsa milk," Sally said. She took Bahé's scarred hand to bring her along to where they could set up camp. Bahé stretched her arms toward the bright hill, a woman at the end of time.

"Pretty nice acorn up along there," she said.

ℰℛ

Law

Law must have thrashed in his sleep and opened something up again, to stir up such a sweat and discharge. He didn't rest well on account of the pain. All he could eat was mush. Hell, he couldn't turn over in the bed. Mellie and the squaw had to turn him. Any teaming to Kaikitsil had to be done by Isaac Tooms, a big dumb man that was a drinking friend of Jeff Thrush. Henry Nott brought over a book on woodworking that helped pass the time. Law never had much use for books before.

He had done what he shouldn't, and was paying for it now. He couldn't tell Mellie all about it, either. The medicine was terrible. His teeth stirred in his jaw like worms in a carcass. He didn't know if his leg would ever bear.

"I know damn well I need help," he told Mellie. "Hardly a man any more. Do what you can with the ranch."

She'd bring coffee and sit a spell and give him the news, and they'd talk about what ought to be done.

"The worst is going to be the calving," Law said.

"We'll manage."

Meaning her and the Indian woman.

"Nothing's worked out the way we planned," he said.

Bahé was building a house under redwoods up above the creek, the Indian way, Mellie said. She laced poles in a circle leaned together at the top, scraped up the earth to make a sill to keep the rain out, covered the frame with bark, chinked with moss. Law would have let her have some boards, but she didn't trust them to keep out the water. She didn't like seeing hogs get the acorns. She liked potatoes, though, and made them nice and crusty, fried in a skillet. She looked terrible, her skin a ruination, but she was not the worst thing to happen along, not by a long shot. She had a quietness about her.

"Good thing that woman showed up," Law said to Mellie. "How else were you going to flip me over in the bed?"

Some of the settlers were using strychnine on the coyotes, Mellie told him. They'd wrap it in meat. She found it sometimes and got rid of it. Sharper was too smart to touch it, but little Plato came home pretty sick one day. Bahé doctored him with warm tea. Law took the dog in bed with him, and he improved. Law figured somebody might not have been sorry if some Indian got that strychnine.

Doc was still worried about the inflammation. He told Law not to strain himself and not to get too friendly with Mellie, not yet. Made him promise. Anyway, he was a long way from feeling that good. Doc treated Bahé too. Old burned-out syphilis, he said. The child would never be right, but neither one of them was a danger to anybody now, in the ordinary way.

Law started coming out to the kitchen, listening to the talk, especially when Bahé or May Potter was around. Bahé didn't understand the war news everyone worried about. Her whole idea of a war was two or three people getting killed over a salt lick. She thought it was funny, white people killing each other.

"Can't find no more Indians to kill," she laughed. "Got to kill theirselves." Laughed till she had to sit down on the wood-bin.

She came in one day to talk to Law when he was up, sitting at the table. She wanted more money. She had relatives in trouble.

"You were starving," Law said. "We took you in. You got a place to live and all the food you want and 60 cents a day. You're coming to me for more?"

"Not give for land. You not give nothing."

"I paid my filing fee and $1.25 an acre, fair and square."

"Not give to Indians."

"You never paid nobody for it neither."

"Indian first. Indian not pay first."

"Let me think about that," he said.

"Sharp customer," he told Mellie. "Look at that. Well, she takes work off you, and she's not a yapper."

He made it 70 cents, and if there was a big job, he gave her a sheep. She collected a nice little herd.

Sheep take care of you twice, Law always said. Meat and wool.

႘

JANUARY 1865

Bahé

Morning and evening, Bahé prayed in the water of the creek.
She stood in the flow and lifted her hands and the water trickled and poured. All the voices of earth come from the sound
of running water, as everyone knows.

"You're learning," is what she heard. "You got yourself. I'll
keep you alive. I'm looking out for you."

Snow fell on everything, wet snow on leaves and branches.

This thing called work, it was just living. Living another way.
Bahé and Mellie worked together. They moved cattle, put out
salt, fed hogs, lambed out, skimmed and churned. Bahé didn't
like to ride a horse. She never felt right that far above the
ground, but with her feet so bad, she had to try it, at least until
they healed. Then she saw the point of it. Through the time
when the wind breaks branches, through the ice moon, she
and Mellie rode around to help the cows, sadly unintelligent
creatures, lacking in self-reliance. On a windy morning they
found one in the near pasture, moaning, ready to drop her
calf, and urged her toward the barn, where she could keep
warm. They talked her in, legs stiff and wide, and Mellie raked
up a pile of straw.

"Do you miss the old ways?" she said.

"Same."

"How can you say the same? Things are so different now."

"Spirit the same."

"Is that who you worship? The spirit? Or is it Coyote?"

"Worship?"

"When you lift your hands."

"Maker," Bahé said. "Make trees and rocks, make sky, wind, people. That one. What his name?"

The cow strained and bulged. A trail of slime glistened under her tail. The two women leaned their heads against her sides and stroked her.

"We call him God," Mellie said. "Or Father. Lord."

Bahé shrugged. "Call him Coyote, Grandfather."

"Why Coyote? He's not an animal. God has no tail."

"Got to call something." This never ceased to amaze Bahé. Mellie was grown, a mother, yet did not know how it is, the true name too powerful for every day. How tell her a thing this big if she did not know? "Call me Bahé. I got leaf? Got branches?"

Mellie laughed. The cow's belly gripped. She stiffened into her knees and stretched her neck and moaned. A slippery transparency bulged out her hole in back, gleaming purple and white. For a moment the calf showed inside, hoofs gathered neat under the nose.

"I called you Bahé," Mellie said, "because I loved that tree."

"Good." Bahé watched the cow. "Come easy."

The calf dropped out with the next push. The caul was in

one piece, and the cow bent around to it, licked at it with her yellow tongue. Smart enough for that, at least.

"Old Man Coyote live a long time," Bahé said. "Watch. Know how it happen."

"He doesn't seem *good*," Mellie said.

"Not good." Bahé said. "True."

The calf struggled and kicked free and managed to get up, shaking. The mother licked the wet off.

"It's a bull," said Mellie. "What shall we call him?"

"True."

When spring got warm, people came from all over to see the old man, for his doctoring. Mellie didn't say anything about it, but Bahé saw her often at the creek, listening to the water. Bahé never told where she'd been all those months, never asked any questions either about Mellie's children, the ones not here. But one day, making her milk thing in the pan, Mellie told it short, how they died from a sickness that they couldn't breathe. Told it without crying. So Bahé told too how her littlest girl went away after the burning time, when they fled down the mountain and hid in the *síl* trees in the rain.

"Lost from me. Flew out. Too cold, too hungry."

ℬↄ

Mellie

Bahé fatted up on wheat and beef and looked almost her old self. When she used to teach me about acorns and baskets, she never said much. She just showed me, this is how I do it, so I showed her that way too. We rolled up our sleeves, got help from Jakob and the Potter boys, and butchered a couple of cows that hadn't calved, sold meat to the crew working on the road, and jerked some for the logging camps.

She wanted me to teach Rose to read. I made a little book about the valley, about the cricket and the squirrel and hawk and crow and snake. Sally was too young to read, but she could listen. Rose was smart, and we went on to McGuffey's Reader. Every so often Bahé and I took an afternoon to get acorns or willow sticks for baskets or to dig lily roots. She wanted Rose to know about those things too.

There came a day when Law was well enough to get out and see his stock for himself. He stumped down the kitchen steps with his leg splinted straight and hopped to the rail fence. Somehow, Bahé and I got him lifted up on Joe.

"Don't worry, girls," he said, "I ain't going to fall off. Now we'll see how you done."

He was that cocky, feeling good at last.

Bahé went two days a week to May Potter to churn butter. May had been persuaded of her cleanliness, and Bahé came to trust May, though she didn't approve of our working with food at all times of the month. During her monthly times, she neither worked nor touched food. Rose fed her. May and I grumbled about it. We were jealous, I suppose. Bahé was a good worker, skilled at needlework, though she wouldn't wear a thimble, but drove the needle with her thumbnail. Sam had muslin at a good price that spring, so we made a lot of shirts and shirtwaists. I made Bahé a new dress, though I never thought she looked right in white clothes.

I brought a chair outdoors to sew one afternoon. Bahé preferred to sit on the ground. A second petition was going around for the removal of the Indians. *All Indians, wild or tame,* it said. Sam was a County Supervisor, one of the three, and dependent upon Indian help in his store, so we hoped to defeat the petition. But it troubled me. I said nothing to Bahé. She believed her people were made specially for this country and even kept it going by their life and prayers. That's who they were, the people of this place.

"Killing each other still?" she said. "Them whites?"

"It's almost over. The captain in Washington will win."

"White captain dream for people?"

"Well," I said, "yes. He dreamed a house divided cannot stand. Dreamed men are equal, not one better than another."

"Got to dream that?" She laughed, wiped her hands in her apron, and took up a new length of thread, setting a sleeve for Law.

The light sparkled in the different greens of oak and pine

and alder and emerald grass, and the creek spun among the stones. I'd never asked about her son, the boy who'd brought me water the first day.

"People can't be equal," I said, "if some aren't free."

She shrugged. "Not free?"

"Not able to choose for themselves."

"They dead then?"

Sometimes it was hopeless, talking to Bahé. I tucked my needle into a hem and let the shirtwaist fall to my lap.

"Are you free?" I blurted out.

"Do what we know, same like always."

"We took up your land. We took everything. You told me so yourself. There's not a bit left free or wild. We own it all."

"Own nothing."

"It belongs to us."

"Not belongs. Land not belongs. People belongs to land."

I gave up. No point arguing with her. Anyway, she had a certain reason on her side. Grandfather got tears in his eyes watching floodwater cut away the bank, not for the lost value but because it was his country. Law sat in the barn door of an evening, gazing at the hills where he meant to lay his bones.

In the morning, Bahé and I boiled laundry on the creek bed in a light amethyst air, the oaks full of yellow shoots, red and green sprouts coming from the pepperwood boles. I'd noticed that Bahé took her new basket in to town, a flared one with lightning marks, and came back without it.

"Aren't your baskets meant to be burned with you at your death?"

She fished with the stick, lifted a steaming shirt and plunged it in again. "Give good money, Sam Brandt."

"We don't pay you enough yet?"

"Sick woman, west ridge. Chwilen hungry."

I took a stickful of washing to the creek to cool and brought it to a rock and scrubbed, head down, hair in my face. It was easy to forget how much trouble pressed always on Bahé. I called to her for a bucket of rinse water, and when I got no answer and sat back, pushing my hair up with a soapy wrist, she was gone. Yet there was movement in the brush. I followed into the shade and was almost upon them before I could see them in the dark. Two young men, one pale as a white, his right hand gone, the stump dressed rough with moss and bark.

"Kaáika," Bahé said. "Cousin."

The boy who stood on his hands, clowning. The limber dancer. After we fed the boys, and she listened to what they had to say, she told me his story. He and his friend had gone north to winter in the woods, but game was scarce. There was little to eat. When the yellow mustard flowered, they came down to a valley for the new shoots of bracken fern and surprised two white boys sitting by a stream, who jumped up shouting, ran for their guns and horses, shot Kaáika and rode off, leaving their beef sandwiches. This was five days before. The Indian boys ate the sandwiches. When Kaáika began to burn with fever, the other boy built a fire to clean his knife and cut the hand back to the wrist. They had come along slow to the medicine man. It was the first I understood that the old blind man who helped Bahé pound acorns was a doctor.

While we washed up that evening, she told me about her boy.

"So tall, about eleven year boy, go with men down Big River, get salmon, abalone. Plenty fish. Come up Red Ridge, see horses, stranger men come down road there, stranger white men, three four boys tied up together. Come down that way. Keep boys like that, tie up that way."

Bahé poured a kettle of boiling water over the coffee cups. Her voice was quiet.

"See my boy, them white men. Shout, 'give us boy.' Call out, them tie boys, call to Indian men, 'Go back in woods. Go back!' 'Give boy,' them white men say." Bahé scoured out the cups, one by one. "Give boy? Not give? Not know, them Indian men."

Over on the Red Hill stood a big tree that had lost its top to lightning, once much taller than the rest.

"Shoot, them whites. Shoot Indian men. Steal my boy. One not dead come tell me after, say that boy gone." Bahé stacked the cutlery and poured rinsewater over it. "See him no more. Die maybe, maybe live." She spoke as though from a root that went far down in the earth. "Same boy still. Same boy."

ဢ

APRIL 1865

Law

Law went out early Easter Sunday to harness for church. His leg was taking weight pretty well and bent about halfway at the knee. With a good cup of coffee in him, he felt fine. He was backing the pair into the traces when a boy rode up along the fence.

"Lincoln is shot! The president is shot!"

"Best not joke about a thing like that, Seth."

It was May Potter's boy, the one apprenticed in Kaikitsil.

"It ain't no joke. A wire come in to San Francisco. Shot Friday night."

Could it be true? Friday night, and today only Sunday. It gave Law the strangest notion of the country. No distance to the east at all.

When he and Mellie got to church, there was a knot of folks outside.

"I hated that President," Myra said.

"The North will kill them all now," said Jeff Thrush. "All the Dixies."

"Shut up, Thrush," said Sam. He went over to the new hotel and put the flag at half staff.

"Friday night," May said. "And we know already. It takes my breath away. When we were so many weeks coming across the country."

Law heard later that a Kaikitsil man was jailed for hallelujahing and throwing his hat in the air. In the saloon, when Cal Tooms said, "That damned old son-of-a-bitch should have been shot long ago," Law turned him around, knocked him out and threw him in the street. An American ought to have more respect.

Sam voted to table the petition to remove the Indians, with the shortage of labor, and so did the Supervisor from Kaikitsil, and that was enough to bring it down.

Law liked the look of one of the Indian boys that came to stay with Bahé, called him Red, gave him work with the sheep. He was good at wrestling them into the dip and learned to use shearing tools, but he ran off, so Law had to make do with the one-handed one. Called him Jack. There's plenty for a one-armed man to do on a ranch. The Indian doctor healed him a clean stump, and he carried buckets of milk, churned, pitched hay, coaxed animals into the chute. He understood some English, but he didn't talk, except to Sally. In Indian.

Law was breaking a black one afternoon to pull a hay bale on a rope, and the horse wouldn't. Jack hung to the fence on the danger side of Sally, bad wrist stuck in his pants, and laughed. It made Law mad to have an Indian watch him get beat by a horse, so he was short with the black, and the horse bucked and screamed and threw himself sideways.

"You try it, if you're so smart," Law said.

Jack took the bridle and talked to the black, talked his nostrils small, walked him through the job, leaned with him when he felt the weight of the bale. By the third day, he had him pulling the bale into the corral like he was proud of it. Law had to know a good thing when he saw it. He let Jack work with the horses, and pretty soon he was driving a wagon.

Law could ride all right, but he couldn't get up or down off a horse by himself or walk worth a good goddamn. He got to thinking he might not stay with stockraising, seeing the politics anyway wasn't good, with the big men muscling over the land. Maybe he could make a thing of the freight business. He went into the kitchen in the middle of one morning.

"Get the coffee and the cookie jar, Mellie, and hear me out."

If he sold the stock and went to teaming, a lot of the ranch would fall to her.

"We'll keep some sheep and a few cows, grain and hogs. That'll be enough, with vegetables and the orchard. Nobody in New York with this Delmonico's they talk about can eat the way we do. Are you with me, Mellie?"

"You going to be happy without your stock?"

"I like mules and horses."

"It's a lot of traveling."

"I reckon Jack can do some of it."

Mellie was happy outdoors, a thing Law understood, the way the mountains changed from blue to green to purple and the grass spears burned gold, catching the flicker of morning bluebirds, the way grasshoppers danced up under your feet with a thwack of wings. She had only the one child, and that child mad to ride the range.

Law got Henry Nott to build him a new wagon, got Carter to bind the wheels with iron, and bought four big honey horses in Vallejo. Sally sat on the fence, only three years old, to watch him train them. She'd hold her hand out, and they'd reach their heads down for her to pet their faces.

But when he had to let his stock go, Law's cup of bitterness ran over. That was a bad time. Crippled, washed up as a stockman and a man. He gritted his teeth and set up a regular schedule. Kaikitsil one week and the coast the next, and then he'd make the triangle. He picked up around the valley, butter for the dairy men, meat for the stockmen, grain. He brought in whatever Sam wanted for the store. Soap, salt, hardware, yard goods, liquor. On the long runs, he sought comfort where he shouldn't. He set up a freight office in town. Near everything that came in and out came in his wagons.

Nobody ever knew how Jack managed a team of four with just one hand, but people in the saloon used to invite visitors to the door to watch. The sight of that one-armed Indian boiling down the hill into town, hair streaming, got to be something everyone looked up to see.

ॐ

MAY 1865

Bahé

Bahé was tired all the time, up at all hours with the little blind, lame boy, Kekawí, two-hearted and troubled, bound to be a Dreamer. He couldn't eat sometimes, woke screaming with nightmares. It wasn't the white sickness they had taken white medicine for. It wasn't that. He dreamed for the people. The old man held him on his lap for hours at a time, singing what songs he thought could help. The boy ought to be taken to the Roundhouse, into the heart of the people, to be named and guided by the ceremonies. No people and no Roundhouse now.

"What's wrong?" Mellie said.

Bahé could not explain. She was living two lives, and Mellie only one. But the Spirit spoke to her out of a thicket where a red bird sang.

"Why don't you tell her about it? Tell her what happened, what you been through."

"I don't want to even remember it myself."

"She's here, and she's no stranger."

"White people so ignorant, you don't know where to start."

"That's why you have to tell them. Where you going to get a better chance than her?"

"All right, Grandfather. Maybe you can fix her ears. Sometimes she don't hear too good."

So Bahé told Mellie about the bad time, told it piece by piece as they dug roots for making baskets one long, warm day. She told how, when the village was burned out, the people hid in a high valley toward the coast, without *melé*. They ate bark. Bahé's husband, Matuku, went with the young men who had killed the cattle, those that still lived, to try their skill at hunting. They meant to keep to the mountains and bring food to the others, but game was scarce.

"All sick. Half us dead, before longest night."

The old man insisted that they stay together, but Matuku said he would work at the white places. That is how he would live. Bahé went with him, and in time the old man and a few others followed to the coast.

The sawmills, where the trees screamed, wouldn't hire them. Indians from the reservation worked there already for one meal. But Matuku got lucky. He found work on a ranch, watering and harnessing stage horses.

"Sleep in the barn. Let him sleep there."

The willow roots she and Mellie were getting pleased Bahé. They comforted her as she told the story. She showed Mellie how to follow them through the earth, getting their whole length.

Matuku, she went on, got money, brought food and blankets to Bahé and Rose, the son, the half-dozen others. The winter was bad, with cold sleet on the rocks. Bahé and the others fished north up the coast, where smelt runs in the winter, hid well, slept in shallow caves dug in the dunes, got through. They fished for steelhead and silver salmon in the creeks after the spring rains, took chickens off farms at night. In the summer, they gathered roots and seed and *bahé* nuts in poor little mountain valleys, not daring to be seen by whites. Whenever there was trouble with cattle or horses, white men went hunting Indians. They kept moving.

Matuku was still working on the coast, but he was lonely. He could not take care of his family. He was not the man he thought he was. He began to buy whiskey. When Bahé learned this, she and the old man came to take him away, but he did not wish to go. He was angry with the quick and also the long anger. He had no more dollars. He took the little baskets and arrow points and rabbit skins Bahé had for trade and went into a filthy bar in town that would serve Indians. She left the children and followed him inside. He said things. Men laughed and pushed him. They touched her. She pulled him outside, though he was almost too drunk to walk, and someone seized her from behind, her skirts lifted. She fought, but there were two men. She fought and yelled. Her children ran to her. The men pulled them off. She yelled for them to run. Her head was slammed down on the road. Matuku, hearing her cry and trying to come to her, was beaten and thrown into the ditch. When he tried to get up, one of the men threw coins at him.

"Go drink yourself to death, you crazy Indian."

Bahé didn't care what happened next. Her head hurt too

much. The men did their filth and took their horses from the rail.

"Take her along," one said. "That squaw is worth money down at Elsie's."

Out of the corner of her eye Bahé saw Matuku coming. He was hurt and drunk, but he came fast and cut one man through the wrist. The other shot him in the head and wrestled Bahé toward his horse, but the cut man was bleeding fast.

"Let her go," he said.

The other shot a few times, wild, and they rode away.

Bahé could not burn Matuku the right way. She dug a hole for him and hid the old man and children in the hills. Then she went back to town and asked for Elsie's. It was a place where men paid to have women, and Elsie took her on. She was handsome, tall for an Indian, a curiosity, and Elsie paid her almost as much as she paid white girls. Bahé was able to buy meat and bread and take it to the children and the old man in the hills, or in the caves of the dunes. She worried what would happen if those men ever came to Elsie's. She stole a knife from the kitchen and kept it under her mattress, but they never came.

"Would you have used it?" Mellie said.

"Sure." Bahé followed a willow root through the deep earth, softening around it with her fingers, pulling gently, freeing it. "Full of poison them days. Kill how many white people I can find."

Mellie cried easily, Bahé noticed. Like now.

"What you going to do?" she said. She came to the end of

her root, began curling it in a coil, shaking the dirt off. "Never killed nobody. Got sick. Kicked out of Elsie's. Went back in the woods till this child, pale blind little white child, bent legs, born second winter. *Kekawí.* Moonchild."

Bahé tied her coil together in three places and laid it in her basket.

"Grandmother kill child like that. Mother too."

"Why didn't you?"

"Not lose no more chwilen. No good thing. Dream come to me. Say, go home. You're still Indian. Live how I tell you. Throw away the knife."

5

SHE'S NO STRANGER

ༀ

NOVEMBER 1865
Mellie

Everyone crowded into town one warm November day to vote. The big ranchers were running a candidate against Sam for county Supervisor, hoping to move the Indians off faster. Flags hung outside the post office. Union, Confederate, Bear flag, all three. A little desk on high legs was set up in the hotel lobby with a curtain run around it on a wire, women and children not allowed too close. Gamblers in white shirtsleeves worked the logging camp greenhorns on the hotel porch.

"No ladies of the night, I'm glad to see," said May Potter. She told me an old Tooms pony had been found dead in front of the store that morning. Throat cut. Sure enough, I could see the blood stain in the dust. Of course it would have been the Haskells that did it.

"I wonder they're not worn out with hating each other," May said.

I spread out my dishes on one of the trestle tables set up in the road with cornbread and green beans, pickled beets and fried chicken. May had brought some of her ribs. More than fifty sat down to eat and celebrate. Doc Gray was over from the coast. Pete Waps had made mince pie, and Indian Jake kept bringing beer from the saloon.

"You've been lucky with your Indians," Doc said. "Haven't had the trouble we've had."

Bob Meenan said he'd like Doc to remember that he, Bob, had lost a cow, shot on his own acreage.

"Well," Doc said, "you can send the malefactors up to Round Valley now."

"Thirty thousand acres of the best land in the state," Bob said. "Free to the Diggers."

"Cheap at the price," said the doctor. "Cheap at the price."

"Ain't no bargain if you lose your farm hands," Wes Haskell said. "You and your damn petitions, Meenan."

"Once they're gone," Cal Tooms called up the table, "we won't have to smell Indian when the wind blows over from your place, Wes."

"You damn horse thief," Wes said. He had a meat knife in his fist and he brandished it at Cal. "You said all you ever going to say on that."

"Now boys," Doc said. "It's Election Day."

I'd heard enough. I left Sally with Law and made for the creek to sit awhile, sick at heart, watching the water trickle. In this very place not long ago, a circle of women had sat weaving, telling tales. A child was amused with a straw, dogs bit their fleas in peace, and the breeze came over with a warm pine taste. All gone. And so fast. So fast.

From the valley came a sound of thunder, and I climbed the bank to see. A scratch horserace, Tooms horses winning. They favored Morgans. A few people that were betting on it set off firecrackers. The picnic was breaking up. Going back along the road to pick up my dishes, I passed by the saloon, where Wes Haskell on the sidewalk wagged a finger at Grant Duncan.

"I don't want to fight you about it," Grant said. He was a handsome boy, black-haired, a Tooms by marriage.

"You Rebels still as yellow as ever?" Wes backed Grant to the rail, where he'd have to fall backward or fight.

"You only licked us because of the railroads," Grant said, and dodged away, but Wes broke a pistol over his head, and Grant went down heavy on the boards. Too heavy. As I picked up my skirt to run to him, I heard horses pound up behind me on the road and Sally cry out from somewhere on my left.

"Mother!"

Crackers went off again, and I tried to gather her in my arms as she ran to me, but tripped and fell over her in the dust.

"My God," someone yelled.

Sally was in one piece, and so was I, but Wes was down. So was Pete Waps, folded so's nobody had to ask if he was dead. Another man lay with his face in the road. Ezra Haskell, the old Yankee, stood in the street, pistol smoking. A horse reared with an empty saddle.

"Isaac shot first."

"Who got Wes?"

"Ten seconds, and three dead!"

Grant twitched on the sidewalk.

"Stand back," came Law's voice behind me, and when people moved away we could see three bodies, two more Haskells

303

and Bob Meenan, all dead too. The Tooms boys on horseback got them. Ezra shot Cal Tooms – that was him lying in the road – but Abner and Isaac rode clean away. Some wanted to go after the Tooms boys, but Sam stood on the hitching rail, holding on to a post, and argued with them.

"I say, let it go. The Haskells had more killed, but everybody knows they started it, and we all can see how poor Grant is suffering. We never had to build a jail in this town. Let's keep it that way."

"Pete Waps never ganged with the Haskells," Law said. "He just run his mouth for the Union. But we don't want no more killed."

They found Grant's wife in the store. She rushed out, wringing her hands in her skirt, too scared to touch him. I got water in the saloon and tried to help him drink, but he was struggling in some far place of his own. Ezra Haskell lost a son and a nephew. Another son, Wes, wounded. He mounted and rode off, and nobody touched him. Wes lived till noon next day, left a widow and two children. The rest, except Bob, were single men.

The preacher from Kaikitsil said eye for an eye and tooth for a tooth would never settle this. He insisted on one funeral, but Old Ezra never came to it, he was that sorry to be alive.

Sam got the credit for calming the crowd at the vendetta, and he won the election.

"Wasn't I there," Law said, "getting people to act right?"

"He made the speech," I said. "It's what he's good at."

"What am I good at?"

"Doing right."

He pulled me down on his knee. "There'll be a lot to do for Arabella, now Bob's gone," he said. "We'll all be helping her make out."

&

Bahé

A man stood in Bahé's doorway. An Indian man, but like a stranger. She knew that man from big time dances long ago, but he was fat now. Didn't look good. Called Charley now. Come a long way, from a ranch over by Hastings where he used to work. No work now. Said he'd marry her if he could. She said no, and he went off but came back another time. She had to tell him again. Another time he brought a knife and tried to stab her, surprised how she fought him and got the knife away.

"What he's thinking?" Bahé said to Mellie. "I'm so good looking any more?"

"You look good to me. Be careful."

"Not many what you call man round here no more."

Bahé had noticed how Mellie told stories out of books. Always the same. Not like real stories. Not so strong. Kekawí went along to listen, weak in his bent legs. Had a hard time to walk, but a strong spirit. Dashuwé, what Mellie called Rose, learned from the books. She knew plenty strange things. They loved horses, all them kids. Kekawí, riding, he was not lame and blind then. Dream told Bahé he would carry on the songs. She made sure he spent plenty of time with the old man.

Sally, she loved ranching, wanted to be always with the plants, the animals, her father. She couldn't do much, only four years old, but her heart was good. She listened when Bahé sang songs for pounding acorn, finding willow roots. She asked if there were songs for grapes and peaches.

"Sure," Bahé said. "Song change to how you live."

Bahé wished Rose would ask such questions, but Rose wanted to go to school. Bahé said no. She wasn't going to let white people take her children.

"Sally sings these songs," Mellie said one day when they were mucking out the barn. "She has a milk song and a song for finding eggs." Mellie leaned on her pitchfork. "Did you teach her this?"

Bahé shook her head.

"Did you learn basket-making from a song?"

"Watch my mother."

"How do you know all those patterns? From her?"

"Come to me."

"Come from where?"

Bahé didn't know how to tell her how things come, if she didn't know. Sometimes Mellie wore her out. A bluejay grabbed a branch outside and made a racket.

"Bird tell me," she said.

Mellie forked cow shit out the door. "She says you know a song to stop the rain. Do you try to stop the rain?"

"It get too wet, you have to do something."

Jakob Brandt plowed a big field, sowed it with winter wheat, and told the Indian people to take the grain when it came time.

307

Wheat made bread, not bad. You get used to it. Plenty of acorn on the hills, but hard to take, too much trouble in the country. Come the rain, Indians began going out to Jakob's place to watch that wheat grow.

ॐ

DECEMBER 1865
Mellie

It seemed to me it shouldn't take all year to put shelves in a corner of the hotel. Sam had promised space for a lending library, and May and I held him to it, reminding him he'd promised a decent establishment, not a hideaway for ladies of the night. In the end we had what we wanted. Several women subscribed, and we sent off for a few volumes, taking it in turns to exchange books Saturday afternoons, at five cents apiece. We let Mr. Parker take books for the school at no cost. *Bleak House* was my favorite. May was partial to *Hard Times*, but I thought Stephen Blackpool far too good to be true.

The Saturday before Christmas, when we were both at the library, it startled us to hear music. Someone was playing the new piano in the parlor across the hall. May sank into a chair, tears in her eyes. When the song was done, we sought out the musician, to our surprise a woman with swept-up hair and a beautiful hat. A stranger. She had cunning pointed-toe shoes and a book on the piano bench beside her.

"How lovely," May said. "I've been starved for music."

"It's only ballads: *Tenting Tonight, Jeannie with the Light Brown Hair.*

"Won't you play on?" I said.

"I've had enough. Are you the book ladies? This must be your *Barchester Towers*. My name is Helen Branscombe."

"May Potter. The books may be borrowed for five cents."

Mrs. Branscombe wore rings on her wedding finger. She took a nickel out of her reticule and dropped it in May's hand.

"What brings you to Oak Valley?" I asked.

"Business. I have an undertaking with Sam Brandt."

"Will you be long with us?"

"Oh, I don't know." Helen Branscombe was beautiful but not quite young. "I may stay awhile."

We had never met a businesswoman before.

On my way home, I stopped to see Grant and Lesley Duncan. They'd had to move back with Lesley's family, Grant was so hurt. She was expecting a child. It was a tolerable day in the winter sun, and Grant let her lead him out along the porch. The Tooms family was proud of that porch that went around three sides of the house, so they always could sit in either sun or shade. We sat, and I picked a piece of mending out of Lesley's basket. Grant was simple and didn't talk, but he could walk two sides of the porch, and she was so proud of that. There was a tenderness between them that made me sad, thinking of Law and me. Since we'd lost the children, all this time, it seemed any sweetness made me cry. Such sorrow was exhausting, and it stood between us. I'd never meant it to be that way.

Lesley's cousin Isaac came across the yard, Isaac Tooms, the one that fired the first shot in the vendetta. He put his bucket down, a sorry-looking man that couldn't get his hair cut the same on both sides of his head.

"I ought to be swilling the pigs," he said.

"Why don't you swill them, then?" I said.

He sat down on the step, too close to me. "I didn't want to kill nobody."

"Why did you, then?"

"Ezra drew his pistol as we rode up, and when Abner yelled, I fired. It went so quick."

"It won't be through with quick, though, will it."

He picked up the hem of my dress and felt it between his fingers. I twitched the skirt away.

"My consolation," Isaac said, "is I done something for Grant. I don't hold his name against him, even though a Yankee general got it."

After that visit, I tried to hold Law a little closer. He wished for another child, if the Lord grant, and looked to me to be a comfort to him, and I was easier and hopeful. I walked every day at first light by the creek to refresh myself in the clean sound of water. I liked to listen to the voices of the stream and feel its mist upon my skin. At a place where an old redwood had fallen and a circle of six young trees stood around its ancient root, I often saw the old man. Slow and frail, with a bent back and blind eyes in a bright face, he set his feet light as dry leaves on the path.

One day Bahé gave me a message from him.

"Old man want you know his doctor name. Tsikinídano,

Owl Mountain. Owl call him on mountain, time he young. Speak to him. Make him strong, happy. You listen *síl*, he say, them big old trees, long time you going to live."

ॐ

Mellie

I fell ill that winter with a discharge and a bad smell, a rash on my palms and soles. Doc Gray called it female complaint, gave me calomel till my gums bled, and wanted to let blood. I wouldn't have it. Father never approved of bleeding, and Law stood by me, though he seemed alarmed. He took Jack off the teaming to help get the ranch chores done. I was very low and couldn't get enough heat on my belly. Women brought food. Some advised fresh air and open bowels, and gave me hot douches that started the blood into my eyes. Others wrapped me tight and closed all the windows. Arabella Meenan was the helpfulest and worst. One day when Law expected to be late on the road, she came to stay overnight.

"Now don't apologize. It's good for me, now I don't have Bob to take care of."

She rustled around in the kitchen, then came to me and proposed frying bacon for Sally's supper.

"That's all right," I said.

"Might I put the milk in the blue pitcher and the syrup in the white?"

"Yes."

"Unless you'd sooner the other way around. A person might be particular about a thing like that."

"Either way." I put my head under the quilt. I had been really ill, with fever and vomiting, and was still all nerves.

"I hate her," Sally told me in the evening. "She made me brush my hair."

"You do have to brush it."

"I hate her."

Rose explained. "Mrs. Meenan told Sally she might die like her brother and sister if she wasn't good."

"The gall! There's one thing we know's not true!"

I knew it, and Rose knew it, but I had to go to work to calm Sally.

In the morning, Arabella apologized. "I'm very cross with myself. I was too talkative yesterday, and tired you out."

"I am much better" I said, "and there must be things you need to do at home."

"Nonsense. I never put my own need ahead of a friend's."

"Only please allow me to correct Sally myself."

"I don't understand. I've always been good at making children mind."

"Nevertheless."

"Well," she said, "there's no arguing with nerves like yours."

When Law got home, I pled with him, and he gave Arabella a lamb and sent her away. "Determined to be alone," I heard him say. "Nothing I can do with her."

When she was finally gone, Rose slipped in with manzanita cider for my sore throat, and I walked out to the Indian lodge on the gurgling, cold wet earth. Bahé was cutting the worms out of last year's apples, waiting Arabella out.

"Not listen to no, that woman," she said. "Yes neither."

I'd missed her laughter.

Rose was crazy to go to school, and she was wearing Bahé down. Maybe the child ought to go, Bahé was starting to think, if she felt like that about it. Talk about removal of the Indians had subsided, and everyone liked Rose. She could read simple books and loved to hear *Oliver Twist* aloud, though *A Child's History of England* was hopeless, since everything had to be explained. I still had a foul discharge and no love of life, but my fever broke, and I said I'd speak to the teacher.

It wasn't difficult to persuade Mr. Parker, once he heard Rose read. I made two school dresses for her, a red one and a green. She looked beautiful in red, with her shiny black hair, so keen for learning that her eyes danced. The only difficulty was Kekawí. He never complained, but he suffered deeply every day when Rose climbed up on one of the old mules to ride away to school.

In the spring, I still didn't feel right. Law was full of the anxieties of business and frequently on the road. I guessed I would pick up when the weather dried, but I had fever again and cramp, and I wanted to cry sometimes with weakness. I wondered if it was serious and whether I should consult Doc Grey again. Then I was sicker still and had no will to think or act. Things fell to pieces in my mind.

One afternoon when Law was in Kaikitsil, Bahé made a soup from dried fruit and persuaded me to drink it till my bowels

315

ran empty. Toward morning, she came with Jack. Kaáika. They wrapped me tight in blankets, ran poles through the wrapping, and carried me outside. We'd slid back into winter in the night. The sun came up sparkling through frost flowers, and a little fresh snow fell in pats off the trees. They carried me up a quiet draw where the old man waited by a pit of coals. They laid my poles in forked posts either side of the pit, suspending me to soak in the heat.

The three went around me singing, rattling, beating clapper sticks. The dry heat loosened everything. Comforted by the fire, and softened, I couldn't follow any plan of thought. The fragrant smoke brought back the lemon tree where the lady with fever rested in white lace, looking always at Father. It recalled the sweet timothy hay the rabbits ate, when Bessie wanted to hold the soft bunny just a minute, and the dog came, and the rabbit jumped out of her arms and the dog took it very fast in its jaws and shook it once, and the rabbit lay still and grew cool under our hands.

The clapper sticks exploded, vigorous, irresistible. They got in deep and loosened me. Weak and safe, I laughed and cried. I recollected listening on the stairs to silver clinking on the plates and grown-up talk and laughter, watching the ladies pass into the parlor in their lovely dresses, the gentlemen in stiff shirt fronts. Red-bearded, merry Mr. Andrew Puckett handed around the bottle of gas they breathed from, silly with laughter. He took a hammer to his great toe, just to show it didn't hurt, and the ladies shrieked. Mother's voice went all singing. When Mr. Andrew limped into church the next day, Father looked satisfied.

Bahé took me away from the fire and made me drink strong herbs and shudder horribly. Then back again to the fire. So she would have cooked Matthew, had Law allowed it, newly born out of my warmth. All around, the bodies of rabbits hung, spitted on sticks. I was turned toward the creek, then toward the mountains, my weakness complete. Safe behind the hedge of sticks, in the protection of the rabbits, proud now to be able to think reasonably, I made a great discovery. The fire outside was bigger than the fever within, and so could draw it out. The sickness flowed to meet the beating of the split sticks and grew thin and insubstantial in the wind of the song. I was inside the cocoon rattle with the little stones, in the midst of the fire.

Grace and Matthew ran, sun-splashed, in a field. I wept and reached for them, but they would not have my grief. They ran ahead, away. Stay, stay, I cried. Take *me*. But they had no more to say. I turned from them without meaning, without wanting to. Impossible to resist the fierce letting go. It might have been a heathen ritual, but I understood there was no white or Indian any more. Neither Jew nor Greek, as it says in the Testament.

Then, leaving its English name, Briggs Mountain, miles away, Kenaktai came to me. Old Woman Mountain, capped with snow. She opened her top and swallowed me, drenched me with icy water. And then I was a bird flying over the mountain and the valley. I was winter and spring, the mouse in the grass, the acorn on the tree. I fell asleep and woke in my own bed, weak as a new-hatched chick, but whole and mending.

℀

Jakob

Jakob Brandt was in trouble, and he knew it. No money and no health. He held on, sure the Indians could learn farming and in time that would set them right, if he could go on working and they could get through this bad spell. He made the most of every moment there was light, and then he'd take a lamp out to the barn, mend something, finish something. Some of the Indian men went off drunk, others tried to work. He took care of a girl with one foot cut off in a trap, and others. There were always others.

His pleasure was to go over to the school and talk about butterflies and birds and how the animals made their homes. It cheered him to watch the children discover the dewdrops on the spiders' webs, see in the creeks how everything is flowing. He showed them through a jeweler's loupe the huge, amazing flowers, the thick gold star on the forget-me-nots, the shining orange walls of poppies, and how the blue flags and lupines made doors and corridors and rooms for bees.

It pleased him that Mellie's Rose distinguished herself at school. In no time she'd become a reader, and she asked curious questions without losing a quality of quietness she had, like her mother. She asked why the warmest weather came after the longest day and the coldest after the shortest, so that he had to think a bit and make up a lesson about the sun and planets. She was to recite the Declaration at the spring exercises.

One afternoon when they'd been out looking at the eagle's nest on the Red Hill and examining the Spanish moss that hung from the oaks and lived on air, he asked her if she was ready with the Declaration.

She stood looking down. "I don't want to go to school any more."

That was all Jakob could get out of her. He had a talk with the schoolmaster, Mr. Parker. Rose was quick, a pleasure to teach, but there had been an incident. Two older girls who couldn't keep up with her in reading had complained they didn't want to sit next to a Digger Indian. They likely were saying worse things to Rose herself. Mr. Parker looked weary. His solution was to give Rose a desk near his own and let her teach the younger children. Between him and Jakob, they persuaded her to carry on with school and with the recitation.

"You're going to do fine," Jakob told her.

Rose made a beautiful job of the Declaration, but her success got people going. Arabella in particular.

"It's not right," she insisted one day in the store. "Right there at the exercises. School is not for Indians."

"No law against it," Sam told her. "If she's under white guardianship, which she is."

"Why do we need a law against it?"

"Well, you ain't got one."

319

"Just because nobody's got around to making one yet."

Jakob didn't hear any more because he had to hot-foot it out to the privy. That was the way these days. He had to sit and grip his knees and let his guts turn him inside out. It wasn't easy to stifle the groans. He was shitting blood.

The school business inflamed enough people that a third petition went around, demanding that the Supervisors call upon the Army to remove the Indians. Down in Kaikitsil, the *Sentinel* wrote that Indians in the schools would have a demoralizing effect upon the health and morals of the rising generation. As far as health and morals were concerned, Rose was beating people at their own game, but Jakob knew that folks set on a thing will say whatever is necessary to get it. With the other two Supervisors divided, it would all come down to Sam. Jakob braced himself, sweating in the privy many times a day, weak and gray. He needed more sleep, he figured. But he couldn't sleep.

ꙮ

MARCH 1866

Mellie

When the third petition went in to the Supervisors, Jakob came by to let me know. He said he wasn't good for much, and his color was poor, but he didn't want to talk about it. We hoped the petition would fail, like the others. Sam thought the labor provided by the Indians was useful. All that was needed was for him not to act.

I went in to town one Saturday, to relieve May at the lending library. Bahé came along to sit on the hotel steps and sell some little baskets she had made, and Rose came too. As we got to the porch, May ran out laughing.

"Thee will never guess, Mellie."

"What?"

"Helen Branscombe." She covered her mouth with one hand, like a girl.

"What of Mrs. Branscombe?"

"I got it out of Luke. Who she is."

"Well?"

"Oh Mellie."

"Who is she, then?"

"She's everything we've been trying to keep away from.

She's a…. What a joke on us, Mellie. Don't make me say the word."

I went into the hotel with May.

"She's setting up a group of girls to work at the saloon and the hotel." May clutched her waist as if she'd swallowed something awful. "Oh, Mellie, isn't life just too *gruesome?*"

I suppose we thought we could ignore Helen Branscombe. Not absolutely cut her. Cool and polite would do. Some packets of books had arrived, and we were unwrapping them when the piano began to play *Betsy from Pike*. I looked at May and she at me. What would we do? It would have been one thing if we hadn't liked her. The song ceased, and in came Helen, elegant in a yellow hat.

"You're packing," she said.

"Oh no," May said, "unpacking."

Of course she saw from our faces that we knew. "Oh dear," she said. "And now I suppose we can't be friends, seeing that you're good women." She sighed. "I liked you very much."

May went red. Embarrassed, I looked out the window to see if Bahé was ready to go. She was talking to a man on horseback who held his hat in his hand, and I wondered what sort of man would take his hat off to an Indian.

"Can't we get over this somehow?" Helen said. "I don't want to impose on you. I'm a businesswoman. Here's my proposition. If you'll give me the time of day, I'll make sure my enterprise is clean, and I'll teach any children dancing on Thursdays between four and six."

"Oh goodness," May said. She swallowed hard. "That seems fair."

We shook hands on it, and all the while it was dawning on me about the man on horseback, who he had to be, and I ran out, calling to Rose.

"My whiskers didn't throw you off, Mellie? The lad at the livery stable looked as if he'd never seen a General Albert E. Johnson beard. And who is this handsome young lady? Is this Rose?"

It was. It was Father!

🕉

MARCH 1866

Law

It would be all talk, Law reckoned, with her father come. The old man turned up just after the heavy spring work, the calving and shearing, was done. Mellie couldn't take her eyes off him, a tall man with a big head, all knees and elbows. She even served tea under the old oak, lady-like. Tea doesn't taste of nothing, and if you put sugar in, still worse.

"You're not still shooting each other, are you?" the doctor said. "What's the politics up here?"

"Pressure's coming on the County Supervisors for Indian removal," Law told him. "However, nothing going forward. Quite a few Indians work on the ranches."

"What you got? Three Supervisors?"

"The one from the coast been through the depredations there. He's for removal. The Kaikitsil one lost twenty head of stock from natural causes, none to Indians. He thinks they'd be all right if we let them alone."

"You're set, then," the doctor said, "if your third holds on."

"That's Sam Brandt. The diehards are after him, and they don't quit. They say the Indians may be few now, but they will breed and start up all the annoyances again."

The children came along with a fish they'd caught, swung in a bucket. That suited Law. He wanted to get off the subject of Indians, which was sure to stir Mellie up, and her father would only make it worse. Law figured to be preached at by the both of them.

"Who are you?" Sally asked the old man she'd never seen before.

"Sally!" her mother scolded.

"No, no," said her grandfather. "She's within her rights. You know what, Sally? I'm your mother's pa."

At supper, her father stood while Mellie took her seat. He talked of sleeping in the room off the barn where the sheep-shearer stayed.

"I like solitude," he said, "and my wants are few."

Law figured there'd be wants aplenty that would come out later, including the want to exercise the jawbone.

"How'd you all come through the war?" the doctor asked Law after supper.

"A man on the Kaikitsil road had peaches for sale," Law told him. "When anyone stopped he'd ask, 'What's your politics?' If they said, 'We're Union,' he'd cry, 'Drive on!'"

"I'll tell you something worse," the doctor said. "A woman at Big Flat had a baby die, and her breast caked. She was awful sick. I asked around for a puppy, because they'll suck and draw the milk off, you know. We found a litter, and the owner was delighted to give a pup, and the young woman improved."

Law got up and put a stick on the fire. He offered his father-in-law some whiskey. Might as well prime the pump.

"Then the owner came back to say he'd heard the young couple were Secessionists and he wanted his dog. The husband pled with him. His wife was better, but not out of danger. But the man was determined to have his pup and took it, saying, 'She can die for all of me.'"

"By God," Law said.

"I'll tell you another story," the doctor went on. "We had a stage robber operating at the mines. They called him the Rattler because he struck from behind rocks. He wore a mask, of course, so nobody knew what he looked like. Now it happened some men were snowed in around Tahoe lake in a hotel one night, so many they had to double up, and one of them was a preacher. Who was going to share a bed with a man of the cloth? Nobody wanted to, but one of the men looked like a real gentleman, dressed in a nice suit, so they picked him."

The old man took a pull on his whiskey.

"Found out next day, when he robbed an express in the same suit, he was the Rattler."

"Be darned," Law said.

"This fella that told me about it, he said, 'By-gad, if'en that preacher would a woke up to the fact that he was a sleepen with that er Rattler, he'd a done some tall prayn I betch'a.'"

Law laughed. Her father could talk, all right.

✺

APRIL 1866

Mellie

Father helped me dig and wrap my seedling fruit trees in straw and manure and burlap and take them to town to sell. He took Law's plow to the blacksmith and got the split haft bound. He worked with Law to fix a wagon sprung at the corner. They pegged and glued it and drew the edges together, twisting a stick between two cords. They had the smith make an angle iron to strengthen it.

Father gave Jakob a hand as well. They worked together a day or two.

"Most of his Indians don't know how to sharpen tools or cut wood," Father said, "or they've given up anyhow. I like Jakob Brandt, but he's driving himself sick."

Pretty soon, Father was working his magic in town. He walked in to enjoy the talk at the saloon or the hotel. He made lists of books to discuss with May. He took up with Helen Branscombe. When I saw them strolling arm in arm, I thought perhaps I ought to warn her, but I guessed she must know what she'd got herself into.

We had a quiet time between storms, with warm afternoons and deep morning dew. The moon was cold, the nights damp.

There came a fresh smell from the hills of growth and mist.
Last year's food was tiresome, and I longed to bite into the first
radish. I thought Father might be itching to travel, but he
began to be comfortable and feel at home, and I was glad to
have him. I asked him one night why he'd left the mines, how
he'd left Nannie.

"Couldn't bring myself to speak of it," he said. "It's a hard
thing. Nannie was carried off by scarlet fever in the fall."

"Oh no! I never thought..."

"I didn't either. It's generally the little ones that sicken, and
she nursed so many without taking harm. But she worked herself to skin and bone, so thin you could see through her."

Never to see Nannie in this world again! I'd hoped she'd
have a life of her own one day.

"They called her *Sor*," Father said, "the Italians at the mines.
As if she were a nun. She was the picture of devotion. I don't
know how I'll do without her. Will you keep me a while, Mellie?"

"Of course I will."

"I might stay until the January term of the legislature. Might
stay forever."

But I knew he would never stay anywhere forever.

Late in the spring, Tsikinídano failed. He gave up walking
by the creek and sat against the lodge wrapped in blankets in
the afternoon sun, his old face cobwebbed with wrinkles. He
slept by the fire all morning, and in the evening sang for hours,
sometimes all night, and Bahé and the little boy listened to it
all. One raw morning, I took some clabber milk up to her lodge

and found her working a basket, the Indian doctor asleep on the ground beside the fire. I wondered if I should bring bedding, but she said old people were fond of lying on the earth. They took strength from it.

"End his time," she said. "Pretty soon dream no more."

She sat coiling quietly, a red and black pattern, thunder and lightning. In the triangular space of the lodge's door, a snowflake or two fell diagonally on the wind and melted in the grass.

Snow in April. After milking, I made a custard and sent it up with Sally. Back came a request for more thick milk. I taught Rose how to make it, and Father took it up. He was curious, but Bahé was not inclined to speak to him, and the old man knew no English.

"He's frail," Father said. "He enjoys the custard but is taking off weight. Yet he might last a while. He will choose his time."

Bahé seemed distracted. The little boy had pains in his legs. She was dreaming. Houses tall as redwood trees, crows flying at the speed of shooting stars. I'd had a troubling dream myself. Three horses waited by a fence, in a stark emptiness hardly to be borne.

"What shall I think?" I asked her.

She had trouble enough with her own dreams, let alone mine. "Ask," she said.

"Ask who?"

"Spirit. Ask him, this dream good? This dream from You?"

I asked, but I could never be sure of the answer.

During the summer, Father rode around the country and

found a girl in a back-away valley that had her private parts eaten away with syphilis. He talked Doc Grey out of a supply of calomel and made a nuisance of himself applying to the Indian Agent for more medicine, pushing the coroner in Kaikitsil to make accusations.

"I'm *persona non grata* down there," he told me with satisfaction.

One night I rolled out dough for rhubarb pie, and while they all waited for it to be ready, Father and Law told stories. Law spun a tale about crossing the plains, the wagons drawn in a circle, redskins whooping and riding around, bullets flying, clouds of smoke, braves dropping down on the far side of the pony to shoot arrows into the hearts of men defending their wives and families. Rose and Kekawí and Sally listened with the terror and admiration the whole country was sick with, till a funny look came over Law's face.

"Don't quit now," Father said.

"It only just came to me, two out of the three I'm telling it to are Indian."

It was when the oaks were turning yellow that Joe fell in the pasture and lay breathing heavily, sides heaving. I cried out to him, and he got up and bumbled into a tree. Then he seemed all right.

"Heart, I expect," said Father.

We sat late by the fire that evening. The moon shone full above the fir tops, casting their shadows down the hill. Law dozed on the settle after a hard week with the pig scour. If I waked him, he'd feel he had to go down to Joe in the barn.

"Can't you give me something to do with my hands?" Father asked.

"Feeling restless?"

"I'm an old wanderer, Mellie. Can't help myself."

I gave him some rag strips to twist for a rug. "What made you leave home in the first place?"

"I was neither the eldest nor the favorite son. I thought I could do some good by doctoring, but at the medical college in Philadelphia I had a shock. I met blacks I could see no other way than as men. It followed that the whole theory of the inferior race was a cheat."

He stood and threw a big log on the fire. Sparks showered upward.

"When I came back to Mississippi and fell in love with your mother, I tried to see again as I was raised to see, but though I made a trial of it, it didn't take. I wanted to change things." He began piling the fire logs beside the hearth, by size. "I've tried to see clear, but I've made a mess of it, Mellie."

"You haven't."

"We so often do more harm than good, we doctors. I did have an idea once. There was a gas we breathed at parties. It made you laugh, and it took away feeling, made you numb. I thought to try it in surgery. Dacey's daughter had a fistula, and sure enough, after she breathed this gas, I could cut and stitch and couldn't hurt her. No thrashing and suffering. I meant to write an article, but your mother thought it a waste of time."

A coyote barked far away. Otherwise, only the crackling of the fire and Law's snoring from the settle.

"I wasn't sound," Father said. "I treated slaves, you see. I couldn't buck that."

"It was a bigger thing than you. There was a whole war fought about it."

"If you could stop the pain in surgery, I thought, that would be something. Well, someone else had the idea soon enough." He bent to pick up the rug twists he'd dropped on the floor. "I've talked too long and too late."

"You never married again," I said.

"Your mother. There was no one like her." Tears came to his eyes, and he quavered like an old man. "Still, there was one I might have forgotten her for. Can you guess?"

"Mrs. Morse, on the ship?"

"Oh no," he laughed. "Good Mrs. Morse, with her highland plaid."

A flurry up from nothing beat on our ears. Hooves tore along the valley floor, pounding hard, and rounded the big rock. Boots slammed on the porch, fists battered at the door. Law shook himself, looked to see where we all were, and let in one of the Nott boys.

"Indian attack," he shouted, "Meet at our ranch," and turned to plunge away.

"Whoa." Law shoved his good foot across the door. "Slow down, boy."

"I'm sent to rouse the south valley. A woman's been attacked."

Law met my eye a moment. "Sit and talk, Seth. What woman."

"Mrs. Potter. We had quilting at our ranch. She came to help."

"What? May?" I said.

"Passed Indian Charley on her way in, sitting on a stump, whetting a knife. Said something to him. When she came out, he followed her and pulled her off her horse."

"Is she all right?"

"She cried out, and Charley run off, but she's cut up. Ma and Mrs. Brandt are taking care of her. Mrs. Meenan says she can't breathe when she thinks how near Mrs. Potter was to scalped, with the Indians raised up like that."

"Diggers don't scalp," said Father.

"I want to go to May," I said.

"Stay with the children," Father said, "and Bahé. We best find Charley, Law, before they kill every poor Indian in the valley."

The men got weapons and rode off, and the moment I couldn't hear them any more, I took a lantern and went to find Bahé, threading the big trees in the dark. She sat with the fire out, peering into the night. The old man breathed badly and she couldn't move him, wouldn't leave him, but I brought the children down to the house. Thrilled with a dark excitement, wrapped in blankets, they walked back with me, the little blind boy leading Rose and me where the woods were darkest, seeing with his skin. They curled up by the fire, and I watched over them, listening for every sound and worrying for May. She was nowhere near to scalped, if I knew Arabella, but I hated to think of her frightened and in pain. Cock crow came at last. I made coffee, and dawn light restored the world we know. We walked back along the creek, heartening at the water sounds and the fog shredding upward. Bahé took a cup of coffee, and the old man enjoyed a taste and fell asleep. He'd sung all night, she said.

Down at the little beach, the sun set gold flecks humming in the air and warmed the day. Bahé and I washed linen on the rocks, and the children built a dam across the stream and waded for fish. After a time, Bahé climbed up to the lodge and came out singing a hoarse song. Tsikinídano was dead.

"Who will dream for the people now?" I asked. But I knew who.

She squatted by the water, loosed her hair over her face in a dark flow, and cut it close with a flint knife. Her black hair floated away on the stream.

ॐ

APRIL 1866
Law

Law had been surprised to find that Mellie's father could work as well as talk, but still, it was only a courtesy to bring him on the hunt for Indian Charley. They joined up with the other men south of town, where the road went down to the Nott Ranch. Somebody had a dog, and he trailed the Indian toward Kaikitsil. They caught up with him about midnight, drunk, making for Two Rock Valley. He took a step into the brush. No real attempt to hide.

"Carry him to the Justice of the Peace, boys," Law said.

"Don't waste my time," said Jeff Thrush, and threw a rope over a tree.

Law saw how it was going to be. Charley made faces at them. He was not too drunk to know what was happening, but almost too drunk to care.

"Dirty Indian," Jeff said, and kicked him.

Charley spat back. Law wished himself anywhere but here. Don Haskell had a whip, but Mellie's father dismounted, went up to the Indian and looked him in the eye.

"Why did you do it, Charley?"

"Ugly white woman."

"Just for that? Lack of feminine pulchritude?"

"Not like looks of my knife. What goddamn business of her? Not sorry I do her like that."

"I'm afraid you've got to die, Charley."

"Okay. No good here anyway. Damn you all."

Thrush and Haskell set Charley on a horse and noosed him. It seemed to come easy to them, like they had done it before.

"He ain't no Christian," Thrush said, "so we ain't going to waste no prayer on him."

The doctor stood between Charley and the whip. "God is no respecter of persons," he said, speaking quietly, but this Law clearly heard. "But in every nation, whoever fears Him and works righteousness is accepted with Him."

The men spooked the horse, jerking Charley's neck. They shot him seven or eight times and let him hang while they got out their tobacco and had a smoke, then shoveled him under and rode for the Nott ranch where May was being taken care of. Law felt middling sick.

"The crowning glory of creation," Mellie's father said, "though we don't look that way."

"One thing you can say for Jeff Thrush," Law said, "he does his own dirty work."

"Poor Charley. Yanked to his reward in a drunk like that, shoveled into a grave still warm. But when you've seen as many as I have, son..."

ॐ

Bahé

Bahé dug a pit up near the broken roundhouse. She heaped brush in there, manzanita and other dry stuff that burned hot. A few people came. Kaáika, called Jack. Tomacaak. Kaikai and her husband. Mellie and her father. Jakob Brandt. A few others. In the time before, the old man had been the leader of a thousand. They carried him to the pyre with his shell ornaments, his flicker headband, the crown of fur with flags of bright shell and feather that had danced with him.

Bahé lit the fire at dawn. It burned fast, in a roar. Feathers and beads danced in the fire wind. She sang.

"Tsikinídano, he is coming to You. From under the clouds he comes, from the light of the sun, from the abalone rocks, from the caves in the dunes he comes, from the little running water, from the *síl* mother and six children, he comes to You."

She sang his true name, by which he was known in the spirit life. She had melted a basket of pitch. She reached into the ashes, mixed them with tar, and smeared a wide band around her head. She sang and beat a clapper stick. Kaáika blew a bone whistle and danced.

"Creator," Bahé prayed, "we're trying to keep this up so we'll remember who we are. We understand how to live. We know our trees and streams are family. We understand the ways of the poison people. We know to take nothing from them and walk the other way. But this is a new world. Evil don't leave you alone. It comes after you. Charley been poisoned, that's all we know, and we don't have Tsikinídano to lead us. You'll have to find us a new way."

After the fire died down, a flock of crows flew into the clearing and perched on top of the ruined roundhouse, cawing and strutting this way and that. Twelve of them.

"Grandmother," Bahé prayed, "I believe the crows are helpers. Thank you. But we lost a lot of knowledge here that the old man had, and I don't know so much. You're going to have to give us a lot of help."

She threw into the dying fire Charley's tobacco pouch, that Mellie's father gave her.

After the funeral, she waited a long time for a new song. Nothing came. More nothing. When fog covered up the world, she was glad. She didn't want to see nothing. She was tired. Looking at nothing, though, she saw shreds and streamers and heard in the withdrawing fog a song. "Still here. I've got a new place for you. Still here."

Bahé did not understand this. They had their place. The valley. How could they be who they were in any other place? It might be good land up there in Round Valley, but they did not belong there. All kinds of Indians there. Strangers. Anyway, people were too sick, too hurt to go.

When the first snow came on the mountain, a Dream came to her.

"Get ready," the Dream said. "You're going somewhere."

"Live here, die here." This is what Bahé knew.

"Get ready."

"Is this You? Did you forget me? Don't you know who we are?"

"I know you. I've always known you. Get ready. In a little while."

Bahé took Rose out of the school.

"But I'm up to nine times nine!" Rose protested.

Bahé was firm. Rose must help her. She must remember herself, Dashuwé. Bahé listened to the silence, staring off over the churning or ironing, watching the hills.

"Rose is beside herself," Mellie said. "Must she be so unhappy? If she can read and write, she can help you."

Bahé didn't listen. She listened to the Dream.

"Go up to the mountain, and I'll show you more about it. Where you got trout with your father when the fish kill came in the lake that time. Above that. Where the water flashes down the rocks. I want to show you something."

The mountain rose blue and far. The new moon set over its shoulder, sharp against the sky. Snow had been deep up there, this winter, lying in patches still.

"Go to the mountain," the Dream said. "I'll tell you when. When you get up there, I'll show you."

OCTOBER 1866
Mellie

The mourning cries for the old man, the bitter wailing, tore the air for weeks. People complained, especially Arabella. Since the attack on May Potter, anything Indian was a fresh affront to her. She and her friends agitated for removal, hounded customers in the store, beseiged Sam, demanded that the Supervisors act.

May was shaken but not badly hurt. Her poor cut hands suffered for a time with anything sharp, like vinegar, and the scar on her neck would always show.

"I shouldn't have said anything to him," she told me.

"What did you say?"

"I didn't like the looks of his knife."

"Brave of you."

"Foolhardy."

"You had the presence of mind to cry out at the right time."

"Mellie, it was luck. I bluffed him. 'Man on the road!' I yelled, and by chance there was a man. I don't suppose he meant to kill me, and certainly he should not have died for what he did. I don't believe in that. Anyway, it wasn't him. It was the liquor. Poison."

I was concerned for her, and for Father, who was getting restless. One evening when we were alone he gave me a pair of stockings to darn, big holes worn in the heels. He wished he could have a little cottage near Bahé, he said, and stay forever.

"As if you'd be satisfied with a cottage."

"I suppose not."

"Or stay anywhere forever."

"None of it's forever," he said. "*We are such stuff as dreams are made on.*" He bit into one of the apples off the smokehouse tree. "I'm sorry you lost the children, Mellie. Diphtheria is terrible. You do everything you can, and it isn't enough. But your little Sally is lanky already. There might have been two or three more by now."

"It hasn't turned out as we hoped," I said, bending the wool double to get it through the needle. "A long time Law and I were strangers, and afterward I was ill."

"Female complaint?"

I nodded, struggling to fit the thread through the eye.

"Flow and burning? Fever? Gray must have known about this. What did he give you? Calomel, I don't doubt. Leave fussing with that thread and tell me how you are."

I told him how the Indians cured me.

"Put the poles right through? Rabbits, did you say? She must have hunted quite a time for you, Mellie. How was it in the wrappings over the fire?"

"It was warm, subtle, fragrant. I felt complete trust. I wept from gratitude, not to have to sustain myself in any way."

"Strange how belief has power to heal," he said. "Or hurt." He looked stricken. "But it won't reduce internal scarring."

341

I thought I knew what he meant. I'd never spoken my thoughts to Law, hardly put words to them myself.

"Do you know what you've had?"

"I've wondered."

"Venereal disease."

"I thought it might be so."

"I don't know how Gray managed not to tell you. It's burned itself out, but I wouldn't look for another child now, Mellie."

No use crying over spilt milk. Especially when I must have almost known already. I rolled the pair of socks together and tossed them into his lap. "These will take you another piece of the way," I said. "We mean to butcher some hogs when the weather cools. If you don't stay to help, I'll slaughter you too."

He laughed and promised.

When the day came for the hogs, Law and Jack stuck them, hung them, bled them, washed them down and split them. We had three fine hogs, and it was work. Rose kept the fire going under the kettle and helped me scald and scrape and cut. Father scrubbed the guts and salted. The little ones kept the flies away. Law cut meat and Bahé made sausage. At the end of the day, we roasted some nice cuts, everyone hungry and eager for a feed.

I was sitting down with my first taste of pork, Law beside me with a mouthful of chop, when Father said he meant to take the stage out after lunch tomorrow. We'd begun to protest, when Father came over to Law, urged him to stand up, and hit him hard, full in the face. Laid him out on the ground.

I sprang to my feet, frantic. "What do you mean? Are you mad? What example is this for the children?"

"Law can explain," Father said. "He should have told you about it long ago."

The children scattered. Jack and Bahé made themselves scarce. The dogs went after the meat. I tried to shoo them off and burst into tears.

Law came up on one elbow, feeling at his jaw. "Your father's done right, Mellie."

"What!"

Law brought me down to the creek with him to wash up his bloody cheek, and that's when he told me he'd been with a woman in Santa Caridad.

"After we lost the children. Not at first, when you didn't know what to do with yourself. After. When you didn't want me. I never meant to make you sick."

"Why did you do it, then?"

"We'd been apart so long, and then you come to me and I didn't know how to say no."

"I knew you had an inflammation, but I thought it was the leg."

"I thought it was done with. Hoped so."

The blood was still coming. Tears washed it down his cheek. He was swelling up under the eye.

"Say something, Mellie."

"Are you sorry?"

"I was sorry from the first minute. Then I went back again when I shouldn't, and I wish I hadn't. 'Fore God, it was just a gal in a red dress."

ஒ

Mellie

"Come quick!" Sally said. "Bahé is leaving."

I reached for my shawl. The day was gray and windy, dying. I found her sweeping the earth floor of her lodge, everything neat and glowing, her tools and pans around the circle, a clean fire, blankets hanging.

"You can't leave," I said. "Where are you going?"

"Old Woman Mountain."

"Kenaktai? There's snow up there."

She shrugged.

"There might be slave traders. Must you go?"

"Dream tell me."

"What about me? How can I do without you."

"Few days. Them kids pretty near grown."

It was never any use telling Bahé what to do, or trying to stop her. A wet snow fell that evening, sticking a while and melting. I wrapped some jerk beef, easy to carry.

"Show this letter if anyone troubles you on the road."

Law had signed it under the lamplight.

This Digger Squaw is a good worker and belongs to my ranch. She has permission to visit her old mother near Tysonville. Kindly help her on safe to me, Stanislaw Pickett, Oak Valley, California.

Next morning, Bahé set off with a staff over the Red Hill to the saddle of Kenaktai. She wore an old blue dress and moccasins, with skins wrapped up her legs and a warm cape woven of twisted rabbit fur. Twilight closed down early.

❧

DECEMBER 1866

Sam

Sam knew Mellie would be coming. She burst into the store in a drenching rain, looking like a drowned calf.

"You changed your vote," she said.

"Who said so?"

"Arabella heard the Army's set to march them to Round Valley. She's all satisfied about it."

"Arabella's jumping the gun," said Sam. "All right, I'll talk to you. In the back room. Private."

Once he had her in the office, she burst out again. "You can't send them away. Rose is the best scholar of all the children in the valley. They don't have any kind of school up there."

"Calm down," he said. "We haven't had the vote yet."

"Near as makes no difference.

"How long you going to fight this fight, Mellie, after you lost already? I thought of every plan I could to keep our Indians here, but after what happened to May, you can see which way it had to go. You and I both know there never will be peace till they are gone. Here, you're all wet. You need a towel."

"You call it peace? What'll it be for them? It's sixty miles into

346

the mountains. How will they walk it? What about the old people?"

"The soldiers are experienced. They'll have wagons and food."

"Nonsense. It's bitter cold, and the settlers attack the Indians in Round Valley, as you well know. Plenty die that go in to that reservation."

Mellie rubbed her wet hair with the towel. Sam hoped she didn't know the actual number that died there in any year. It was about half.

"The Army won't come till the weather improves," he said. "But they'll come. We had to do it. So many signed the petition. Luke Potter, of course. Ezra Haskell, Tom Carter, Isaac Tooms."

"Isaac Tooms! He's a half-wit."

"Now Mellie, don't lose your head. Folks want it settled."

"You're the one talked so big about how we were going to be friendly in this valley. You're the one has a brother sick to death with trying to act like a neighbor."

"You have to change with the times. Jakob couldn't do it."

She said things no white woman should say. The valley would be desecrated, its spirit wasted like milk poured on the ground. Worse for us than the Indians. Losing something better than ourselves. Sam hated to see the way she was going. Cursing her own race. He felt more than ever that the thing had to be settled. Uncertainty was too hard on people.

"We're stone blind," she said. "We'll be haunted forever by their shadows."

She'd never got over losing those children. Gone right over

the edge, and poor Law was tied to her. She dropped the towel and went.

"Don't think we won't go through with it," Sam called after her.

༂

FEBRUARY 1867

Bahé

Bahé looked over her things. Her baskets. Baskets inside baskets. Her acorns, many the right age, ready to grind. Just a taste was enough to remind her who she was. Cocoon rattle. Split clapper stick. Rabbit fur blanket. Feather cape. These things were important. For Kekawí one day.

She went to every place she loved, which was every place. She climbed the west ridge to the ocean, a blue spot far away. She had not seen it in four winters. She stood in the field where wildflowers bloomed in summer, lupine and blue flag and poppies, blowing in the wind.

"I'm here," the Spirit said. "I didn't go anywhere. Wait and see how it turns out."

In a few months, meadowlarks would flash their yellow breasts, flying to nests down in the grass to feed their young. They would sing, hovering, a high, woven song like a creek running over stones.

"See?" the Spirit said. "It goes on."

Bahé's skirt dragged heavy in the wet, in the cold morning. The earth was in its beauty of green hills, red berries, and a dust of snow. The deer came and looked at her. So did raccoons and possums and the horses in the fields.

"You're part of me," the Spirit said. "Where you're going, I'll still know who you are, and you'll know me."

Later that day, when the sun was bright, Bahé and Mellie's Rose dug in the deep, earth-smelling loam and drew out strands of redbud root for baskets. This was to pull her back, Dashuwé. The white world tugged her like a big salmon pulling a child too small. The little ones helped a while, then played, throwing stones in the creek. The live oaks took up water, loosening their angles. The turkey buzzards hunkered in the bare-branch oaks that glowed orange in the evening mist. Soon, in spring, spangling the edges of the woods, would come the little blue flowers with yellow star eyes. Mellie called them not-for-gets.

৪০

APRIL 1867

Mellie

Joe fell again, down and senseless. Then he got up and grazed quietly through the rain. We waited. The Supervisors had called upon the Army to remove the Indians, but there was no further sign. I read with Rose. She was ready, now, for *The Legend of Sleepy Hollow* and for Whittier. Each day unfolded, perfect as a lily in bloom.

One morning, jewel-green and bright with rainwater, I took coffee with Helen Branscombe at the hotel, and we talked of Father. He had written from Rich Bar and Challenge, and then Grizzly Flats.

"He's back at the mines, doctoring sick Indians," I said. "He won't stay put."

"It's temperament," said Helen. "Poor old dear, he can't help it."

"I hope you're not..."

"Oh," she said, "for me it's business. But I was fond of the old coot."

So I was in town when Law came in with news that the south-bound stage to Kaikitsil had been held up at Top Rock. He was on his way with some of the men to hunt the bandit, who couldn't have got far.

"Seth Nott was driving. He's hurt. You might want to get over to the livery, Mellie, and see can you do anything for him."

The passengers crowded the stable. Seth had his scalp grazed, with a lot of blood, but nothing serious. The others were all right, except for what they lost, the rings, the watches.

"Stepped out from behind a rock."

"Seth pulled up the minute he fired."

"I got religion fast," Seth said, "when I got that haircut."

"Black suit."

"City suit.'

"'Can I trouble you for your pocket watch,' he said, like a gentleman."

Lesley Duncan was among the passengers. She had never left Grant's side in all these months, till her cousins in San Francisco wanted to see the baby. She'd lost her wedding ring and felt it was a judgment.

At lunchtime, Joe staggered in the pasture and went down. When I called to him, he picked up his head, but that was all. I sat stroking him a long time, until Bahé came out in her blue dress.

"Old mule, Mellie. Can't no more."

Her hair had grown out, threaded with gray.

I swabbed my face with my skirt. "Everyone's deserting me."

"Got to, Mellie."

"You can't go. Not everyone. Not you."

Rose came down with water for Joe, talked to him and

scooped away the flies. Bahé looked around at the blackberry thorn, the tangle of grass heads, the lizard on the stone, the *bahé* trees with their old wrinkled fruit and new blooms.

"I'm in all this," she said. "Got a squirrel here, a bear. Got hills, got trees. Long as you got those, got a Spirit, got a Indian people here."

"But what will I do when you're *not* here? What will I do then?"

"All place now," she said. "All time here."

I needed a spell of hard work to take my mind off the world. It was warm and only mid-afternoon, so I took out the suit Law was married in, been folded in the chest all these years, the one with shiny blue stripes that Nannie said only a common man would think fine, and gave it a soak, scrubbed and rinsed it and hung it on the line. Then I rubbed the kitchen table down with sand. I was beating out the rag rugs when a traveler came walking around the rock, dressed decent but road-weary, coat over one shoulder. He'd got off the northbound stage, he said, a little seasick from the mountain track. Thought he'd walk into town.

"Just passing through?"

"I'm in business in the City, selling shirts. Left my samples on the stage. They're going to put them off for me at the hotel."

A well-spoken man.

"If you're hungry," I said, "I can have biscuits in twenty minutes."

I brought him in and fed him. He had seen Edwin Booth in *Hamlet* in the city.

"A melancholy story, but how beautifully he spoke. *Words, words words.* The Booth family should have stuck to acting."

What if life had worked out another way and Law were a man like this? Thoughtful. No doubt a reader. I had to speak to myself a bit sharp, pulling my biscuits out of the oven.

"I don't wish to be curious," the stranger said, "but you seem a little low."

"I'm not myself at all. My mule is dying."

"I don't wonder, then. Our best friends are animals, for they recall the happiness of Eden." He pushed back his chair and thanked me for the biscuits. "I hope a little excitement comes your way sometimes, Ma'am."

"Oh my," I laughed, "I don't know if I can stand any more excitement. The southbound stage was robbed here just this morning. You want to be careful."

"Much obliged. But excitement is what people want, you know."

I wondered as he walked toward the road what it might be to love a man like that.

APRIL 1867

Law

Law found a strange horse, saddled, on the south ridge. He thought the stage robber must have come in that way. Probably stole it somewhere. If the men got word to Kaikitsil, maybe they could find out where. There wasn't much else to go on. Maybe he'd hidden the takings and was walking cross country, looking to pick up a mount.

Law went home at the end of the day with a note from Sam to give Mellie, and he wasn't looking forward to how she'd take it. He waited till she finished frying the chicken and stood back from the hot fat.

"Sam came over to the freight office. The Army will send soldiers to remove the Indians."

She never turned a hair. She opened the note and read it out.

"*The Indians must go. It is certain. Sorry, Mellie. Sam.*"

If he hadn't seen the note shake in her hand, Law might have thought it didn't matter. She was full of surprises.

"Bahé knows what she's doing," Mellie said. "Never mind the Army. Have you seen that suit? I had your suit on the line, and it's disappeared. Must be the children teasing me."

"Sally," Law said, "have you seen my suit?" Sally was perched on a stool, mashing potatoes. "I looked pretty handsome in that suit."

"No, Papa."

Mellie went to pull her cake out of the oven. "Oh God," she said of a sudden, dropped the pan, and fell in a chair.

"Did you burn yourself?"

"I'm such a fool! Shirt samples at the hotel!" She laughed until the tears flew. "If you'd come home early, Law, you could have talked Shakespeare with the Rattler. And now he's wearing your suit up to Long Valley or wherever he's really going, which is not the same as what he says. Excitement is what people want! Oh my goodness."

Law went to wash up, feeling peculiar. He didn't know what to make of Mellie, never had, and he anticipated feeling pretty low to have to tell Sam and the others that while they were hunting around the hills, the Rattler was eating biscuits in his kitchen. After supper, Mellie flung her arms around him and said he looked pretty good to her. He couldn't figure that out either, but he liked it.

"But oh Law," she said. "It's Joe."

Law felt sick to have to do it, but he had to. It looked like Joe wasn't suffering, but the night would be cold, and it wasn't no good, him lying there. He took his big old Colt he'd had so long and went out to the pasture. Told Joe what a good fella he'd been, working with you like he always knew what you were doing. Joe raised his muzzle up to Law, still soft between the bristles, and after a minute, because if he didn't do it now he never would, Law got up and stood behind Joe and shot into the back of his head. He was sick when he'd done it. Had to walk out among the willows and weep like a woman.

In the morning, he hitched a team and dragged the carcass out behind the rock and into the south valley. The head bounced over the grass, with the eye gone dull and sunken, trailing strings of blood and brain. Buzzards hung over the place all day.

Best mule he ever had.

∞

JUNE 1867
Mellie

We expected the soldiers to come up from the south. They would collect the Indians at Kaikitsil first. Bahé had been storing up food and clothes. I didn't like the waiting. I tried not to think about it. If I thought at all, I thought maybe the soldiers would see how few Indians we had and let them go.

"It'll soon be over," Jeff Thrush told me in the street. "Marched away like bedbugs when you light the lamp."

I went to Law in agony. "I'll keep Rose. I'll hide her."

"Of course you won't. You can't drive yourself mad, nor her neither."

We heard the Rattler held up a stage in Soda Springs wearing Law's wedding suit. The papers described it exactly. Helen Branscombe had a laugh over that.

"He must have been very attractive. The Gentle Bandit. Like your father."

"Cheap suit," Bahé joked. "Not have to buy from Sam Brandt."

"You can't go," I said. "I can't do without you."

I held every day in the palm of my hands. We put beets and carrots down in the root cellar. We stuffed a tick with feathers.

"If you got yourself," she said, "got what you need."

One day there was no Jack. Jake was gone, too, from the store, and Tom from the livery stable. The Indian men had taken to the woods. Jakob and I agreed on our story. We'd seen no Indian bucks, and it was true. Let them hunt and feed the column on the march. Let them come and go.

Bahé cut open the doors to the acorn granaries. "Squirrels' luck," she said.

Alder leaves dipped in the creek in the early evenings, and the late light came up under the lichened branches of the big oaks. The nights passed quiet. In the mornings the fog burned off slow. So I was ready and not ready when a little company of mounted soldiers appeared on the Kaikitsil road, seven of them, with a rag-tag band of Indians, forty or fifty dusty women and children and old men. Some had walked too far already. Our place was the southernmost in the valley, so that was where they came first, that bright morning at the start of summer.

The children were up the creek fishing, Bahé in the smoke-house. Stay where you are, I prayed. Somehow I would keep them. Meantime, I must get Law back. We had a mare that was randy and would go to the horse Law had with him fencing. I cut her loose and she streamed over the hill. Law would know to come.

"What the hell?" the lieutenant said, dismounting.

"Nothing for it when she takes off," I said. "Isn't she a beauty?"

The lieutenant took off his hat and said he'd come to collect any and all Indians, with intent to march them to Round

Valley for their protection.

"Ma'am," he said, "do you have water?"

"Help yourselves at the spring."

"Some of the people are hard used up," he said. "Been on the road three weeks."

He seemed stiff in the shoulder, couldn't turn his head to the left. Behind him, a few old people hobbled toward the spring. There weren't as many children as there should be, seeing he'd been over the whole of Kaikitsil Valley. Nor women.

"Take time, Lieutenant. The people are tired and hold you back. Let them rest and eat."

He could brook no delay, he said. There was danger to his charges on the march. He had limited provisions. More would die if he dallied. He would graze his mounts and rest an hour.

Something about him struck me as familiar, maybe only the wiriness of men who live a long time on the trail. I took water to the people under the oaks. How had they come thirty miles over mountains with these rags binding the legs, these sores on their bare feet, these pitiful burdens of washed cloth? A woman tried to take away something from a thin girl who cried and held on to it. A dead baby. I unwound an old man's foot rags and the foot came too, in layers of thick paste. And the smell. I wrapped it back and touched his forehead. Blazing.

I accosted the lieutenant, where he stood smoking in the dooryard with his men.

"These people cannot walk. They need wagons. I was told there would be wagons."

"I have no wagons. My orders are to march and I will obey them. I believe it to be the determination of certain settlers to exterminate these people, and I see no way to prevent it unless I can collect them on the reservation under strict orders."

"Those who survive."

"Don't you think a chance is better than certain death?"

I recognized him then from a look in his eye, blue and calculated. "Corporal Jakes."

His eyes strained, trying to place me. "Lieutenant, Ma'am."

"Of course. We met at Big River reservation. You're the one requisitioned beef and blankets."

"I'm not a young fool any more."

Where was Law? Where was Rose? I had to hide her. I could not lose Rose.

"Your men could do with a rest," I said. "How long since they've had good ham? In the morning, when it's cool, you can move on. I'll bet they've never tasted peaches like ours. I have jars and jars of them."

"I'm clearing this valley out today."

"Send your men around the valley to collect the Indians here. I'll feed you."

I ducked into the smokehouse, where Bahé stood, listening.

"Where is Rose?"

She shrugged.

"I'll kill them. Shall I kill the soldiers?"

She laughed.

"What shall I do?"

She touched her two hands to my cheeks, and after a moment we went out together. Law was riding down the steep hill, kicking up dust.

"Where are the others?" the lieutenant wanted to know.

"Fishing."

"Call them in."

Law fetched the little ones from the creek, Sally and Kekawí together. But no Rose. During the afternoon, while Bahé and I dug potatoes and picked beans and cooked and fed, the lieutenant sent soldiers out around the valley, to bring the Indians in. Ruth and Essie from Point Ranch. Mary and her two children from Edsel Valley. Jane, who worked on the Nott ranch. Ella drove Jane over in the buggy and hugged her before she let her go.

"Jane's too fat to walk so far," she said, biting her thumb.

Jakob came along with the Indians he had living on his place. They sat up under the trees, a few ragged browns and blues against the white, hot grass. Some of the old people curled, asleep. A few stragglers limped in. In the crowd around the horse trough where people were drinking, a soldier shoved an old man, who fell, and I went to the lieutenant in a blaze.

"Look sharp there," he told the soldier, then turned to Jakob and me. "It's no use. We will find them. Where are the men?"

"It's hard to tell," said Jakob, with a wave of his hand. "They go off."

The lieutenant sent riders to hunt the men.

"Stay the night," I said. "We'll make room in the barn. You need the rest."

I followed Bahé to her lodge. She stood her big basket up and packed it with a skillet, willow roots, a dress, a rabbit cloak, needles and thread, a feather cape. She made a place in the top for Kekawí. Meantime, Law and Jakob had persuaded the lieutenant to remain the night. I took clothes off the Kaikitsil children and went to the wash house with a basket of things I could have clean and dry before they left, keeping my eyes peeled for Rose. She often went into the hills alone. I didn't want her to come in suddenly and be put under guard. The sun drew out the shadow of the barn. We pretty near emptied the smokehouse, feeding everyone.

At supper, the lieutenant told how he'd been disciplined for insubordination at the reservation and sent east to the war, fought at Antietam. He showed us a fan of white scar where minié balls chewed up his shoulder. It made him irritable. He slept badly. He didn't like this job, either, but he was damn well going to do it right. Conditions in Round Valley had improved, he said. There was no longer open warfare between the settlers and Indians.

"It should never have come to war," Law said.

"I agree with you. This whole thing's been bungled from the start."

Bahé went around all evening, speaking to the people, assuring them that their life would go on. Whatever the Army thought it was doing, she was leading them in the spirit. Rose was still hiding somewhere. Where? Dear Lord, I thought, what shall I do?

I treated blisters, sewing a white thread through them, leaving it in to drain. Most people were not so badly off that food and rest didn't go a long way, but Jakob and I found an old woman coughing and wheezing, and though we tried to raise her head and ease her breathing, there was little we could do. With the baby, she made the second death. Jakob doubled up and barely made it to the bushes, came back with a stain of blood on his pants. I'd had no idea he was so ill.

About midnight, some of the soldiers began drinking behind the barn and bothering the women. Law went down and made a lot of noise with a hammer, and that broke them up a little. He spoke to the officer, and Jakes went out to the men.

"Act as you would at home, men. Price of the ham."

I never went to bed. I made bread, kept up the fire in the washhouse, found blankets. Soon after dawn, there came a cry of women from under the pepperwoods by the creek. The lieutenant started up from his hammock outside the kitchen window.

"I'll whip them if they lay a hand on the squaws," he said.

But now there was great laughter at the creek. The Indian women had captured a poor soldier's trousers and driven him into the water, where he crouched freezing, cursing himself blind. Bahé held the pants. The lieutenant drew a pistol.

"Go on," he said. "Give him his trousers."

"Drop gun," Bahé said.

"Take him his pants. March, or I'll shoot."

"Not march," Bahé said. "Walk. We walk. No gun."

"Damn it, Jackson," the lieutenant said, "you're a fool."

"Sorry, sir," the boy shivered.

The lieutenant had to shoot Bahé or agree to her terms. He agreed. Bahé could lead the column of Indians. They would walk and not be marched. The soldiers would not hold guns on them. She gave the pants to the soldier.

I made coffee. Most everyone had some, gathered now ready to go.

"My orders are to burn her lodge," the lieutenant said.

"It's my property," said Law. "I won't allow it."

The lieutenant shook his head. "Orders," he said, and detailed a couple of men to do the burning.

"Let the soldiers carry their saddlebags the sixty miles," Jakob said, his weak voice strengthening as he went on. "The horses can carry the Indians' gear."

That plan was met with laughter.

"I have a wagon," Law said, "belongs to the Indian woman. And mules to pull it. It can carry their bundles and anyone too old or sick to walk."

"Where we're going there'll be no wagon road."

"Part way, anyhow."

"It's not in my orders."

"You used to like breaking orders," Law reminded him. "Take the wagon."

"I can't get your mules back to you. No, I won't do it."

We were smelling smoke. As Bahé came toward us along the creek, I realized she must have set fire to her lodge herself. I had a moment to look for Rose, hunting quick in the spring-house, the barn, smokehouse, shed, even under the house. She'd slipped into the washhouse behind the clothes baskets, streaked with tears.

"Thank God!" I clutched the child. Her thin arms gripped me, like someone drowning.

"Hide me," she whispered. "Let me stay."

It was what I wanted most. It stopped my heart. I sat on the floor and pulled her into my lap. "What about your mother?"

"She is strong."

"Not by herself. No one by herself is strong."

"She has Kekawí."

"She has the people to take care of."

"Why do I have to help her?"

"You belong to her."

"You don't want me!" Rose sobbed.

"You are the Rose of the world, my heart. But who will make the baskets, sing the songs? Who will read for the people?"

"Don't make me go. Don't make me!"

I held her tight. The lonely horses of my dream were coming true, the empty land, the useless fence, the silence that would go on forever. Rose stilled in my arms, so I heard the sound of her heart breaking, and she heard mine. We rocked together, and when we could, we went out and found Bahé.

We all tried to make it go quickly now. Law and I petted the little brother, cheerful as usual. Sally gave him the little folding knife her grandfather had given her. The soldiers mounted. Rose stood by her mother, pale and straight. I ran to find a book and put my hand on *Great Expectations*, stuffed it with paper and a pen.

"Use pokeberries for ink," I told her.

Bahé and I had already given each other everything.

I watched her lead the people out, beating a split stick on her palm, singing a harsh song. It was a clear, dry day, for luck. They were in no state to walk, many of them, but she lifted them up, and the valley emptied of its spirit, like wine poured out upon a stone. Their way curved around the big rock. When they came there, that would be the last of them, the horsemen and the line of ragged marchers. It came very soon. I watched the whole time, and Bahé never looked back.

ACKNOWLEDGEMENTS:

I am grateful to these publications, institutions and individuals, all indispensable in imagining this novel:

Elsie Allen, *Pomo Basketmaking*; *Alta California*; P.M. Angle, ed., *Lincoln-Douglas Debates of 1858*; S.A. Barrett, *Ceremonies of the Pomo Indians*; L. J. Bean, ed., *California Indian Shamanism*; Sarah Bixby-Smith, *Adobe Days*; D.J. Boorstin, *The Americans*; V. M. Bouvier, *Women and the Conquest of California*; W. H. Brewer, *Up and Down California in 1860-1864*; Dee Brown, *The Gentle Tamers*; R. D. Brown, *Knowledge is Power; The Diffusion of Information in Early America*; Brown & Andrews, *The Pomo Indians of California*; Carranco & Beard, *Genocide and Vendetta*; *California Historical Society Quarterly*; W.J. Cash, *The Mind of the South*; Mary Chesnut, *Civil War Diary*; Walter Colton, *Three Years in California*; S.F. Cook, *Conflict Between the California Indians and White Civilization*; E.S. Curtis, *The North American Indians* (photographs); R.H. Dana, *Two Years Before the Mast*; Vine Deloria Jr., *God is Red*; Bernard DeVoto, *The Year of Decision:1846*; I.R. Egli, *No Rooms of Their Own: Women Writers of Early California*; *Five Views: An Ethnic Historic Site Survey for California*, www.cr.nps.gov; J. D. Forbes, *Native Americans of California and Nevada*; Goodrich, Lawson & Lawson, *Kashaya Pomo Plants*; R.E. Heizer, *The Destruction of California Indians*; Heizer & Kroeber, *Ishi; the Last Yahi*; A. L. Hurtado, *Indian Survival on the California Frontier*; A.L. Kroeber,

369

Handbook of the Indians of California; J. F. de La Pérouse, *Life in a California Mission;* Jack Larkin, *The Reshaping of Everyday Life, 1790-1840;* Lucien Lévy-Bruhl, *How Natives Think;* Levene et al., *Mendocino Country Remembered; An Oral History;* Lucy Maddox, *Civilization or Extinction?,* www.georgetown.edu; L.F. Maffly-Kipp, *Religion and Society in Frontier California;* S. Magoffin, *Down the Santa Fe Trail and Into Mexico;* Malcolm Margolin, *The Ohlone Way;* Jerry Mander, *In the Absence of the Sacred;* F. Marryat, *Diary in America;* Frederick Merk, *Manifest Destiny and Mission in American History;* Doug Monroy, *Matters of Race in 19ᵗʰ Century California,* www.sscnet.ucla.edu; *News of Native California;* William Osler, *Principles and Practice of Medicine;* T. C. Owens, *The Yokaia;* C.E. Pancoast, *A Quaker Forty-Niner;* Julia Parker, *It Will Live Forever;* Stephen Powers, *Tribes of California;* F. P. Prucha, *The Indians in American Society;* Harvey Rice, *Letters from the Pacific Slope* http://memory.loc.gov; Glenda Riley, *Women and Indians on the Frontier;* W.W. Robinson, *Land in California;* Alan Rosenus, *General Vallejo and the Advent of the Americans;* Rupe family letters; Greg Sarris, *Mabel McKay: Weaving the Dream;* Page Smith, *The Nation Comes of Age;* Swann and Krupat, eds., *I Tell You Now;* J.L. Stratton, *Pioneer Women;* G.T. Strong, *Diary;* D. and B. Tedlock, eds., *Teachings from the American Earth;* Lucy Thompson, *To the American Indian;* Mark Twain, *Roughing It;* Gerald Vizenor, *Manifest Manners: Postindian Warriors of Survivance;* Jack Weatherford, *Indian Givers;* W. P. Webb, *The Texas Rangers.*

Bancroft Library at UC Berkeley, California State Indian Museum, Grace Hudson Museum, Kule Loklo at Point Reyes, Library of Congress, Marin Museum of the American Indian,

Mendocino County Museum, Mendocino Historical Society, Miwok Archaeological Preserve of Marin, Missions of San Juan Capistrano, Santa Barbara, San Juan Bautista, San Carlos Borromeo, San Francisco de Asís, & San Francisco Solano, Museum of the City of San Francisco, National Library of Medicine, National Museum of the American Indian, Olompali State Historic Park, Petaluma Adobe State Historic Park, Pomo Cultural Center Coyote Valley, Round Valley Indian Reservation, San Francisco Public Library.

Bernice, Herman & Albertine & the ranch, Nancy on Tuesdays, Dolores & the writers at Edgemont Ave., Darnella, Greg & Gerald, Susan, Gareth & the E.E. Ford Foundation & the WIS class of 2008, Robbie & Bob, John V & Larry & SAC, Fr. Downing, Laurie & the Biscuit Eater, Patch & Jester & Jack.

Washington Writers' Publishing House

Washington Writers' Publishing House is a non-profit organization that has published over 100 volumes of poetry and fiction since 1975. The press sponsors an annual competition, featured in *Poets & Writers*, for writers living in the Washington-Baltimore area: The Jean Feldman Poetry Prize and The Washington Writers' Publishing House Fiction Prize. The annual winners of each category, one each in poetry and fiction, comprise our set of published works for that year.

WWPH has received grants from the Lannan Foundation, the National Endowment for the Arts, the D.C. Commission on the Arts and Humanities, the Nation magazine, and the Poetry Society of America. Many individuals have also assisted, encouraged, and supported our work through the years.

Look us up on the web at http://www.washingtonwriters. org/, "like" us on Facebook at https://www.facebook.com/ WashingtonWritersPublishingHouse, and follow us on Twitter @WWPHPress.

ॐ

The typeface used in this book is 11 point ITC New Baskerville.

CPSIA information can be obtained at www.ICGtesting.com
Printed in the USA
LVOW12s1746201014

409617LV00006B/1022/P

9 781941 551028